t wishes to my good friend
Lewis Van Cannon. Thanks
all the great work you
for United Methodists.

Bill Johnson
November 18, 1996

Moon over Purgatory

Moon over Purgatory

Bill Johnson

VANTAGE PRESS
New York

Copyright © 1995 by Bill Johnson

Published by Vantage Press, Inc.
516 West 34th Street, New York, New York 10001

Manufactured in the United States of America
ISBN: 0-533-11265-6

Library of Congress Catalog Card No.: 94-90516

0 9 8 7 6 5 4 3 2 1

In memory of my late mother-in-law, Evelyn W. Cox, whose love
and knowledge of local history kindled my interest in this story

Contents

Author's Note

Growing up during the 1950s and '60s on a farm in central North Carolina was a trying experience to say the least. My friends and I often hunted and hiked in this desolate rural area even though we were warned by the locals, "Y'all stay off Purgatory Mountain, heah? Them moonshiners might shoot you fer mess'n round their licker stills."

Those bootleggers' favorite ploy for scaring us away was to launch rumors about wild beasts such as mountain lions, panthers, and bears inhabiting the area. They even talked about ghosts lurking in the dense foliage on the mountain.

So many stories circulated about weird happenings on Purgatory Mountain, that we didn't know which ones to believe. However, the tale that intrigued us most predated the bootleg whisky era. It told of how a group of boys used that mountain to hide from a vindictive Civil War recruiter back in 1865.

This story aroused my curiosity and ignited a search for facts about the incident. Over the years I talked with several people who claimed to be descendants of the group of young men in this book who were illegally drafted into the Confederate army in late 1864. They managed to escape being pressed into military service and sneaked back to their homes in rural Randolph County. Upon their return, they found themselves in a battle for their lives with a harsh recruiter who was hell–bent on forcing them back into military service.

In researching this tale, it soon became apparent that my information was long on curious facts but short on details. Thus, I decided to make it into a novel. This book pieces together the stories I extracted from several people, but remember, this information came to me ninety years after the fact.

That's why I make no claims as to the accuracy of places and incidents. I have randomly named the characters. Therefore, the book does not necessarily reveal their true identities. If I have correctly named a character, it's pure coincidence.

I admit that Purgatory Mountain is not a household name even in Randolph County. It has little historical claim to fame, except for this story which heretofore hasn't been widely told.

At just a thousand feet above sea level, Purgatory is indeed a puny mountain. Located near Asheboro, it was part of a 1,370-acre tract chosen to build the North Carolina Zoological Park in the early 1970s.

Zoo animals and plants from across the globe now inhabit the land where the action took place back in 1865. For more than two decades artists and craftsmen have labored shaping these rock outcroppings and ledges into natural-looking animal and plant habitats.

Thus, this mountainside, which 130 years ago was covered with briars, vines, brush and trees dense enough to hide twenty boys from a psychotic Civil War recruiter, is now a well-kept zoological park.

I admit to taking liberties with the facts. My apologies to any descendants of these characters who may dispute the details: But that's why this is a novel and not a history book.

Hopefully, reading this story will strike a nerve in you the way it did for me as I researched and visualized happenings in the Civil War period. This was, no doubt, one of the darkest periods in our history.

Those four years ripped our nation apart and put it back together leaving us a drastically changed society. However, I do not feel that this, the bloodiest of all wars, defined us as a people. The way we've remolded America during the 130 years since, did.

It is my contention that even after that disastrous war, America was yet to fully understand itself. The average American probably spends more hours contemplating the sex life of alligators than in trying to comprehend how humans can coexist without war and violence. Therefore, I invite you to join the characters in *Moon over Purgatory* in pondering these questions:

Will humans ever progress beyond war as a way to settle their differences? Why are there nearly thirty shooting wars in progress at all times on earth? Will the descendants of slaves ever fully forgive the offspring of those who once enslaved them? Is living free harder than living as a slave? Is the burden of freedom too heavy for many of us to bear? What lasting lessons did that war, which nearly ripped our nation apart at the seams, teach us about ourselves? What are the chances of such a war-from-within happening again?

Moon over Purgatory

Chapter 1
Father Was a War Victim

Nathan slapped Bess gently across the rear as she stepped into the chilled waters of Bachelor Creek. She glanced briefly in his direction but mostly ignored the gesture as she ducked her head under the briars and honeysuckles. Then Bess began sipping water from the sparkling clear stream.

The handsome young lad stood motionless on the stream bank, choking back a tear as his mind raced back six months. "Papa died trying to save your life right here at this very place," the sandy-haired boy muttered in a low, quiet voice. Old Bess, the family milk cow, just kept drinking.

"It wasn't you he died for, though. Papa was trying to save our family from starvation," Nathan grunted in a muffled voice. "Guess you could say the war killed my father even though he never saw a shot fired," Nathan mumbled, with a slight quiver in his voice. "This dreadful war may kill us all before it's over. Whether it's bullets or starvation and sickness that kills us makes little difference. We're just as dead either way. In fact, death by bullets might be less painful."

For several minutes he sat quietly contemplating the thought he'd just uttered. It was as though he expected a reply to come from somewhere. "Why am I talking to a dumb ole cow?" he whispered to himself.

There was another pause as Nathan listened to squirrels thrash about in the falling dry leaves. "But I have this need to tell somebody how I feel," he said after a long thoughtful wait. "And it hurts too much when I try to say what I'm thinking to a real person."

For the next half hour he sat motionless, gazing into the rippling water while Bess nibbled dried grass and honeysuckle along the creek bank. Small shafts of sunlight trickled onto the forest floor through the barren maples and fox grape vines overhead.

Nathan York was just one of the thousands of farm lads whose life had been totally upset in his teenage years by the start of the war between the North and South. This cruel outbreak of violence had changed his life in more ways than he could ever count. Civil war and the hardships it brought now tainted his every thought.

Little did he realize what lay ahead in his innocent young life or what this dreadful war had in store for him. Nor could he know that the next few months would test him to the very core of his being.

Nathan's most troubling memory of the war thus far was rooted in this very spot where he now sat watching Bess graze the last forage of autumn. For it was here that his father had made his last valiant stand in his own battle, aimed at saving his family from starvation.

It was on mornings like this, when he would lead old Bess down to the creek for a drink, that Nathan's mind often raced back to that dreary day in March 1864 just six months earlier. The ordeal that began on that day had now thrust him into premature manhood and changed his life forever.

On that fateful early March morning, Nathan's father had spotted six blue-coated riders galloping down the long muddy road toward the York farm. Such incidents had become familiar and quite commonplace. Ever since the war began three years earlier, roving bands of both Union and

Confederate soldiers had made frequent appearances on the York farm looking for food.

Like all southern farm owners, he knew that these men were coming to confiscate everything edible from the place. It was general knowledge that both armies lived off the food and materials they scavenged from farms across the South. Thus, hiding food had become priority number one with all of them.

The York farm was particularly vulnerable for two reasons. First, it was located just a few miles off the great North-South Trading Path. And second, prior to the war there had been thirty head of fine cattle roaming here. But now the cattle had all been taken, except Bess.

Every member of the York family had been carefully drilled in how to hide their belongings from these search parties, which they referred to as "buzzard squads." Hiding a live animal such as Bess, who could be used for food, presented the biggest challenge of all.

When Nathan's father saw that band of bluecoats coming down the lane that dreary morning, he quickly tied a rope around her horns, grabbed a bucket of oats (her favorite feed), and led Bess to her prearranged hideout down by the creek.

He knew she was his family's most precious source of food and possibly even the link between them and starvation. Her ability to eat grass and leaves and produce milk, butter, and cheese made her extremely valuable. He also knew that if those Yankees got their hands on her, she would quickly become stew beef for a bunch of soldiers.

Old Bess's prearranged hiding place was the thicket of briars and honeysuckle where Nathan now took her to water each day. Mr. York was able to silence her by offering her occasional bites of oats from the bucket he took along.

The search party quickly fanned out across the farmstead looking for anything edible they might grab.

"You got any livestock here, boy?" the blue-coated captain leading the group shouted at Nathan.

Glancing quickly toward his mother as if seeking her approval to lie, he yelled back, "You army people took them all a long time ago."

"We have no food that we can spare," pleaded Nathan's mother. "We are scarcely making it here and cannot help you. So please leave us alone."

Nathan and his mother could see these soldiers didn't believe them. They knew from experience that these human vultures would search the place over, scratching for every last bit of food. Their mission was to find food, and it didn't seem to matter to them whether the farmers from whom they took it survived or not.

The six men methodically searched high and low. They scrounged through first one building and then another. They looked in the barn, smokehouse, chicken coop, house, root cellar, and granary, gathering up small morsels wherever they found them.

Nathan and his mother had no choice but to step aside and watch them. They only hoped these rude intruders would not find all the foodstuff they had so cleverly hidden the previous summer. And they especially prayed that these thieving bluecoats would not find Father and Bess hiding in the thicket down near Bachelor Creek.

The soldiers' exhaustive search seemed to go on for hours. A steady rain continued to fall, while the temperature hovered just above the freezing point. Occasional wind gusts made the raw weather almost unbearable.

When the search finally ended, the soldiers had stolen a ham from the attic of the smokehouse, several bunches of onions they found hanging beneath the granary floor, and seven chickens from the yard.

Despite their losses, Nathan and his mother were quite relieved just knowing that marauding band had not discovered Father and Bess hiding down at Bachelor Creek. However, this escapade had forced Mr. York to sit out in a cold, steady rain for nearly two hours while the troops did their dirty work.

As soon as the bluecoats rode away, Father quickly parked Bess back in the barn. He was soaked to the skin and felt as though he was going to freeze to death. So he quickly headed for the house to find a warm fireplace and some dry clothes.

This ordeal had taken a toll on his undernourished body. Later that evening, after he finally stopped shivering, he began coughing and sneezing. The next evening chills and fever set in. For several days his pain, chills, and fever grew worse. None of the herbs or tonics he tried seemed to help.

Nathan's father lived only twelve days before the chills and fever caused his frail body to collapse.

The loss of his father hit Nathan hard. He was now the oldest male at home, meaning a load of responsibility had instantly fallen into his lap.

Even though he was approaching his sixteenth birthday, this soft-spoken young man of moderate build didn't feel troubled by the pressures of the war recruiters. He was a Quaker, which meant that when he reached the draft age of eighteen he would be allowed to serve in some role other than that of a combat soldier. Being a conscientious objector to war, Nathan believed he would be allowed to exercise his right not to bear arms against his fellowman.

At the time the war broke out in 1861, Nathan was a

mere boy of twelve. The farm where he lived was in the southern part of Randolph County in central North Carolina.

He was being raised in the Quaker religious traditions that had been brought to this area two generations earlier. His ancestors had first emigrated from Europe and settled in Pennsylvania. A generation later they pulled up stakes and moved south, spending a few years near Cole Creek, Virginia, before venturing farther south to the rolling foothills of North Carolina.

Even at the young age of twelve, Nathan could read the anger, concern, unrest, and stress in the adults around him when news of the Civil War came to Randolph County. These emotions scorched indelible pictures upon his impressionable young mind. He quickly learned to fear and despise nearly everything about the war. He often wondered at the term *Civil War*. "How can any war where human beings form lines and march with guns blazing toward other humans for the sole purpose of killing each other be called civil?" he often asked.

Whenever his father and mother talked about the war, he could read both fear and disgust in their voices. At the monthly Society of Friends (the church of the Quakers) meetings, he'd hear men talk about the slaughter and killing that was taking place on faraway battlefields. They often described the dreadful battle scenes in gory detail. They would tell about men being shot in the foot and then having their legs amputated at the knee simply to keep infection from killing them. Such tales upset him even though he didn't always fully comprehend their meaning.

And when he'd go to the gristmill with his father to have grain ground into flour or meal, he'd overhear men of the community speak about the death and maiming of their relatives and friends. But these battles were taking place in Virginia, Georgia, and other distant places with strange-sounding names. Names like Bull Run, Gettysburg, Vicksburg, New Market, and Bristoe Station all seemed so distant, as though they were part of another world.

Nathan had a good understanding of the slavery issue, which he'd been taught to believe was a major point of conflict among his southern neighbors fighting in the war. Most Quaker families did not own slaves because their religious beliefs forbade it.

Before the war, he and his family had been part of the Underground Railroad. This was a movement that helped slaves escape from the South to the North, where they gained their freedom. In fact, some of the Quakers even bought slaves and set them free.

One of his uncles had married a wealthy woman from Georgia who had brought a half-dozen slaves with her when she came to live with him in North Carolina. Upon arrival in this Quaker community, the couple agreed to set the slaves free and gave each of them land and livestock. They even helped them get started farming.

But even slaves who had been set free sometimes ended up back in the hands of slave owners. They would occasionally be captured by bounty hunters trying to make a quick buck and sold down at the Fayetteville slave auction.

Nathan's most vivid memory of slavery, though, was of an incident that took place when he was eleven years old. The experience had burned a lasting message into his young mind that wouldn't go away.

His father had allowed him to go along on a trip to the slave auction in Fayetteville. There he saw Negroes of all ages, who had been cleaned up, slicked down with lard, and dressed to look their finest. They were placed in the center of a large room and auctioned off like cattle or swine.

Before going to the slave sale, Nathan's father had received a message written on a piece of parchment. It came from a middle-aged slave named George, whom he had befriended down at Kemp's Mill several years earlier.

George had belonged to a neighbor and had become a trustworthy wagon driver for the farm. He would regularly drive loads of grain to the mill and bring them back home ground into flour or meal. Nathan's father had talked with George many times at the mill and had gotten to know him well.

Three years earlier George's master had died unexpectedly. His childless widow had then sold off most of his possessions. George and the other male slaves from the farm had been hastily sold in a group to a large plantation owner near Fayetteville.

The message Nathan's father received from George had been written by a traveling leather merchant. This man had written the letter in his own words at George's request and personally delivered it to Nathan's father.

The message read:

Mr. York:

I am writing to beg you for help. I'm not asking you for money, just a favor that would make my life less miserable.

Since I've been here on the Robertson plantation, I've been sick a lot. My master says I'm not as good a hand as when I first came. He has not beat me none, but he plans to get rid of me and buy another slave in my place.

He says he aims to sell me in the second September slave auction over at Fayetteville.

If Master Robertson sells me, Lord knows where I'll be going next. I might be hauled so far away that I'd never see my woman Samantha and our four younguns again. I ain't seen them even once in the three years I've been here.

So, Mr. York, I'm begging you to help me. I know you

Quakers don't own no slaves. If you did I'd ask you to consider buying me. But since you don't, I'm pleading with you to talk to somebody in your community who is a slave-owner into coming to the September sale and buying me. That way I would at least be close to my Samantha and our younguns. Then maybe I could see them sometimes. Lord knows how much I miss 'em, and the thought of not ever seeing them again is almost enough to kill this poor old black man.

I would be forever in your debt if you'd talk somebody into buying me and bringing me back to Randolph County so's I might see my wife and younguns again before I die.

Your humble friend, George

Nathan had seen his father cry only a few times and that was at funerals. But he couldn't help noticing him sobbing aloud as the leather salesman finished reading George's letter.

For two hours Nathan's father sat silently pondering the message. This note from George had cut him deeply and he was struggling for a response to the old Negro slave's request.

Early the next morning Nathan's father started preparing for his next move. He dropped all his chores and began making plans to go to the September slave auction in Fayetteville and buy George. He didn't know just how he'd do it, but he would somehow raise the money.

First, he sold a horse and several head of cattle. He didn't know how much money a slave would cost at auction, but he had soon raised a substantial sum. He believed that this money, along with his savings, might swing the deal.

Nathan and his father arose early that morning, hitched the team to their big buckboard wagon, and headed toward Fayetteville. His father remarked several times how uneasy he felt going to a slave auction when he didn't believe in owning slaves. He felt that he was somehow lending support to an evil practice, which was unacceptable to his fellow Quakers and his Lord. But he reasoned that under the circumstances, he would be forgiven if he went through with his plan.

When they arrived at the auction house a couple of days later, a large crowd had gathered. Slave sellers from all over the eastern part of the state had lined up their sales offerings in rows along the wall outside the auction house.

Prospective buyers would walk by and ask to feel the muscles and examine the bone structures of those being offered for sale. Some would open a slave's mouth to look at his teeth. Others would carefully examine their backs for scars made by bullwhips, which might indicate discipline problems.

At noon a large bell rang and sellers began to move their slaves inside the building toward the auction floor.

By now Nathan and his father had located George. He was among a group being held for the early part of the sale. They had a chance to speak just briefly with him before the auctioneer began talking. They didn't even have time to tell George they had come to buy him. But they could see a glimmer of hope in his weary old eyes, indicating that he knew relief might be in his future.

Soon the auction hit full swing.

"Whadd'um I offered for this strappin' big niggah heah?" the auctioneer chanted. "He's young and vigrus and can chop cotton from sunup to sundown without much restin'. Don't eat much neither.

"Sold to the man ovah theah from Harnett County for eight hundred and fifteen dollahs," he said, after several minutes of chanting and wrangling.

Then Nathan watched as one slave after another was

sold to the highest bidder. Every buyer would fetch his money to the treasurer's desk. He would then exchange it for a registration paper for the property he'd just bought at auction. Then the new owner would take his registration paper out back and pick up his newly purchased slave.

Soon it was George's turn at the auction block. Nathan's father didn't join in the bidding immediately. He waited until just two bidders were still offering and the price had gone to $790.

"One thousand dollars," shouted Nathan's father, just as the auctioneer raised his gavel to signal the completion of the sale.

"Thank you, mistah," the auctioneer shouted with renewed enthusiasm. "Anybody else want to bid on this ole niggah? All in, all done, sold to the gentleman ovah heah on my right. Who'd you say you are, suh?"

Without another word, Nathan and his father finished the paperwork and took possession of George.

Soon the three of them were seated on the buckboard wagon headed west.

"Thank you, Mistah York," George shouted over and over as the team trudged off down the dusty road from the slave market. "Law me. How in the world is I evah gonna make it up to you fer comin' all the way down heah and payin' a thousand dollahs fer an old broke-down slave like me? And heah I is headed up the road toward Randolph County with you good Quaker folks what don't even believe in ownin' slaves."

Nathan's father put his arm around George. "Just take it easy and don't get too excited," he told George.

"Does this mean that I'm gonna git to see my Samantha and our younguns agin'?" he asked, with tears in his eyes and a tremble in his voice. "I has been prayin' fer somethin' like this ever since I left Randolph County three years ago. But I never dreamt it would happen. Thank the Lawd."

"Just hold on a minute, George," Father interrupted. "First, no, you're not going to see your wife and children in Randolph County. We're not taking you back there at all.

"Second, we Quakers don't ordinarily own slaves. But this day is different. Today I bought you and three days ago my brother, Hiram, bought your wife, Samantha, and your four children from the man who owned them.

"We know that if we take you back and put you out to live as free Negroes, you're likely to be captured and resold," Father explained. "So we have decided to move you to a place where we know you can live free and stay together for the rest of your lives.

"Hiram has already slipped Samantha and the children into the Underground Railroad. They are now being smuggled to Indiana. We're taking you to a farm north of here where you, too, will be put into the channels and moved to Indiana.

"Most of the Quakers who lived around here have moved to Indiana and Ohio to escape living in a society that condones slavery. Most of the Friends meetings in South Carolina, Georgia, and Virginia have been closed because the people have all left to take up a new life out West. Our family has even considered it. But we believe it is better to stay here to help put an end to this dreadful practice than to run from it. May God help us to do it.

"If all goes well, in two or three weeks you and your family will be united. You will also be free. Here is enough money for you to make a new start as a free man. We have arranged with a white man we know in Indiana to give you a job in his blacksmith shop if you want it. You will know the man when you see him."

George sat quietly listening to the words he'd never

dreamed of hearing. Nathan could see that he was a bit un-easy with his newfound freedom.

Then his father interrupted a long period of silence. "George, being a free man is in some ways harder than being a slave. You'll have to work as hard as ever to make a living. Being free has a lot of burdens attached to it. The big difference is that you now have the chance to be whatever you want to be. You're now escaping the chains that have bound you all your life. But by gaining freedom you're accepting a heavy load of responsibility to go with it. Do you think you can handle it?"

George sat quietly for a long time. He broke the silence with, "Yes, suh, Mistah York. I knows this is not gonna be easy. But I is willin' to do anything to get my Samantha and my four girl childrens back. I'll work day and night if I has to."

"I have one bit of advice for you, George," said Nathan's father. "Do everything you can to see that your four daughters learn to read and write. They will have many chances in life that you and Samantha never had. But they need to be educated to take advantage of them.

"Your daughters may resist. They may say they don't want to study and become educated. They may prefer to sit back and blame the white society, which once made slaves of them, for their poor circumstances. But you, George, must not let this happen to them. Otherwise, your children and their children's children will forever be in bondage.

"You and your children are about to gain your freedom. You have no control of the fact that you were a slave most of your life. Your children cannot help the fact that they were born slaves. But what's done is done. You're all now free to fit into society as best you can. It won't be easy for white folks to accept you as free people in their society. Many will resist.

"I believe down deep in my heart that our loving God will somehow bring an end to slavery all over this country. There may even be a bloody war before all the slaves are set free.

"After you're all freed, it may take years, possibly even a century or more, for the children and great-grandchildren of slaves to fit fully into society. It's important that you understand, George, that in the future the children of former slave owners and the children of former slaves must learn to live together in harmony. It is unlikely that once all slaves are freed any of them will go back to Africa. In fact, I doubt that most of you would ever want to go back because the opportunities as free Americans are so much greater than living in tribal Africa.

"So, George, do you understand what I'm saying? Do you realize that Nathan and I are risking our lives and spending our entire family savings to plant a seed with you and your family? You all must begin as quickly as you get settled in Indiana to make yourselves citizens of a free country. You must be ready when all slaves are freed to help plant the seed with them.

"Begin immediately when you're settled to find someone who will teach your daughters to read and write. Then have them read to you or maybe even teach you and Samantha to read. From books you'll get an understanding of the world around you. But, remember, George, those who *don't* read are no better off than those who *can't* read."

A long pause ensued.

"Suh, I thinks I knows what you is sayin' to me," said George, placing his big black hand on Mr. York's shoulder. "I only hopes I can live up to what you expects of me and my kin."

Another long pause.

"I sees what you have done for me and I wants to cry.

I even thinks about just askin' you to take me back to that auction and let me stay a slave. But I knows you is not doing this just for me. You is doin' it for all black people who live in America now and for all times. You is givin' me and my family a head start on those who may git free later. If we don't takes our freedom seriouslike, we's no better off than bein' slaves.

"Mistah York," George said after a thoughtful pause, "if you is willin' to risk the lives of you and your boy here to bring your hard-earned savins' down here and set me free for such a cause, then I must takes your advice. I'll do my best. I promises to study and pray about it ever day. I only hopes I's up to doin' all them things you said."

With few words and much contemplation, they continued down the rough dusty road, resting only long enough to water the horses.

The next night Nathan and his father left George at the home of a prominent farm family near Cane Creek in Alamance County. They had helped this family route others through this station of the Underground Railroad. George would stay there a few days and then make his next connection through the underground movement that was destined to deliver him to Indiana. There he would be free at last.

Nathan's young mind still flashed back to this incident often. He had observed and tasted the true meaning of slavery and freedom. He knew unequivocally and was sure in his own mind that slavery in America was wrong. He knew deep down in his heart that somehow the practice must be forced to end, yet he had no idea of how or when it might happen.

Despite the fact that the Yorks and these North Carolina Quakers detested slavery, none of them approved of war as a way to settle the issue.

Soon after the cry for war went out across the South, there came a plea for every able-bodied man to join the Confederate army. "We'll whup them Yankees' butts and end this thing once and for all. We'll send them packing back up North in short order" was their rallying cry.

The Confederacy sent a recruiter to southern Randolph County to speed up the military drafting efforts. John Stone, the first recruiter sent to this area, was quite successful at getting the men and boys to join the Rebel cause. During the first year of the war, he enticed more than three thousand men from the county to join the Confederate army. That was nearly one-fifth of the county's population. He'd failed to sway many of these stubborn Quaker men to leave their farms and go off to war though.

Most of the men John recruited signed up for one year or less and half of them returned home within a few months. They had expected the war to last only a few days or weeks.

John was a well-bred Southern gentleman from Alamance County. He respected the rights of the Quakers to be conscientious objectors, thus his job was quite a challenge. His instructions were to make a soldier out of every Quaker he could and then try to convince the rest of them to serve in noncombat roles.

He had coaxed and convinced many of them to accept support jobs to help "end this war in short order." And he encouraged the ones who chose to stay home to plant additional crops and work extra hard to grow food for the soldiers.

The Randolph County Quakers were glad to help in this role. They were good farmers and proud of their agrarian abilities. So they plowed, planted, and harvested their own land and even tended the fields left vacant by their neighbors, who had gone to fight the war. The women worked long hard hours spinning, sewing, preserving food, and tending the crops and livestock. Their lives had been made extremely difficult by these extra chores. But they were willing to endure the hardships in order to shorten this war, which they so openly detested.

Early in the war Nathan's older brother James had yielded to John Stone's plea for help in a noncombat role. James left home back in 1862. He had written letters home several times telling his family that he was helping tend the Confederate wounded in Virginia. But for the past five months there had been no word from him.

The family wasn't sure if James had been killed, wounded, or was ashamed to communicate with his family because of his involvement in the war. They even wondered if he may have yielded to demands of the Confederate officers and taken up arms to fight the enemy.

Naturally his mother despaired greatly at not hearing from her son for so long. But she now had even greater worries occupying her mind most of the time. Like most Southerners, she had expected the war to end in just a few months. It had now dragged on for more than three years and there seemed to be no end in sight.

Nursing his father through his sickness and death back in March had been a very trying experience for Nathan's mother. Following the funeral she became silent, hardly speaking to anyone. Whenever friends called on her, she just didn't want to talk. Her depressed state of mourning left her listless and she spent much of her time in bed.

Her despondence had become a burden for Nathan, his brother Calvin, and sister Rebecca. They, too, mourned their father; but their mother's state of depression was becoming more than they could bear. They tried to console her, but nothing they could say or do seemed to help.

Finally after several weeks she called Nathan to her bedside. "Nathan, I just don't know what we'll do," his mother said to him in a low, weak voice. "I sometimes feel that I don't want to go on living but I know that I must. God has seen us through this far and I'm sure He'll be with us as we try to survive this hardship."

Nathan tried to console her, but it was difficult to find words to fit the occasion. So he stood in silence, touching her hand and trying to fight off a big lump in his throat.

"You're fifteen now and we don't know if James is even alive," she continued. "You've worked with your father and brother in the fields. Now it's up to you. With the help of your brother Calvin and sister Rebecca, we may be able to plant a crop this spring. It's almost time to begin planting. Do you think we can do it?"

Chapter 2
Caught and Hog-tied

The first Sunday of each month always found the Yorks and their friends gathered down at the meeting house. Most of the Quaker families took lunch and stayed after the monthly meeting to catch up on the news. They often ate together in the churchyard and exchanged news of significant happenings from the previous weeks.

Since the war had started, these Sunday lunches had even become a time for food sharing. The kindly Quakers often used this time to share what little food they had left with less fortunate families. In many cases they would use the event to barter one commodity for another, even though they didn't believe in doing business on the Sabbath. One family who had a surplus of potatoes, thanks to a good harvest, might swap for dried beans or cabbage with another family.

Of course, some commodities were not to be had. Coffee was something that people remembered before the war. Now anyone who wanted coffee drank a substitute brewed from parched grain or some other commodity.

Salt, spices, and dry goods of all kinds were impossible to get at any price. And there was nothing made of metal to be bought anywhere in the South.

Everyone had come to accept this situation as one of the many hardships of war. They lived on what little they had while clinging to the hope that someday the war would end and their lives could be put back in order.

The Sunday meetings were about the Quakers' only chance to get away from their farms as a family each month. Even then, most families felt they had to leave someone on guard to protect the farm from wartime scavengers.

The other source of news about what was happening in the community was down at Kemp's Mill. Most people in the community took grain to the mill once a week or more to have it ground into flour or cornmeal. They would usually exchange grain for grinding services with Raymond Kemp, the miller.

Raymond was more than just a good miller. He could be depended upon to keep all these tidbits of news straight. He would hear many wild stories about the war and about the troops who'd been out scavenging that week. But this bearded, heavyset, knowledgeable man repeated only the significant tales or the important parts of stories. He usually left off the trivial and meaningless details. And gossip was not his forte.

For several weeks now, Raymond had been portraying the war in a rather grim light. The Confederacy was not faring well in recent battles, he would relate to his visitors. Union troops were winning in most confrontations and the Confederates were suffering from lack of manpower and supplies.

The beastly marauding General Sherman was leaving a trail of mass destruction all across Georgia and other parts of the South. There were tales and speculation that he might even march his vast army back across South Carolina and into central North Carolina. Of course, Raymond was always quick to point out that this was purely uninformed conjecture.

There was also talk that Confederate Gen. Joseph Johnston was trying to raise a large army to confront General Sherman somewhere in central North Carolina. And there had been talk that General Sherman intended to burn North Carolina the way he burned Georgia. Reports had come in that this ruthless Yankee general not only burned farmsteads to the ground, but he even torched the fields of standing grain before they could be harvested. And he took no mercy on women and children as he burned their houses, barns, and crops.

Raymond had heard these questions a hundred times but each new visitor repeated them: "Is General Sherman headed this way?" "Will he send North Carolina up in flames the way he burned Georgia?"

It was at the first Sunday meeting in October that Nathan and his family first heard a disturbing rumor. Initially it seemed only small news compared to reports of how the Confederate army was being whipped into submission in nearly every confrontation with the Union forces.

"The Confederacy is replacing John Stone as the recruiter for Randolph County," Samuel Brown told the Quakers as they ate their meager lunch that Sunday. "A traveling merchant told me there's a real tough man coming over from Moore County to take his place. I don't know his name. Some people call him 'the Hunter' because he works so hard at hunting down draft dodgers and war deserters. Others say his real name is Peter and they call him 'Pete' for short. But I've heard most people just call him 'Skully' because he once nailed the skull of a man shot stealing horses to a big oak tree. Most people believe this man Skully did the killing, so that's why they gave him this name."

There had been a contingent of military men left behind in this area to enforce the draft and to try rounding up draft dodgers. However, they had not been nearly as enthusiastic about sending men off to war as those in most North Carolina counties. In fact, many of them outright opposed the war.

A few months earlier these uniformed soldiers, who had been the enforcers back home calling themselves "the Home Guard," were shipped out to help on the war front. This left only John Stone and a couple of older men to help him do this unwanted recruiting job.

The news of a new war recruiter was confirmed by everyone who went to the mill that week. They learned that John Stone had already packed up his belongings and headed back home.

On Thursday of that week a tall, ruddy-faced man wearing a tattered gray uniform came riding up to the mill. He was accompanied by two younger men who looked to be showing signs of suffering from three years of wartime wear and tear. They dismounted and headed to the mill's front door.

"I need grain and hay for these horses," the tall middle-aged man shouted demandingly to Raymond as he kicked the door open. "We've been on the road for several days and we're tired as hell," he said in a deep gravelly voice.

Raymond responded by lifting a bag of wheat bran and handing it to him.

"I don't believe we've met before, have we?" Raymond asked. "Are you new around here or just traveling through?"

"We've come from another county to help straighten you people out," the tall, rude man said to Raymond. "I'm the new war recruiter and these here are my helpers," he grunted. "All you draft-dodging sissies and war cowards are going to have to shape up, and we're here to see that you do."

Raymond never doubted for a minute that this was Skully. This gruff, uncouth man didn't give his name nor did he introduce either of his two sidekicks. But it was obvious that things were about to take a turn for the worse in this community. Raymond smelled real trouble here.

Skully was six feet two inches tall and weighed almost two hundred pounds. It was obvious that he'd not suffered from lack of food as many of the Southern families had during the past couple of years.

His two partners, Ralph and Floyd, looked as if they had not weathered the war as well as Skully. They seemed to fear Skully's commands the way a slave loathes his master. But their obedience to him was similar to the way a rabbit hound responds to his owner. They kept their steely eyes zeroed in on him most of the time as though they feared and mistrusted his every move.

Skully wore a pistol in his belt on his right side and a knife on the left. His gruff mannerisms gave most everyone he approached the impression that he was the kind to reach for either weapon without second thought. And no one doubted for a moment that he might use them at the drop of a hat.

It was very obvious that all three of these new faces lacked the social graces found in most of the kindly rural families living in Randolph County at this time. In fact, Raymond described them as having "the poise of a grizzly bear, the manners of a hungry hound after an all-night fox hunt, and the disposition of a Purgatory Mountain rattlesnake." Their language was atrocious.

After an hour or so had passed and the three men fed their horses the wheat bran Raymond had given them and watered them from the creek out back of the mill, they then demanded a sack of cornmeal and a bag of bran to take with them. They didn't bother to pay Raymond for any of the grain they took. They only gave him a note saying the Confederate army would pay. Raymond knew this was worthless script. He already had dozens of notes like them, which he'd received from many other soldiers passing through. But he was helpless to refuse anyone who demanded grain in the name of the Confederate army.

Like wildfire in a tall pine thicket, the news of Skully and his henchmen spread throughout the community. And it soon became obvious why John Stone had been replaced by Skully as the recruiter for the area.

"This county has more draft dodgers, war deserters, and no-good scoundrels hiding out from the war than any other county in the Confederacy," Skully declared on several occasions.

He insisted that two hundred or more men and boys were hiding out from the war somewhere in the county. "We aim to find 'em all and send 'em off to the war," he declared. "They're no better than the rest of us and the army needs them so we can whip them Yankees. We aim to find 'em all and put 'em in the army or hang 'em."

They wasted no time getting started.

John Stone had failed to catch the two Macon boys who were both of draft age. They lived over near Deep River and had managed to elude the recruiter every time he went after them. They would slip out the back and run down to a thicket at the riverbank each time he tried to capture them. They would disappear into the thick underbrush and John could never get close, much less apprehend them.

Skully and his two henchmen, Ralph and Floyd, made quick work of rounding them up. They slipped in before daylight one morning. Ralph and Floyd scouted out the back side of the farmstead and stationed themselves along the path that led toward the river. Then Skully kicked in the front door.

As the two young men ran out the back of the house like a pair of scared rabbits, Ralph and Floyd intercepted them.

They tied the two boys with ropes and led them into town. They were forced to walk behind the horses like a pack mule tethered to a rope. Such a public spectacle would surely put everyone on notice that Skully and his boys meant business.

News of Skully's capture of the Macon boys spread quickly. Several other young men who had escaped being drafted began to get uneasy. Some left their homes entirely so they could not be flushed out at night the way the Macon boys had been. Two young men even turned themselves in and were sent off to Raleigh by Skully.

Another young man, who had been living in the cellar of his house, began spending his evenings digging a tunnel that led to a secret opening down near Deep River. He felt the need for an escape tunnel leading from his house. His neighbors say he was never caught.

Slowly but surely, Skully and his men rounded up nearly all the young boys sixteen, seventeen, and eighteen years old who had not been drafted. Those who weren't conscientious objectors were sent to Wilmington, North Carolina, for training or to work for the navy. Some of the older ones were sent directly to join a company of soldiers already in action. The conscientious objectors were sent to labor in the salt works or aid troops needing medical care.

Skully delighted in going after the Quaker boys. He had a particular dislike for people who spoke using words like *thee* and *thou*. He would harass them unduly and scorn them in public. By so doing, he had managed to get a couple of them to abandon their religious beliefs and join the regular army. But most of them held out for noncombat roles.

By the time Skully had been there a month, he and his men had rounded up nearly every boy in the southern end of the county who was sixteen or older. In so doing, he had established himself as a terrorist to be avoided. He seemed to take great delight in making a public spectacle of his activities.

There was now talk of lowering the draft age to fifteen. Nathan knew this meant that he could be Skully's next target. And Skully would be delighted that he could round up another Quaker boy and send him off.

It was now late in November. The county had already experienced several killing frosts, and Nathan and his family had finished harvesting their corn, beans, and pumpkins. They still had a few dried peas to pick. Harvesting of anything edible required more than just picking the items from the field. A good hiding place had to be found for everything or it would be looted and carried off by either the Northern or Southern armies.

Earlier they had dug their potatoes and turnips and hidden them in underground straw hills. Prospects for having ample food to get through the winter now looked pretty good.

Nathan and Rebecca sat on the pile of firewood they had just hauled in from the forest out back. The last golden maple leaves of autumn floated to the ground, and they could feel the air getting colder as a slight breeze rustled in the nearby grass.

"When do you think this old war is going to end?" she asked. "I'm getting terribly worried and scared, too."

"Don't fret, sister," Nathan consoled her. "There's no fighting anywhere near here. So far, there has not been a single battle fought in this county or even in nearby counties. We've hidden most of our food. They can't steal it all, so we won't starve.

"Folks are telling down at the mill that General Lee is almost ready to surrender," Nathan explained. "Surely the war can't last much longer."

They both sat quietly watching more withering leaves float to the ground.

"It's not the war that scares me anymore," she said. "It's Skully and those ruffians who ride with him. They don't seem to have a compassionate bone in their bodies. I'm afraid they'll try to harm you and send you off to the war. They don't have the right to do that, but there seems to be little to stop them. It's as though we don't have any laws that apply to them.

"I'm afraid of what might happen to Mother and me, too," she continued. "They have been bothering some of the girls over at Flower Hill. One of the men tried to get Malissa Brown to let him in the house while her family was away last week. She and her little brother were home alone. But she threatened to shoot him through the window if he didn't go away.

"And it gets even worse. I heard that Ralph forced one of the Wright girls to let him have his way with her. He caught her when she was walking home from Cox's Mill and threatened to send her fifteen-year-old brother off to the war if she refused his advances," Rebecca said with a tremble in her voice.

"They might make the same threat to me," she said. "What could I do if that happened? I would do anything to keep them from harming you, but I know it is wrong to compromise my virtue."

"We must not let that happen," Nathan explained. "Just be sure you're never in a place where one of them might confront you alone. We all need to stay as far away from them as we possibly can. Maybe the war will end soon and they'll go home. From now on we must all try to watch every move they make and be extremely careful to stay out of their sight."

"What do we do if Skully comes to take you?" Rebecca asked. She could not hold back the tears. "If Skully takes you I don't know what we'll do," she sobbed. "Mother hasn't been well since Father died. She worries a lot about us, the farm, and the war. Sometimes at night I hear her crying in her room. I think she's as scared as we are."

There was a long pause as Nathan collected his thoughts.

He tried to be strong as he consoled her. "We all have a lot to be worried about. But we'll pull through somehow. Surely this torment can't go on forever. Peace will come again, but only God knows when. The war will end and James will come home, I believe. Then we'll start to rebuild this farm and put our lives back together again. It won't be easy without Papa, but we'll manage somehow. We must be as strong as we can."

"I hope you're right," Rebecca said. "But right now I'm so confused and scared that sometimes it all seems hopeless. Just trying to rebuild our lives without Father is bad enough. But now having to worry about the war and trying to stay away from Skully and his men makes life almost unbearable."

Nathan put his arm around Rebecca to console her as she wept. He said nothing as they sat there on the woodpile for several minutes. He felt helpless, yet his upbringing told him to appear strong. He managed to fight off a large lump in his throat that made him want to cry with her. There seemed to be no words appropriate for the occasion that hadn't already been said.

News of the war grew worse. General Sherman was

making quite a name for himself as he destroyed the lives and sustenance of hundreds of innocent Southern families. And reports said he was coming to the Carolinas as soon as he finished his dirty work in Georgia.

Reports of further harassment by Skully and his men kept coming in, too. After finding most of the eligible boys sixteen years and older, he was now having a heyday rounding up war deserters. His reputation had now grown to the point that he was dreaded by the people of southern Randolph County the way a group of small animals feared a large predator.

He sent most of the deserters he caught back to the army. But he threatened to hang one of the Davis boys living in the northern end of the county. The young soldier had slipped in from his fighting unit in Virginia to see his wife who was expecting a baby soon. He planned to stay until the birthing and even had a note from his commanding officer.

However, Skully had a different idea. The hanging was set for next Monday if Davis didn't return to his unit by then.

Skully and his men were also turning their attention to looting. They called it "war procurement" but they were taking everything edible they could find on any farm. No one knew for sure if they were sending it off to the war. And reports of their forcing sexual favors from women were becoming more numerous, too.

This caused everybody to fear for his or her life in more ways than one. And naturally it called for every ingenious scheme imaginable to hide property. Several people built false chimneys in their houses. They sealed all their valuables behind these rock structures. After the war they would tear the chimneys down and retrieve their valuables.

One evening in late December, Nathan and Calvin had finished hiding everything for the night. They both felt a sense of fatigue and fear as they sat down for supper.

"I don't feel like eating," said Calvin. "I had a dream last night and it's been bothering me all day. I dreamed that James was killed and that Mother was very sick. Then I dreamed that just the three of us were left and Skully was coming to get us."

"Try not to worry," Nathan consoled, patting him on the shoulder. "You're upset. We're all upset. The war and the stories about Skully have all of us on edge. But we must have faith in God. We will survive and peace will come someday."

Over and over again Nathan had told his family, friends, and himself that peace would come again. But at times he doubted it. It was now getting harder and harder to console anybody.

That night Nathan lay awake for what seemed like hours. "Should I keep trying to convince people that things will be alright?" He asked himself this question many times as he tossed and turned on his straw tick.

It was very late when Nathan finally dropped off to sleep. Little did he realize that this was to be his last night as a free man for a while.

Just before dawn he awakened to a commotion outside. The dogs began to bark and it wasn't even daylight yet. This warning meant that somebody or something was approaching the house.

Nathan and Calvin sprang quickly out of bed and pulled their pants up as they ran to the window to see what was happening. They stepped in front of the window and peered into the darkness. It was too dark to see anything except a torch burning at the edge of the front yard.

Before either of them could get downstairs, they could

hear a heavy pounding on their front door. Then Skully's loud, gruff voice pierced the crisp predawn air.

"You two Quaker boys get your clothes on," the voice boomed. "You're coming with us. Get you a change of clothes and a blanket. You'll be needing them where you're going. Don't try to run out the back. My men are waiting there and will catch you."

A combination of fear and anger raced through Nathan's young mind. Should he do as Skully commanded and come out peacefully, or should he and Calvin grab their hunting muskets and try to fend off Skully and his men?

Perhaps they should try to convince Skully and his men to leave.

It took him only a few seconds to realize that he and Calvin would be no match for these thugs if they went for their guns. And he quickly realized that somebody could be killed if they chose to confront them. He also knew that he'd be placing the lives of Rebecca and their mother in danger if shooting broke out. Their choices were indeed limited.

So Nathan and Calvin did as Skully commanded.

By torchlight Skully tied Nathan's wrists together. Ralph did the same to Calvin. Then they tied a long rope to each of them and draped it onto their saddles.

"Now don't try to get away," Skully warned. "You're both coming with me to the recruiting station at Flower Hill, so don't try anything foolish. If either of you get away, we'll hunt you down like a fox and bring you back dead or alive."

Nathan pleaded with Skully to take him and leave Calvin. His mother and Rebecca begged him to leave both boys.

But it was no use.

"Shut up, and start walking," Skully yelled. "I aim to have you both." Then he mounted his horse and began walking, pulling Nathan along behind. "You can either walk behind the horse or I'll drag you," he said with a diabolical chuckle in his voice.

Neither Nathan nor Calvin resisted.

Their peaceful Quaker upbringing and fear for their lives combined to tell them not to fight back. Rebecca and her mother watched sobbing as Skully and his men led Nathan and Calvin down the driveway as if they were cattle headed for slaughter.

Chapter 3
The Long, Hard Walk

Nathan and Calvin both walked at a brisk pace as Skully's ropes tugged around their shoulders. Skully kept them moving at a rather uncomfortable stride all the way to Kemp's Mill, but there was nothing they could do but walk fast as he commanded. They took him at his word when he promised to drag them if they refused to walk.

When they arrived at the mill, six other young lads about their own age were waiting. These boys had also been captured and hog-tied before dawn by another recruiter from the northern end of the county. They were being guarded by a single gray-coated soldier and, like Nathan and Calvin, they were scared half to death.

Skully dismounted and demanded that Nathan and Calvin join the other boys where he ordered them to sit in a half-circle facing the guard. Then Skully demanded that Raymond Kemp fix the boys something to eat.

"These boys have got a lot of walking to do," he scowled. "They'll be marching to the recruiting station at Flower Hill today. Then they'll be walking on to Wilmington, so fix 'em plenty to eat, old man. We wouldn't want any of them to die on us, would we?"

"Wilmington?" whispered Nathan. "That's nearly two hundred miles away. Does he plan to make us walk all the way to Wilmington?"

"Shut up that mumbling back there, boy," shouted Skully. "From now on you'll be told when to talk. And somebody else will do the thinking for you. So keep your mouths shut and your ears open.

"And you, Quaker boy," the gruff Skully scolded, "I don't want to hear another word. You draft-dodging Quakers ain't no better than the rest of us. And where you're going it ain't gonna make any difference who you are."

Steven Lynch was one of the boys in the group waiting at the mill. He and Nathan had attended the subscription school together where they had been friends for a long time. They had visited several times in New Garden where their fathers had been delegates to the yearly meeting. Calvin and Rebecca had also attended the subscription school and become friends with Steven's sisters.

Soon Raymond returned with a large bowl of corn mush and a platter of salt pork. The boys all ate rather timidly. But they were glad to have their fill of familiar foods because they realized this could be their last decent meal for a while. They had no idea what the next meals would be like.

After the boys finished their breakfast, Nathan noticed that Skully and the Confederate guard were engaged in conversation over at the edge of the mill. So in a low voice, he began talking to Steven.

"What do you think is happening to us?" he asked. "Why do you think they've captured us like wild foxes and hog-tied us to walk behind their horses?"

The conversation ended quickly as Skully caught a glimpse of them talking and shouted in his harsh voice, "I told you boys to shut up. I'll tell you all you need to know when you need to know it.

"Back on your feet, Quaker boys," he yelled gruffly. "We're going to march over to Flower Hill now and meet some more poor wretched souls just like you." Then he cracked his long, black whip in Nathan's face, almost striking his right cheek.

It was quickly becoming obvious to Nathan that Skully had singled him out for special attention. This provoked both fear and anger in his young mind, yet he knew his best response was to simply follow Skully's orders, at least for the time being.

The frightened boys quickly hopped to their feet and began a very brisk walk right behind the Confederate guard's horse. Skully brought up the rear on his large chestnut-colored horse.

They arrived at Flower Hill a little before noon. And just as Skully had promised, twelve other young boys were waiting for them. They, too, had been rounded up before dawn and herded like animals headed for a cattle drive. They were sitting in front of a blacksmith shop. Two gray-coated guards watched them like a hawk eyeing his prey.

A third Confederate soldier wearing private's stripes on his tattered gray uniform was talking to a man who looked somewhat familiar to Nathan. As they walked closer, Nathan could see several faces he recognized among the boys. Thomas Cox, Herman Johnston, Joseph Steed, Edward Pugh, and others were familiar to him.

When they arrived at the blacksmith shop, Nathan recognized the man talking with the army private. It was Herman's father and by now the conversation was turning into quite a heated debate.

"That man over there will deal with you," the private shouted to him as he pointed to Skully. "He's in charge of this whole business so go ask him all your questions."

Skully rode over to where the two had faced off. Quickly jumping off his horse he asked Herman's father, "What seems to be the trouble here?"

"These men here have roped and hog-tied my boy, Herman, like he was some kind of wild animal," he explained with a tremble in his voice. "Then they marched him and these other boys over here to this blacksmith shop. What's this whole mess about anyway?"

Skully walked to within two feet of the man. He towered at least ten inches over Herman's father and looked down as he told him, "We've got orders from the Confederacy. They've got to have more men. Them Yankees is whupping our butts real bad and we have to send more fighting men or we're gonna lose this war. Gen. Joseph Johnston is trying to raise a big army to face up to that no-good Yankee General Sherman.

"That scoundrel Sherman is burning and killing everything in sight down in Georgia and he's coming back across South Carolina headed this way. He's killing women and children, burning barns, houses, and wheat fields. If we don't get ready to whup his tail when he gits here, he'll probably burn us all to the ground the same as he's done to them folks down in Georgia."

"But you can't take these younguns here off to the war," the man said. "They're still children. My Herman is just thirteen years old. And some of them boys over there are only twelve. Why, there's nobody in this bunch who's yet sixteen years old. Nathan York over there won't even be sixteen until sometime next year.

"The law says you can't draft boys until they're sixteen. And, furthermore, some of them are Quakers, meaning they're conscientious objectors. The law says you can't make them be soldiers if they don't want to fight. So you're breaking the law in more ways than one."

"They're already drafting boys fifteen years old and younger in some states," Skully said. "And things are getting grim in the South, so we gotta have more soldiers or lose this war.

"Law or no law, I got my orders," Skully scowled. "Jefferson Davis has done said he wants every boy big enough to tote a gun brung into the army and I'm here to do just that. I've already rounded up the scum of this county that's been hiding out in caves and under rocks. Seems like all you got around here is a bunch of war deserters, draft dodgers, and peace-lovin' Quakers too skeered to even shoot back at somebody trying to kill them."

"Well, I've already been in this war and got my left arm shot off," Herman's father pleaded. "And I don't aim to let you take my boy, what ain't yet dry behind the ears, off and git him killed. So, give him back to me so we can go on home."

"If you can still shoot with your right arm, then you oughtta be coming with us, too," Skully chided. "But either way you might as well forgit about your boy because he's one of our recruits now. He's going with us."

"Look, man, I aim to take Herman back with me," his father warned insistently. "Two of his older brothers have already been killed at Gettysburg. That should be enough for one family."

Then he stepped toward the group. At the same time Herman took several steps toward his father. Clearly a confrontation was about to take place. Nathan held his breath as he watched them.

Just then Skully reached into his saddlebag and brought out his long, black bullwhip. Instantly he lashed Herman's father across the chest with a loud snap. The keen blow cut into what was left of his severed left arm and knocked Herman's father to the ground. Blood began to ooze from the stump of his left arm. It had been a rather severe whiplash.

A deep groan followed by a very defined hush came over the crowd of boys. Herman's father lay on the ground, grimacing from pain and seething with anger. He stood up and started for his horse to grab his musket but quickly thought better of the idea when he saw Skully's guards raising their guns and pointing them in his direction.

Meanwhile Herman, who had stepped out of the group and headed toward his father, stopped dead in his tracks as Skully lashed his father with the whip. He quietly eased back toward the group as the incident between his father and Skully played out. He felt almost uncontrollable anger that quickly gave way to fear as he watched the incident. Then he reluctantly rejoined the group and waited to see what would happen next.

"This boy's ours now," Skully insisted. "We're taking him whether you like it or not," Skully shouted as he reached under his belt and pulled out his pistol. "The quicker you accept that the better off you're gonna be, old man. And as for you, boy, stay right where you are."

Herman's father began walking slowly back toward the blacksmith shop. The mixture of anger, fear, and hate that came over his face left an indelible impression on Nathan's young mind.

This man Skully is a beast, he thought. *He has fear and hate in his heart. He's not just an army recruiter doing his job. He harbors a feeling for all of us that will be hard for us to deal with. He'd just as soon kill us as look at us.*

Skully then instructed the guards to gather the boys into a large circle.

"Y'all saw and heard what happened," he shouted as his voice pierced the autumn air. "Let it be a lesson to you. You're all going off to war whether you like it or not. The quicker you all accept that the better off you'll be."

As he paced up and down the roadside, Skully shouted orders to the boys. "It's time you learned to march. For the next several days, you're going to be walking to Wilmington. You're all going to learn how to be soldiers sooner or later, so you might as well start now. Now form two lines out there in that road facing me," he commanded. He then showed them how to stand at attention to receive their orders.

"We've brought you here to make you part of the Confederate army. We need fighting men real bad. All of you are still boys, but after a few days at Wilmington, they'll make men out of you real fast. That's why you'll be sworn into the Confederate army and sent to the war. Now everybody stand at attention and raise your right hand. Higher. I want to see every hand in the air. I know you Quaker boys don't take oaths, but that makes no difference now. Just answer my question. Do you agree to help defend your families, friends, and land from them who want to take it all away from you? Y'all answer with a yes. Louder. I can barely hear you."

A weak yes came from the lips of several of the scared young men.

"Okay, that's it," Skully hollered. "I'm now going to declare you all soldiers in the Confederate army. You now have all the rights, responsibilities, and privileges of soldiers.

"Like it or not, you're now officially in the Confederate army. The army is at war. That means that any one of you who tries to git away will be shot as a war deserter. So don't try no funny business. If any of you happen to get away, then me or some other recruiter will hunt you down and hang you for deserting.

"It'll take you several days of hard walking to get to Wilmington. When you git there you'll be given guns and uniforms, if they have any to give you. Then you'll be trained for a few days, if there's time. They'll show you how to kill Yankees. From there you will be sent off to fight wherever General Lee needs you. General Johnston is tryin' to git up a big army to fight somewhere down around Raleigh or Goldsboro when that scoundrel Sherman comes up here from Georgia. So you'll all probably git to fight for him.

"Corporal Smith and Privates King and Carter here will take you to Wilmington. Private King will drive the horse and wagon up front. Corporal Smith will bring up the rear and Private Carter will guard the flanks. They'll both be on horses and they have guns and ammunition. So don't even think about trying to git away from them. If any of you want to be real troublemakers and try to get away from them, they might even tie you and make you walk behind their horse.

"They'll expect you to walk two abreast wherever the path and roads are wide enough. You'll need to stay bunched up as close together as possible. Remember, you could even meet up with some Yankee soldiers who might start taking potshots at you. So you best be careful and pay close attention to what you are told to do.

"If any of you try to escape, I've ordered these men to shoot to kill. If anybody should git away, I've already told you what will happen to you. Me and my hounds will take special delight in hunting down and hanging you Quakers if any of you escape."

Then Skully ordered Private King to feed the boys. He passed out some hard bread rolls and slices of raw potato. The scared but famished boys ate them without saying a word. The fear that had been instilled in their young minds now held sway over any other motivations they might have.

"It's more than two hundred miles to Wilmington," Skully told them. "It'll take you eight or ten days to git there on foot. Corporal Smith is in charge so he'll tell you when and where to stop, eat, and rest. You should have time to make it over to Cox's Mill where you can stay tonight. I've already sent word that you're coming and that if anybody there tries to break up our little party, they'll be shot for obstructing the army's movements.

"Now, remember, you'll be guarded day and night, so don't try anything funny. We need all of you to be fighting men, and we don't want to have to shoot any of you before you have a chance to become soldiers."

With this, Skully mounted his horse and cracked his big black bullwhip. He rode down the dusty road out of sight as the boys all lined up and started walking toward the east.

But make no mistake about it, his words continued to ring in the ears of the twenty young lads, who just one day earlier were living quietly on their farms with no thought whatsoever of being a Confederate soldier. They knew they were now prisoners of the army that was supposed to defend them and their families.

"My men will shoot to kill if any of you try to escape. If you do get away, I'll bring my men and hounds and hunt you down. Then we'll hang you as a war deserter." These words still echoed in each boy's head.

Each one of them did breathe a sigh of relief, though, at seeing Skully disappear over the horizon. They had all come to detest everything about him. His voice, his commands, his appearance, his manner, and his apparent delight in seeing a bunch of underage boys being marched off to war would haunt them for a long time.

I only hope Skully and his men will not harm Mother and Rebecca now that we're gone, Nathan thought to himself as he began walking beside Calvin. *I fear for them as much as for Calvin and me.*

Corporal Smith was a soft-spoken man just twenty years old. He said he had been in the army two years. He claimed he had been in a couple of battles and was shot in the leg, which caused him to limp when he walked.

Following his recovery from the war wound, Smith was assigned the duty of working with new recruits. He spoke mildly but with a firm sense of command in his voice. The authority he wielded would be enough to keep any of these underage new recruits from Randolph County, North Carolina, from misbehaving. There would be no need to resort to force.

"Stay close together and you can talk quietly," Corporal Smith told them as they began their walk toward Cox's Mill. "When we get to the mill, we'll find a place to sleep. Then I'll tell you more of what we can expect on this trip. If you don't give me no trouble, things will go a lot smoother. But if any of you want trouble, you'll find it."

These new Randolph County recruits arrived at Cox's Mill, located on a creek near Deep River, with still about a half hour left before dark. The surroundings here were familiar to several of the boys because some of them were related to the Coxes and had visited here many times.

Private King took three of the boys to help him and began cooking a large pot of dried beans with salted pork fat in them. The rest of the boys helped Private Carter spread hay from a stack on the floor inside the mill. This was to be their bed for the night.

"We only have six blankets," said Corporal Smith. "That means you'll have to bunch up together to stay warm. In the morning we'll stack this hay back where we found it. Of course, we'll wait until after our horses finish eating. Tonight the three of us will take turns guarding you. So don't anybody try to walk out that door."

After the boys finished eating their beans and pork,

Corporal Smith asked them to gather around him in a circle while he gave further instructions and rules for the rest of the march to Wilmington.

"We must make the trip as fast as we can," he told them. "That means we need to spend every possible daylight hour walking. The days are short this time of year, so we'll be walking only eight or nine hours a day.

"We'll cook mornings and evenings. During the day we'll eat what we have leftover. We'll try to walk two or three hours at a time and then rest for a few minutes. We'll rest near a water hole and near the woods so we can drink and relieve ourselves.

"Talk quietly. If we make too much noise, we might attract undue attention to ourselves. We could possibly even meet a Union army patrol. If we do happen to meet a bunch of Yankee soldiers, I'll give the command to take cover. Then everybody must scatter and take cover in the nearest thicket or brush pile. But when the danger is passed, we'll get back together before we leave. If you try to escape, remember we have horses and you're on foot, so we'll find you."

Then the boys all huddled quietly under the blankets on the hay-covered floor in Cox's Mill. They were too scared to talk except for an occasional whisper. Some of the younger ones could not hold back an occasional sob or whimper.

At daybreak the boys arose, fed the horses, and restacked the hay they'd used for bedding. Then they quietly ate the corn cakes Private King had made for them and repacked the wagon. They paid little attention to the heavy frost and autumn chill in the air.

The initial shock of this whole affair was now gone. Reality was beginning to sink in. What had been initial fright was turning into deep fear for some of the boys. For others a mixture of fear and anger was beginning to well up within them.

And the possibility of escape occupied all their young minds. They all walked quietly for the first two hours. It seemed that everyone was afraid to break the ice and be the first to speak. Then they took their midmorning break.

As the boys fell back into formation following the break, some of them began to whisper quietly to each other. Their guards did not seem to mind their talking.

Nathan noticed that Corporal Smith was trailing well behind them on his horse and that Private Carter stayed well toward the front of the column of marching boys. He figured that if all the boys started talking they would probably be out of earshot of both. And Private King couldn't hear them anyway, thanks to the rattling and clanging of the supply wagon.

Nathan told the boys to start talking among themselves. "If we have several conversations going at once, the guards won't know what any of us are saying," he told them.

Steven was marching just in front of Nathan. "What do you think we should do?" he asked Nathan. "Do you think there's any chance we can get out of this mess?"

"I'm afraid we can't escape without somebody getting hurt," Nathan replied. "They are watching us like a hawk over a chicken coop, so I don't see how we'd ever get away from them."

Neither of them spoke for several minutes.

"Even if we did get away, where would we go?" Nathan asked Steven. "If we go back home, Skully will catch us and kill us. I think he meant it when he said he'd gladly hunt us down and hang us for war deserters."

"But I feel so helpless," said Steven. "I don't think I can stand being put into a war to kill people. Maybe there is

some way we could get away and then go hide out somewhere until the war is over."

"Hiram Thompson has been hiding out in a cave
down at Deep River for two years," Nathan said. "Skully
hasn't caught him. Maybe we could all find a hideout as
good as his."

They marched on for another half hour without saying
anything.

"You may be right, Nathan," Steven told him. "If we
could just think of a good place to hide, we might be smart
to plan an escape. But it's going to take some powerful
good planning to get away from these Confederate soldiers
guarding us."

"Let's think about it for a while," Nathan said. "We'll
have to know every move we're going to make ahead of
time. And we'll have to get everybody organized and sold
on the idea first."

Nathan noticed out the corner of his eye that Private
Carter was beginning to watch him and Steven. He noticed, too, that he was moving his horse a little closer to
them in order to overhear them.

"We'd better stop talking for a while," Nathan told
Steven. "I think Private Carter is a little suspicious of us."
So they walked in silence for a while.

After the boys moved back into formation following
their noon break, Nathan and Steven exchanged places
with a couple of the other boys so they would be marching
side by side near the middle of the column.

"You and I are the oldest boys in the group," Steven
pointed out as they began walking. "If we plan to escape,
someone will have to take charge and keep everything organized. I've already talked to some of the other boys. They
all think you should be our leader. You know most of them
already and they respect you."

Nathan didn't answer right away.

In a few minutes he responded to Steven. "That's an awesome responsibility you're asking me to take. Some of us or possibly all of us could be killed or wounded. Then I'd have their blood on my hands—for the rest of my life."

"If we don't escape and we all go off to war, some or all of us may be killed," Steven reminded him. "Then we'd all feel guilty if we survived and others didn't that we didn't at least try to escape."

"We're between a rock and a hard place, aren't we?" Nathan asked. "Our chances are poor whatever we do. Even if only some of us survive, we may be better off trying to escape."

After a very long pause, Nathan agreed that he would be willing to take charge as the leader of the group, but only if every boy told him personally that he'd go along with an escape plan.

"We'll all have to stick together like cockleburs on a bear hide," Nathan told Steven. "It'll take total cooperation and a lot of guts to make this work. And right now I have no idea how we'll go about it."

"I'll do everything possible to help you," Steven promised. "We've got to make this work. It's going to be a long trip. I only pray that God will be on our side and help us through it."

Chapter 4
The Road to Wilmington

By the end of the second day, everyone was getting rather road weary. The initial rush of fear, which had gripped these young boys for two days, now was beginning to wane. Yet the ugly hand of fear still wove its web through every thought and action. Fatigue was slowly replacing fear as the dominant force for these twenty innocent young lads who'd just been yanked out of civilization and shoved into a whole new world. It was all beginning to take its toll in more ways than one.

The total uncertainty of the situation also made these lads nervous. The realization that their lives had taken such a turn for the worse was grinding at their innards like a bad case of intestinal poisoning.

Nathan could sense their fear because he, too, felt a gnawing inside. It made him feel like a small sapling being choked by a huge bramble briar vine. He could feel the gigantic burden of having agreed to be the group's escape leader weighing him down like a ton of handmade bricks.

As the group walked and took intermittent breaks, the boys continued to talk quietly among themselves. But the conversation usually meandered off toward such trivialities as how far they were from home or how much their feet hurt. Nathan felt a certain pressure. He knew that he must quickly present some word of encouragement about an escape plan.

Nathan continued to walk near the middle of the pack

as the extended trek toward Wilmington progressed. At each break he would ask a different one of the boys to walk beside him for the next part of the trip. This allowed him to question each person and get an understanding of how he felt about an escape plan. He thought it might also help him formulate a plan. He tried to learn as much as possible about each person and about how much the group could depend on each to carry out his part of such a plan. Nathan also needed to know the strengths and weaknesses of each member of the group.

Nathan explained to each boy the need for absolute secrecy. They must not talk among themselves where one of their guards might overhear. "If we fail to get every little detail exactly right, it could mean the death of one or all of us," he told each boy.

Several of the boys suggested that a kind of unofficial decision-making council be made up of Nathan, Steven, and Thomas. Since they were the older and more mature boys in the group, they could serve in such a capacity. As Nathan questioned the boys, everyone agreed that this should be part of the plan.

As he completed his fact-finding mission, things began to look clearer. Nathan could see that everyone was committed to an escape plan, and he also felt that each could be depended upon to hold up his end of the program. And the idea of having Steven and Thomas to help him make decisions eased his young mind considerably.

Nathan could even feel a bit of enthusiasm building within himself. Yet he could still feel a constant inward tugging. *If this plan fails and someone is hurt or killed, the blood will be on your hands—forever*, the small uncertain voice within him kept saying. His Quaker upbringing was now tugging at his conscience stronger than ever. This deeply ingrained belief that to kill another human being intentionally was an unforgivable sin just wouldn't let go of him. And he was uncertain about how his God would judge his decisions, which might lead to accidental death in this situation.

That one Quaker belief complicated nearly every escape plan he tried to formulate. He simply couldn't find a plan that would not risk killing their guards or some of the boys.

"I have no hate in my heart for these guards," Nathan told Steven as they walked along the cold dusty path on the fifth day of their journey. "Can you think of any way that we might capture all three of them and leave them so that no harm will come to them after we escape? If we should capture them, tie them up, and leave them while we escape, they might die before someone finds them."

"I don't know," said Steven. "We'll just have to find some peaceful way to make our break."

"Perhaps we should just keep our eyes open and see what develops," Nathan suggested. Steven and Thomas agreed. They quickly spread the word among the boys that they were working on an escape plan and that in time they would do the right thing. "But for now, everyone must be patient," the boys were told.

By the end of the sixth day, a new enthusiasm spread over the group. Just the decision to make a break for it whenever the time was right seemed enough to reenergize them.

Nathan then asked Thomas to serve as trail scout. He knew that Thomas had a nose for navigation in the woods because his well-developed sense of direction had paid off for them many times when they hunted in the brush and thickets over near Purgatory Mountain. Whenever they seemed to be lost on a hunting trip, it was always Thomas's clear sense of direction that eventually brought them out of the woods and safely back home.

Thomas was already keeping careful mental notes on the group's travel patterns. It was obvious that they were following the river road to Wilmington. He remembered that his father had told him and even showed him a map of how the Deep River and the Haw River flowed together in Chatham County to form the Cape Fear. Then the Cape Fear River flowed near Fayetteville and on to the Atlantic Ocean near Wilmington.

Thomas's sense of direction told him that they were walking southeast most of the time. He kept careful mental records of landmarks, noting where large creeks flowed into the river. He saw major turns in the road and paid particular attention to unusual farmhouses and little villages. He even spotted boat landings along the river.

Thomas asked a couple of the other boys to assist him in remembering certain landmarks. He would ask first one and then another to count steps between various landmarks.

When they came to where Deep River, which they had been following since they left home, flowed into a large stream, Thomas asked Corporal Smith, "Is this where the Cape Fear River begins? Do you know how many miles we've come?"

"No. Why do you ask?" the corporal questioned.

"I was just curious," Thomas replied.

Nathan overheard the conversation. He waited until Corporal Smith had turned his attention elsewhere and walked beside Thomas.

"Do you think he's getting suspicious?" Nathan asked.

"No," Thomas replied.

"Do you think we can find our way home if we do escape?" Nathan inquired.

"I think we can do it if we navigate by the river,"

Thomas said. "The river goes all the way to Wilmington. There is plenty of underbrush and I've seen only a few farmhouses near the river. We can probably stay hidden much of the way home by just walking in the underbrush along the riverbanks."

Thomas's appraisal of the situation was encouraging news to Nathan. Every escape plan that Nathan conceived seemed to have many flaws. He was about to conclude that it would be wise to wait until they arrived in Wilmington to make their break. Steven and Thomas agreed.

By the end of the seventh day, everyone was showing definite signs of physical fatigue. Some of the younger boys showed that their stamina was almost gone as they rubbed blisters on their feet. And their boots were beginning to wear thin.

By this time Corporal Smith as well as Privates Carter and King could see that their troops were becoming quite frazzled.

Up to this time the weather had been good. These early January days were usually quite pleasant as skies alternated between sun and partial cloudiness to keep temperatures within a tolerable range. Cool and sometimes frosty nights made for pleasant sleeping. The boys huddled under their limited supply of blankets on the ground or wherever they could find hay, piles of leaves, or sometimes even an unoccupied building.

But it now appeared that a change in the weather was imminent. Heavy clouds were blowing in off the coast and the temperatures were dropping rapidly.

On the evening of the eighth day, Corporal Smith directed his group to a large barn just a few hundred yards off the road. The farmstead appeared to be deserted.

They bedded down for the night. Everyone welcomed the opportunity to sleep on hay, even though it was dusty with mold, for the first time in several days. Most nights they had gathered dry leaves from the woods to make soft beds for the evening. Hay and a substantial roof were quite welcome as the threatening gray clouds hung heavy overhead.

Shortly after they bedded down, light rain began falling. As the evening wore on, the rainfall became heavier. An occasional leak in the roof caused various ones in the group to have to move their beds a few feet right or left to escape the constant drip, drip, drip. The shingles on this old roof were in obvious need of repair.

As morning broke, the rain was still falling at a moderate clip. Everyone woke up to the patter of raindrops and the security of a roof over their heads.

When Corporal Smith gave the wake-up call, the boys could sense a difference in his voice. They had noticed for the past couple of days that he and his two accomplices seemed to be mellowing a bit. Perhaps this was because up to this point the boys had been model prisoners and travelers.

As Private King and his detail of helpers finished their breakfast chores, Corporal Smith directed them to sit back down on the hay where they had slept.

"We're all worn out from traveling," he told them. "Some of you have blisters on your feet. We've made very good time up to now, so, with that cold rain falling, I think we should just rest here in this barn for a while. Maybe this weather will clear up soon."

Everyone breathed a sigh of relief as most of them thanked Corporal Smith for the favor. "He's a good man, after all," whispered Steven.

There was a small amount of conversation, but most of the boys just stretched out on the hay where they had slept.

The thought crossed Nathan's mind a couple of times:

Is it time to make a break? Could we possibly overpower the guards and tie them up? But as he visually surveyed the surroundings he couldn't see how it would work. Again he felt that his best course of action was to wait.

Soon Corporal Smith broke the silence. There was a warmth and possibly even a touch of empathy in his voice as he began asking questions to no one in particular.

"Have any of you ever been this far from home before?" he asked. Then his questions continued as he asked many things about the boys' homes, families, farms, and feelings toward the war.

"That recruiter back there who rounded you all up—I think you called him Skully—did you know him very well?" Then he proceeded to ask many questions about Skully. Finally he asked, "What was that he kept saying about Quaker boys? Where I live we don't have any Quakers, and I've heard little about them and their beliefs."

After a brief pause, Nathan began to speak. "Several of us were raised in the Quaker religion. Our families came over from Europe to escape religious condemnation. Most of them emigrated from England to Pennsylvania. Then later many of the Quaker families moved to Virginia. Some families then moved on to North Carolina.

"The Quakers were not very popular with the other settlers in these areas. That's mostly because we are a very peace-loving people and take issue with their warlike ways of settling disputes. We believe in turning the other cheek when a fellowman has wronged us rather than fighting back. And we don't believe in such concepts as an eye for an eye, a tooth for a tooth, or a life for a life. Some people call us cowards for that, but most respect us for standing up for what we strongly believe.

"Our families have been persecuted unmercifully ever since this war broke out. True believing Quakers do not join in the fighting but refuse to bear arms against our fellowman. And we've been scorned by many because, as conscientious objectors to war, we will serve only as helpers for the army. We do not support the war effort but we do believe in helping fellowmen who have been wounded.

"Skully kept calling us Quaker boys back there as his way of heaping scorn on us for being conscientious objectors. He swore us into the army without giving us a chance to object. He said that whether we like it or not, we're all in the army and that we'll all be forced to fight in the war.

"We're all under age and eight of us are Quakers. The law is supposed to protect us, but Skully says the law has broken down. It doesn't mean anything, so we can be forced to fight whether we like it or not."

Corporal Smith broke in. "What do you plan to do? Can you demand your legal rights when you get to Wilmington?"

"I don't know," explained Nathan.

"I have a Quaker question," said Private Carter. "I've heard that Quakers talk in Old English; you know they say 'thee' and 'thou.' Why don't you Quakers talk that way?"

"Some of our relatives do," said Steven. "My grandfather who came down from Cole Creek, Virginia, says 'thee' and 'thou.' And occasionally my father will use these words when he's talking with him.

"Grandfather once told me a story about when one of his sons was helping stack lumber. The boy dropped a heavy green board and mashed his finger. He jumped up, shaking and rubbing his bruised finger in obvious pain. Then his father asked, 'Son, what did thee think when thee mashed thy finger?' 'I thought ouch, Father,' came the reply. With this, Grandfather took the boy by the arm and scolded him saying, 'No, son, thee thought dammit.' Then his father found a switch and whipped him for thinking vulgar thoughts."

Thomas chimed in with another story. "I once heard of a peace-loving Quaker who heard a burglar in his house. He came down the stairs with a loaded musket in his hand to find the burglar holding his silver cup in one hand and a ham in the other. 'It looks like thee is stealing from my kitchen, friend. I would not harm thee for the world. But if thee doesn't put my silver and ham back where thee got them, then just consider that thee are standing where I am about to shoot.' Of course, this is just a funny story the older Quakers tell," he explained.

Private Carter seemed thoroughly amused with their stories. He continued to ask questions about how Quakers live and think differently from other settlers in the South. Corporal Smith was also amused by these tales. He even responded to Thomas and Steven's Quaker jokes with a big belly laugh.

By now nearly all the boys seemed to be shaking off most of their nervous anxiety. Perhaps a combination of the kindness their guards had shown them and the time that had elapsed since they left home both helped break the tension. They laughed at the Quaker jokes, too. The boys became very attentive, hoping this conversation might continue.

Soon Private Carter was asking more questions about Quakers.

So the boys alternated telling stories their parents, grandparents, and friends had told them over the years. Thomas told of the time that Lord Cornwallis had brought his men to the Quaker settlement called Cane Creek in Alamance County.

Bad weather caught him as many of his troops headed to encounter Gen. Nathanael Greene. They took refuge at the meeting house at Cane Creek. Members of the Cane Creek Meeting begged the soldiers to treat their property with respect.

However, Lord Cornwallis and his men paid no attention. They rode through the Quaker community taking pigs, cows, chickens, geese, turkeys, and about anything else they could find to eat. They then added insult to injury by using the Cane Creek Meeting house as their slaughter-house. They slaughtered both cows and hogs in the church-yard and laid the fresh meat inside the meeting house using the pews as cutting boards.

The filth and stench made it an almost unbearable sight for the Quakers, as the smell of decaying meat scraps and the stain of animal blood filled the room. But it was not their nature to resist with force. And even if they want-ed to resist, they were outnumbered by several thousand soldiers fully equipped for war.

The soldiers stayed several weeks at Cane Creek. It was partially the snow and bad weather and partly Lord Cornwallis's reluctance to march on to encounter General Greene that kept them in this area so long. The men be-came restless while they waited. So to keep them occupied and to help repay some of the damage they had done, his soldiers carried rocks out of the farmers' fields and built a rock wall.

There was a touch of poetic justice in that story. When Lord Cornwallis finally did march his army into combat, General Greene's troops defeated them soundly. The irony was that General Nathanael Greene was born and raised a Quaker. He later gave up his Quaker religion to fight for a cause in which he strongly believed. After his death, the city of Greensboro near where the battle took place was named for the famous General Greene.

Then Private Carter asked about the Quakers and their

part in the Underground Railroad. The boys all looked at each other as though this might be a subject best left unexplained at the time. Then they all glared at Nathan, as though they expected him to handle this difficult subject.

So Nathan thought for a few minutes. He then answered in a very noncommittal tone of voice. "We've heard about it, but it is a very secret thing. The adults don't talk to us about it much. They are afraid during this time of war that if someone talks to the wrong person about it they might be killed."

With this explanation, the boys all breathed a sigh of relief. They all knew very well that the Quakers played a big part in this movement. Some of them had actually helped their parents hide runaway slaves as part of the operation of the Underground Railroad. They knew that many slaves from several parts of North and South Carolina had been smuggled right through their area on their way to freedom in the North or Midwest. They had seen black families smuggled into their barns or homes at daylight where they would hide until dark. Then they would be accompanied by a couple of Quaker men, often hidden in a wagon covered with hay or feedsacks, to the next location.

The Quaker families had been the moving force in the Underground Railroad. The boys knew that some families were still being smuggled north, even though they were now technically all free.

The boys also knew that this was definitely not the time to explain to these Confederate soldiers what had been happening in their communities for years.

It soon became obvious to Private Carter that the boys would like to change the subject. They had talked all they wanted to about Quakerism.

By now the rain was beginning to slack off. They could

see the clouds hovering above them beginning to lift in the west. The boys were saddened, of course, to see the rain stop because they realized this meant they would soon have to hit the road again.

Corporal Smith gave the word to eat the food that Private King had prepared for their lunch.

After lunch they resumed their march. Naturally they dreaded having to walk in the muddy road ahead of them, but they were all grateful that they had been able to take a half-day off to rest.

The boys relished the fact that this rest stop gave them the chance to get to know their guards and get on better terms with them. Perhaps this would even make their relationship a little less tense. The thought even crossed Nathan's mind that this thawing of relations with their guards might help their chances of escaping. He would continue to look for any break that might help free the group from them.

As their march resumed, Nathan walked beside Calvin. He and his brother had become very close since their father's untimely death the previous year. They had their occasional disagreements, of course, but each understood the other very well and shared their inner thoughts in a way that few brothers do. This whole affair, the capture, the march, and the situation in general seemed to draw them even closer now.

Nathan felt that he must guard against any inclination he might have to be a father to Calvin. He knew he'd have to work at keeping a brother-to-brother relationship. Yet he knew he must guard against appearing to favor his brother at the expense of the other members of his group.

As they walked, Nathan talked with Calvin about several subjects. He told him that even though the boys had selected him as their escape leader this would not affect their relationship as brothers. He explained that he would have to guard against any appearances that he might be showing favoritism toward Calvin.

Calvin said that he understood and assured Nathan that he would not ask for any special favors nor would he do anything that might hamper Nathan's ability to lead the group.

Nathan pledged to keep Calvin informed of everything that he planned to do ahead of time. He also asked Calvin to keep his ears open for any signs of tension or unrest among the boys.

As the group continued its march to Wilmington, it became even more obvious that the three guards were softening their attitudes toward their prisoners.

Corporal Smith alternated letting some of the younger boys with blisters on their feet ride his horse while he walked. He even extended the length of their rest stops, while some of the boys were allowed to take turns riding the supply wagon with Private King. After all, it was daily being lightened of its load as this group consumed the food the wagon was hauling.

As the eighth and ninth days of the march passed, nearly all tensions seemed to have lifted. The guards were now all talking freely with the boys. And most of the boys seemed to have shaken that frightened-rabbit feeling that had gripped them so tightly for much of the trip.

Although no one talked about it, the group's acceptance of Nathan as their leader seemed to be solid. A leadership council composed of Nathan, Thomas, and Steven seemed to have evolved smoothly.

Many of the other boys had begun bringing ideas to them. They would often talk as though they themselves were a small army. They seemed to be planning a strategy for escape, much the same way a Confederate or Union officers' council would plan an attack on the opposing forces.

Nathan was elated that such complete harmony now seemed to exist. He knew that not having to worry about dissension among his followers would greatly simplify any escape plan.

Enthusiasm for an escape seemed to be building. Of one thing they were all sure: "This war is not for us. We'll have no part of it. We are willing to take whatever chance necessary to avoid being put into the ranks of the fighting men. We won't be hauled into battle—period."

With this overall spirit of togetherness, a kind of calm engulfed the group.

By the end of the ninth day, everyone was in total agreement with Nathan's plan. There would be no escape attempt until they arrived in Wilmington. They only hoped that the entire group would be kept together once there. If the group became scattered, they would have to reassemble before launching an escape. They also agreed that if members of their group got separated, they would try to set up a network to stay in touch.

Communicating with all the boys at once was now becoming easier. At night they all slept in a circle with their heads toward the center. Their guards stayed far enough away that the group could talk quietly without being overheard. The boys agreed to try to sleep in this same formation when they got to Wilmington.

Corporal Smith and his two companion guards had obviously decided that their twenty young captives would march peacefully without trying to escape. The boys sensed this and even talked of trying to silently slip away at night. But they decided this was too risky.

At the end of the ninth day, Corporal Smith told the boys he expected to arrive in Wilmington by noon the next day.

The boys noticed that they were now walking through a lot of wet, swampy areas. And the flat land was quite a change in scenery from those rolling hills where they grew up back in Randolph County.

Shortly after noon on the tenth day after the boys left home, they arrived at the Confederate training camp alongside a large body of water near Wilmington. This makeshift compound had been erected in a hurry. It was a shabby encampment to say the least.

As they arrived, they were first stopped to be checked in. They were sent to an old warehouse-type building that had been pressed into military service. There they were crowded into this huge windowless building with several hundred other boys. Most of them were also young and unwilling recruits, just like this Randolph County group.

No one in the group doubted for a minute that they could and would escape. It was possible, but would not be easy. They just needed a few days to figure out the details, but they all knew that it was only a matter of time until they'd be headed back to their homes and to freedom.

Nathan only hoped that none of them became too eager and prematurely tried an escape on his own without waiting for the rest of the group.

Chapter 5
The Escape

Somehow things in Wilmington appeared different than Nathan had expected. There were marshes everywhere and the land was flat and swampy. Tall marsh grass could be seen in every direction. But the thing that stumped these Randolph County boys most was the fact that oak trees still had green leaves in winter. They had never seen live oaks before.

Those trees were hanging full of Spanish moss, another sight that was new to these boys from the hill country. The most awesome sight, though, was their first glimpse of the Atlantic Ocean.

"This land is a far cry from what we have in those rolling foothills back home," Thomas observed as the boys gazed in first one direction and then the other. "We're going to have to think our plan very carefully or we may get caught up in mud and swamps. We might even have to do some swimming."

Corporal Smith marched the boys to an area surrounded by a series of small buildings. These were makeshift storage structures, which earlier in the war had been used for holding guns, ammunition, and supplies. Beside them was a large warehouse-type building. The entire compound was enclosed by a shabby wooden fence made of sawmill slabs. Most of them were nailed vertically to horizontal runners fastened to shaky wooden posts.

With little fanfare Corporal Smith turned the boys over to their Wilmington command. He handed the list of names, which Skully had given him, over to the graycoated officer in charge.

The boys could detect a note of empathy and compassion in his voice as Corporal Smith turned to his group still standing at attention and said, "Thank you all for being so cooperative. You've been a good group. Hopefully our paths will cross again sometime after the war. Now all you Quaker boys stick tight to your beliefs. May God protect you. And let's hope this war is over before you're put to any real tough tests."

With this, he and Private Carter turned their mounts 180 degrees and rode off through the gate. Private King had already left the group and taken his horses and wagon to the stables behind the compound.

Nathan and most of the other boys could detect an uneasy feeling coming over them. As Corporal Smith disappeared into the haze of dusk, they sensed a loss of a friend of sorts. The familiar face they'd come to know and respect was now gone. But most of all, they could feel a tugging inside of gross uncertainty.

"What's going to happen to us next?" Herman asked in a low, muffled voice. "I'm scared and mad, too. For a little, I'd make a run for it tonight."

Nathan, who was standing only a couple of yards behind him, whispered to Herman, "Just take it easy for a little while longer. Everything's going to be alright. You could get yourself shot doing something foolish. We'll all make our break together when the time is right."

But no amount of consoling could do much to calm Herman. He, like all the other young lads in the group, just needed time to adjust. Nathan knew that after being turned over to the Wilmington command, the boys all had

an apprehensive feeling. He hoped it would not completely overtake them.

The guards who had delivered them were now gone.
At least they had managed to build a small amount of rap-
port with them during the days they'd spent together traveling. Now these young men were being tossed into the
hands of total strangers again. They had no idea of what
might lie ahead as these Confederate training officers in
Wilmington took total control of their lives.

Then the sergeant in charge of receiving new recruits
talked with the boys for a few minutes. He explained
where they were to go next and then sent them inside the
large warehouse building to wait for further instructions.

Nathan had told the boys at their last rest stop to stay
together at all times if possible. They would tell absolutely
no one of their plans to escape. The word would come from
Nathan, Steven, or Thomas when it was time to make a run
for it.

There were no windows in the warehouse, only a couple of small holes in the shabby walls. This could certainly
hamper their escape plans. But Nathan had already noticed that security was extremely relaxed around the compound. He observed that escape would be easy if they
were only allowed to stay outside the building for an extended period of time.

The boys sat in a small huddle in one corner of the
large building. There were bedrolls in other parts of the
building indicating that others were also using this warehouse for sleeping quarters.

After thirty minutes passed, the large warehouse door
opened. A short blond man in his early thirties walked in.
His loose-fitting gray uniform had sergeant stripes on the
sleeves.

"I'm Sgt. Alfred Butler," he announced. "I'll be your

training officer while you're here in Wilmington." His voice was firm and his manner stern. However, he seemed calm to these boys compared to Skully's tirades a couple of weeks earlier.

Sergeant Butler commanded his new recruits to step outside the warehouse. Then he asked them to form three lines. As they lined up and stood at attention, he walked down each line pausing in front of every boy to ask his name and age.

After his review of the new troops, Sergeant Butler asked Nathan, Steven, and Thomas to step forward. "You boys are the oldest, so each of you will be a squad leader," he said. "There will be two squads of seven men each and one of six. You will be responsible for seeing that my commands are carried out during these next few days while you're here in training." With this, he had each squad leader step back at the head of his squad.

Sergeant Butler's commands and demeanor abruptly changed and sent a feeling of uneasiness over the group. Nathan was having mental reruns of Skully grabbing him and Calvin. He could almost feel mental flashbacks of the ropes being tied to his wrists and then being forced to march behind Skully's horse.

Nathan could see in his mind Skully and his men harassing his mother and Rebecca. And he even conjured up scenes of these ruffians making passes at Sarah Pugh. Their relationship was not a real serious one, but Nathan had claimed her as his girlfriend. They had often been together at picnics and other outings down at the meeting house. Nathan could even envision one of these men trying to rape her. He knew that if Skully and his men had considered the law null and void in order to capture and recruit twenty underage boys, he would not respect any other laws either.

These unhappy scenes burst from his mind like bubbles as Sergeant Butler yelled, "Ten hut. Now face right. Forward march."

As the group starting marching, they could hear their drill sergeant barking out commands like a hunting hound that had just treed a coon. He was running up and down beside the greenhorn recruits and shouting with glee. "Lynch, get in step. Cox, what's the matter with you? Ain't you ever marched before? No, I don't want to hear any backtalk. Just keep marching."

After nearly an hour, the sergeant called his troops to a halt.

"You fellers are hardly dry behind the ears," he shouted. "But we ain't here to baby you none. We're gonna make men out of you and we're gonna do it in a hurry.

"You're a shabby-looking bunch with those tattered clothes you're wearing. We don't have enough gray uniforms to suit up all of you, but more are on the way. Some women are sewing them now and we hope to have new uniforms for you in a few days. In fact, the sooner you get your new uniforms the quicker you'll be ready to get out of here and join the real action.

"Those old clothes you're wearing smell and look like dog beds. Tomorrow we're going to take them off and wash them. You'll each be given some soap and water and a blanket to wrap your skinny bodies in while they dry. As soon as your new uniforms arrive, we'll throw all these old duds away."

The training drill continued for two more hours. Then darkness began to fall over the camp. Sergeant Butler marched his men to the mess tent and ordered them inside.

Inside the tent the boys sat down to the best meal they'd had since they left home. They were all very tired and hungry, and this was the first time they'd tasted fresh fish in a long time. They even had butter to go with their corn cakes. It was a real gastronomical delight for these tired, famished young men.

By the time the boys finished eating, Sergeant Butler was yelling. "You young punkin'-heads fall in line and march back to the warehouse," he shouted. "As soon as we're finished with you, we'll let you bed down for the night. Y'all got a tough day coming tomorrow."

As the group entered the warehouse, they were surprised at what they saw. Inside were several hundred other recruits. They soon learned that most of them had been brought in for training, many involuntarily, and were awaiting the same fate as the twenty underage boys from Randolph County.

As Nathan's group came into the warehouse, they were each given a blanket. Sergeant Butler asked them to find an area on the side of the building and sit down in a circle. He soon began to talk in a rather stern tone of voice.

"Them Yankees is really bearing down on us," he said. "We've whupped their tails in several battles. But they've kicked us around in a lot of others. We've lost a lot of men and that's why we're gonna train you as quick as we can. Y'all got a lot to learn about soldiering, and we aim to teach it to you in a hurry. We don't have much time. We've gotta get you boys out killing Yankees as soon as we can. After you've been here a couple of weeks, we'll give each of you a musket and send you out to help fight this war.

"There's been some talk about General Lee's being ready to surrender to the Yanks. Don't you believe a word of it. We ain't beat yet and you boys are gonna help run them Yankees back up north where they belong. Them no-account scoundrels got no business being here in the first place. You're gonna help run them home or kill them all trying. Then they might leave us Southerners alone.

"Tomorrow we're gonna show you boys how to kill Yankees. In two weeks, we'll have you hating Yankees so bad you'll want to kill them all. You'll want to make General Lee and Jefferson Davis proud. From now on you have just one thing on your minds. You're gonna eat, sleep, and dream about hating and killing Yankees.

"Anybody got any questions about that?"

Nathan felt the need to speak up. But then he quickly realized that since his group was committed to escape he should keep his mouth shut. Herman, who was standing beside Nathan, squirmed as though he might speak. Nathan quickly nudged him with his left hand, signaling an all-quiet order.

"Now it's time to hit the blankets. The bugle blows at daylight. You boys will all be dressed and ready for breakfast ten minutes after the bugle blows."

As the boys got ready for bed, they each sprawled out on the floor in a wagon-wheel arrangement. Each boy had his head toward the center. They could then talk quietly without being overheard.

"Hate Yankees, kill Yankees! Hate Yankees, kill Yankees!" These words just kept running through Nathan's brain. They tore at his conscience and made him feel limp all over. He could not sleep. *I just can't do it*, he kept repeating in his mind. *We absolutely must get out of here. We've got to have a plan and soon.*

As soon as things quieted down, Nathan began to whisper to Steven and Thomas. They, too, shared his enthusiasm for an immediate escape plan.

"I believe we'll be able to get out of here without anybody getting hurt," Thomas explained. "But we've got to do it in the next two days."

"We're with you," Nathan assured him.

"Yeah, we've gotta leave here before they suit us all in

uniforms and take away our civilian clothes," said Thomas. "If we leave here with nothing but army uniforms to wear, we don't stand much of a chance. We just have to make our break before they put us in those gray-coat uniforms."

"Either of you got any ideas about how's the best way to make a break?" Nathan asked them.

"I believe we can just slip out the back and head for the fence," Thomas said. "Since that door does not close completely, I think we can just slide it back and make a small crack in it. Then we can all slip through the crack one at a time and head for the back fence. There are holes everywhere in the fence.

"There is only one guard out there. He walks the fence only once every hour or so. We could all slip outside this building before midnight and then head for the fence as a group when he's on the other side of the compound."

Thomas was so sure of his plan that he agreed to make a dry run of it that night.

An hour later he returned. "It'll work," he said. "But we'd best wait until tomorrow night to do it. We'll have to wait until the guard has walked past the fence behind our building to make our break."

"Do you think we should try to slip past the guard or can we just jump him from behind?" Steven asked.

"Slipping out past the guard is safer," explained Thomas. "As soon as we get through the back fence, it's only about a thousand feet to the edge of the swamp. If we turn right and walk along the water's edge for about a mile, we'll come to a large live oak tree hanging full of Spanish moss. There's a lot of undergrowth so we can hide. We should go one at a time and wait for the group at the big live oak tree."

The plan sounded good to Nathan and Steven.

"We'll use the buddy system. A younger boy will be

teamed with an older one. This will reduce the chances of someone's getting lost. If some of us get lost, we'll try to hide out and gather down at the big live oak tree the next night. We'll use the whippoorwill call to locate each other at night and the bobwhite call during the day."

Then the three of them agreed to spread the word the next day so that everyone in the group knew all the details of how the plan was to work. They would make their break tomorrow night unless some hitch developed.

It was agreed that each boy would take his blanket with him. He would also take any other supplies, food, or extra clothing he might find.

"We won't have any gray uniforms for several days," said Steven. "I overheard Sergeant Butler telling another sergeant that today. Some of us have holes in our clothing, but we'll just have to risk it. We certainly don't want any of us wearing soldiers' uniforms."

Just as promised, the bugle blew at daylight the next morning. And in ten minutes the twenty new recruits stood at attention as the Confederate battle flag was raised up the crooked wooden pole over the training camp.

Sergeant Butler had his men line up in squads on the dirt street in front of the building. Then he and the other drill sergeants reported to the captain who was in charge of training for the post. The training leader reported to the post commander that he had 402 men available for training that day.

Nathan was standing close to the front since he'd been appointed leader of the first squad of Sergeant Butler's platoon. He could hear all of what the commanding officers were saying. He could hear the training officer tell the sergeants to take their men to the mess tent.

"Feed them and then show them how to kill Yankees,"

he told them. "We've got less than two weeks to get these boys ready to kill Yankees."

"Hate Yankees, kill Yankees! Hate Yankees, kill Yankees!" All day long, that's all the young recruits heard. Nathan felt like he wanted to throw up. How could anyone hate another human being this way? How could anyone want to kill his fellowman regardless of whose side he was on?

Perhaps this was all Nathan and his friends needed to totally confirm in their minds that escape was the only hope for preserving their dignity. It was their only chance of dealing with their collective conscience.

Nathan had once thought of pushing the conscientious objector issue with the training officer. However, this day had confirmed for him that this would not be necessary. Escape was to be their only alternative.

This day had started out foggy but soon turned balmy and partly cloudy. Except for a brisk wind blowing in off the ocean, it was quite comfortable.

As the day wore on and the boys marched from place to place, they all studied their surroundings carefully. The mental maps they were drawing could help them as they escaped.

The boys all saw the big live oak tree filled with Spanish moss in the distance. They also observed that the swamp was almost empty. None of them were familiar with rising and ebbing tides. Thomas had only read about them in school.

Later that day the boys were given a break. Thomas made it a point to talk with a young man he'd talked with at breakfast. His name was Alan James and he had lived along the coast all his life. Thomas knew Alan could tell him about the tides and how they worked.

His newfound friend quickly explained the whole scheme of the seas and the tides. He told Thomas how this rising and lowering of water levels affected the surrounding swamps, canals, bays, and streams.

"Does the tide change at the same time every day?" Thomas asked.

"No, but we who live here know the approximate time of high and low tides each day."

"When is low tide today?" Thomas asked.

"About two hours after dark."

"Will it be the same tomorrow and the next day?"

"Yes," Alan replied.

When Sergeant Butler commanded the boys to fall in for marching, the wheels started turning in Thomas's head. *We can use the tides to help us get away once we leave the compound*, he thought.

Once the group assembled at the big live oak tree, they would quickly head across the swamp at low tide. They would then be able to travel a good distance before anyone could give chase, thanks to the incoming tides. Thomas even chuckled to himself as he mentally compared himself to Moses leading the Israelites in crossing the Red Sea and seeing the Pharaoh's army trapped by the incoming waters.

"I'll bet there are a lot of fish in these waters," Thomas asked his new friend during the next break.

"Yep, if you know how to catch them. There are a lot of fish that are good to eat this time of year."

"How is the best way to catch them?" Thomas asked.

"You can spear 'em, hook 'em, or net 'em," Alan said. "Many kinds will soon be waking up after the long winter and they'll bite almost anything you use to bait a hook. Some kinds will start to lay their eggs soon. They will make beds and lay their eggs near the edges of streams and swamps. You can net or spear them easily at that time."

"What kind of spear do you need?" asked Thomas.

"A sharp stick will work if you know how to do it," Alan explained.

Little did Alan realize that he was giving Thomas a lesson in swamp survival. Thomas knew there would be a tough time ahead and that he and his friends would have to survive off the land as best they could once they sprang free of their military prison walls.

"If you can find the right streams, the herring will run upstream soon," Alan told him. "You can catch them with your hands or a net made from the shirt off your back if you work it right. They are bony little fish but easy to catch, and they taste very good when cooked right."

Thomas went on with his questioning. "What kind of game is good to eat around here?"

"Possums, coons, rabbits, ducks, geese, quail, turkeys, and deer."

"I understand that deer are not as plentiful as they were before the war because a lot of them have been shot by hungry soldiers."

"The soldiers have shot a lot of the big animals that used to be here in great numbers," Alan said. "They've shot a lot of the bear, deer, and even some elk and antelope that once roamed these woods. Why are you asking me all these questions?" he queried.

"Oh, I've heard that it's hard to find food around here," Thomas replied. "When we leave here we'll need to know these things. I've heard that the Confederate and Union troops have both taken nearly all the hogs, chickens, cattle, sheep, and other meat animals around these parts."

Alan then admitted to Thomas that he suspected that Thomas might be planning an escape and needed to know all these things to survive. Alan told Thomas that he and several of his friends had also been illegally recruited.

They, too, were under age. Alan and his friends had not been rounded up like the Randolph County boys were, though. They were simply told to board a train and go to Wilmington. They had not been told they were being recruited into the army. They thought they were going to work to help out some friends of their family who lived nearby. There had not been a brutal recruiter such as Skully to deal with. But Alan and his friends felt they had been tricked into joining the army, and they saw no place for themselves in this brutal war.

"You Randolph County boys planning to escape?" Alan asked.

Before he could answer, Thomas remembered the pledge his group had made not to discuss escape with anyone.

"Looks to me like anybody who wanted to get out of here could do it without much trouble," Thomas told him. "And the way these training sergeants are talking, everyone who stays here is doomed. What do you think, Alan? Would it be possible to escape?"

"I believe anyone who sets his mind to it could walk right out of here with no trouble at all," Alan answered. "However, if anyone does get caught trying to get away from this place, the sergeants would get a lot of pleasure from hanging him as a deserter."

"Yes, they'd probably take glee in making an example of someone," Thomas agreed. "But when it comes to making a choice between being killed escaping, shot in war, or getting killed by a recruiter back home who hates us, escape doesn't look all that bad."

As the troops fell back into their lines for training, Thomas was thinking that he may have talked too much about a possible escape. What if Alan talks to someone about an escape plan?

Meanwhile Alan was thinking of the possible ways he might plot out an escape plan for his group.

Later that evening Thomas felt that he must tell Nathan and Steven about his conversation with Alan. And as he expected, they were both angry. But they soon got over it as they began talking about their escape plan.

"I believe everything is right for us to make a break tonight," Nathan said. "The moon is almost full so we can see the fence and those marshes. Sergeant Butler loaned some new coats and trousers to several of our boys today until the uniforms arrive. And we've gathered up some extra food. It is hidden out by the back fence near those two loose boards.

"After everyone else has gone to sleep, we'll begin slipping out one by one. Then we'll gather outside and wait for the guard to pass. After he's gone by, we'll all head for that hole where those loose boards are. Then it's on to the big live oak down at the swamp.

"If we see a guard anywhere outside that fence, we may have to sneak up and surprise him from behind," Nathan said. "We'll just tie him up and leave him. We'll have to be very quiet about it."

Shortly after dark Thomas, Nathan, and Steven sat together at the end of the building. Nathan and Steven quietly talked over the plans. Thomas sat quietly as they talked.

"Say, is something wrong, Thomas?" Nathan asked. "You're not about to chicken out on us are you? Are you scared that this might not work?"

"No, I'm not scared and I'm not about to chicken out," Thomas said in a tone of voice that could be heard some distance away.

"Shh! Someone might hear us," Nathan warned. "Well, what's the matter?"

"I'm really disgusted that I may have let the word out

to Alan," Thomas said. "I should have kept my big mouth shut. But I've been sitting here thinking. I may be able to turn this whole thing in our favor. Would you both be willing to wait until tomorrow night to make our getaway?"

"I don't know," said Nathan. "What you got in mind?"

"Well, last night when I made that dry run I came back believing we could all sneak past the guard without being detected. I still believe that's possible. But I've been thinking more about that today, and I'm a little worried about twenty of us sneaking by him without being seen. I'm afraid someone might get hurt."

"Are you saying we should try to overpower the guard and tie him up?" asked Steven.

"No, but I believe we can work it out another way," replied Thomas. "Let's stay here one more day. Tomorrow I'll talk with Alan and ask him to help us. Maybe we can get him and some of his friends to distract the guards up at the other end of the compound. Then it'll be easy for us to sneak through the fence on this end."

"Think he'll do it?" Steven asked.

"I believe he will. It's certainly worth a try. And even if he won't help us, I don't believe he'll turn against us," Thomas said.

So Nathan, Steven, and Thomas agreed to delay their escape one more day.

The next morning Thomas spotted Alan outside the mess tent following breakfast. They walked together back toward their drill field, talking as they went.

Thomas explained his plan to Alan. "I don't believe you or your friends would be in any danger. If a few of you could just stage a small argument among yourselves near the guard as he walked by, that would distract him until we all cleared the fence. Five minutes would give us plenty of time."

"I'd like to help you," Alan said. "But after talking with you yesterday, I went back and talked with some of my buddies who came here in my group from Dare County. We decided to try to escape tonight, too. We think we can get away easily. Tonight we plan to jump the guard and tie him up. Two of our big boys, Caleb and Josh over there, plan to hide behind that clump of trees up there. When the guard walks by, they will jump out behind him and one of them will grab his gun. The other will put his hand over his mouth and then tie and gag him."

By this time Sergeant Butler was yelling for his troops to fall in for training.

All during the morning drill exercises, Thomas thought about how he could dovetail his escape plan with Alan's plans. He wondered if Alan's plan would help or hurt his.

Would we be better off to join them or just let them capture the guard and then take off in the other direction? he pondered over and over in his mind.

At lunchtime Thomas asked Nathan and Steven for their opinions on this.

Nathan and Steven both favored the idea of just riding piggyback on Alan's plan. They thought it best to just let the Dare County boys capture the guard and tie him up. Then all the Randolph County boys could just quietly walk off through the back fence as originally planned.

"This way we won't run the risk of being a part of any violence that might take place," Nathan confided.

As nightfall approached the entire group grew quite apprehensive. Hardly anyone spoke. It was as though everyone had his mind stuck in deep concentration on a single thought.

"Everybody just do as we've told you and don't panic," Nathan whispered as they all gathered back in the big warehouse building. The group sat quietly in a huddle and pretended to be getting ready for bed. They were lying in their usual circle with their heads turned toward the center. Each boy listened intently for any and every word that was being said.

Thomas explained that Alan would give a signal as soon as the guard had been captured. He would whistle like a seabird three times as a signal to his Dare County boys to move out. When Thomas heard it, he would tell the Randolph County boys.

Thomas and his buddy would give the word and lead off to the back fence. Then the rest would follow in pairs with Nathan and Calvin bringing up the rear.

Once the group had gathered down at the big live oak tree, Thomas would lead them across the swamp. They would go as far as they could that night. They couldn't afford to be caught on this side of the swamp at high tide in the morning.

Thomas sat in the darkness and looked through a crack in the wall. The moon was almost full. This helped him see the guard patrolling the fence outside. As the minutes ticked away, they seemed more like hours. Quite some time since he'd last seen the guard walk by.

"Alan and his boys must have already captured the guard," Nathan said. "It's been a long time since he last walked by here. But we better not take any chances. We better wait a few more minutes."

Another half hour passed. Still no signal had come from Alan. And still there had not been a guard walking by.

Thomas and Nathan agreed that since the guard had not marched in this direction in such a long time, he must have been captured by now. So they agreed it was time to move out.

Thomas gave the word to move out. Two by two the

boys gathered up their blankets and a few extra goodies they'd squirreled away and headed for the back fence. They all slipped quietly through the fence without disturbing anyone in the compound. Then by dim moonlight they slowly made their way to the big live oak.

The big tree with its flowing Spanish moss formed a silhouette against the moonlit sky, making it easy to locate. A gentle sea breeze blew through the Spanish moss as though it were the flowing hair of a guardian angel gathering her brood beneath the mighty oak. It was as if God was providing an unmistakable beacon under which His children could once again start their journey to freedom through the wilderness.

As the boys huddled under the boughs of the big live oak and formed a circle, Nathan counted to see if everyone had made it. They had cleared their first hurdle. Nathan was about to explain the value of being quiet for the rest of the night when the silence was broken by the distant sound of gunfire.

From the upper end of the compound, a musket shot rang out. Then a couple of shouts were heard. Two more shots were fired, followed by a brief pause. Then a volley of shots pierced the evening air. Once again the evening was quiet except for the occasional sound of ocean wind blowing through the trees above them.

"Oh my God," Thomas said, "Alan and the Dare County boys must be in trouble. I hope they got away. And I hope no one was hurt."

Riders and barking dogs could be heard heading out the north trail. This was the direction the Dare County boys would have been going. Thomas knew they had escaped, and he only hoped they were able to clear the area without being caught. However, he knew that their chances of escaping those dogs would be poor.

There was nothing that could be done for Alan and his friends now. The Dare County boys had done Thomas and his friends a big favor. They had succeeded in decoying the guards and their dogs and heading them in the opposite direction.

Thomas also knew that he'd better make haste in getting his boys across the swamp. Distance and a rising tide now seemed to be his best allies. Somehow he had failed to calculate that dogs might be used to help track them down. He was now thinking that if he and his group didn't have Alan's group as decoys, they would probably not have made it. He also realized that crossing the swamp was the best way to foil the chances of the dogs' being used to track his group. But they had to move out quickly.

Nathan, Thomas, and Steven breathed easier knowing they had now cleared their first big hurdle. But they also knew that enormous hardships lay ahead of this group of unseasoned young men who were now fugitives from the Confederate army. They knew that the obstacles ahead of them were going to try them in ways they had never been tested before.

Chapter 6
Homeward Bound

Thomas quickly led the group across the murky swamp. They waded in water up to their waists part of the way. He had already tested these waters though, because he had walked part of the way across the swamp when he did his trial run for the escape plan. But now he was mostly just following his instincts.

The distant sounds of hounds and riders chasing Alan's group soon died away. "I hope they didn't catch our Dare County friends," Thomas said to no one in particular. "But I suppose we'll never know."

After a half hour of sloshing and slogging through the muddy swamp, Thomas led the boys out onto a small roadway. They quickly recognized it was the same road they had traveled a few days earlier on their trek to Wilmington. Thomas knew the group shouldn't stay on the road for long because the chances of being caught there were much too great. He planned to walk on the road for a couple of hours and then try to find a good place to hide during the daylight hours.

Ideally he would find a way to get his group across the river. This would put them almost totally out of reach of any Confederate patrol that might be sent out from the training camp to find them. Thomas observed back at the camp that there were not many spare men or horses that could be used to hunt for any escaped recruits. He knew any search party would not be gone long.

The mile-wide river would give good protection from any recapture patrol if only Thomas could find a way to cross it at this point.

Thomas recalled seeing several boats docked along the river's edge as they passed this way on the walk from back home. They were only a few miles upstream from Wilmington, as he remembered. His plan was to continue on the road and try to approach the river near that boat landing. But finding that boat landing in the middle of the night could be a problem

Thomas also knew that his group of boys would have to get to the boats as early as possible. The fishermen who owned them would probably start their rounds of gathering fish from their nets and traps at daylight.

For most of the night the boys walked at a very brisk pace set by Thomas. A slight glimmer of light was beginning to pierce the eastern sky as he recognized what he thought was a path leading down to the boat landing.

As the weary travelers approached the river, small rays of light reflected off the rippling water. They could see the outline of a boat dock a couple of hundred yards upstream. They quickly made their way through the entanglement of underbrush and marsh grass to it.

Tethered to the side of the dock were two flat-bottom fishing boats. The boys approached them with caution. There was no sign of life, just the serene ripple of water against the sides of the boats and the pilings that hoisted the pier above the water.

Thomas quickly directed half of the group to climb into one of the boats with him. The other half got into the other boat with Nathan.

"Anybody know about rowing boats?" Nathan asked. "We've got several paddles but we're going to have to practice rowing together. Otherwise, we'll never get across the river."

With Thomas directing the rowing in one boat and Nathan the other, they untied from the dock and began paddling. After a couple of circles and ramming the muddy banks a few times, the group got the hang of it. They were all beginning to row in unison. And they were beginning to move across the river.

Seaworthy or not, they had to get moving. By this time, morning light had broken enough to allow them to see the distant riverbank. They were rowing cautiously and beginning to leave the shore behind.

A few hundred yards out from shore, Nathan could see the dock they'd just left getting smaller. As he glanced back to the path beyond the dock, he could see two men running and waving their arms. Then he heard them yelling.

"Get our boats back here, you thieves," he heard one of them shout.

Then he saw one of the men enter the small shed beside the boat dock and bring out what appeared to be a long-barreled musket. He quickly grabbed the ramrod and loaded. Then Nathan could see that he was taking aim at the boats.

"Everybody down in the boats," Nathan yelled spontaneously. "He's going to shoot."

The urgency in Nathan's voice left no one in doubt of the danger they faced. So they all quickly ducked down in the boats. Just then a shot split the water a few feet behind the rear boat, which Nathan was commanding.

Nathan quickly peeked over the back of the boat, which was now drifting in the calm waters. He could see only one man reloading his musket. So he demanded that everyone grab the oars and row fast and hard until he gave the command to duck again.

"Paddle as fast as you can," Nathan commanded. "It'll take him a few minutes to reload. We're almost out of his reach. Give those oars all you've got. If you don't have an oar, reach over the side and paddle with your hands."

The boat had moved several hundred more yards by the time Nathan yelled to get down again. The second shot landed in the water well back of the last boat. Nathan and Thomas knew they were now out of reach of their muskets.

The motley crews, which only a few minutes earlier had never even set foot inside boats this big, were splashing their oars in unison and making the vessels move rapidly across the stream.

Nathan kept an eye on the men on the bank. He could see that one was reloading. But he knew that they were now well beyond the range of any musket.

By now both boats had reached some swift-flowing water, causing them to drift rapidly downstream as they paddled hard to cross the river. Nathan could see the swift water as an advantage. It would quickly sweep them downstream away from any possible gunshots the men might fire. But the disadvantages had to be considered, too. First, home was upstream; they were headed in the wrong direction. Second, these currents were sweeping them back toward Wilmington and the open ocean. In fact, by the dawn's early light, Nathan could already see the outline of a large sailing ship downstream.

"We must keep rowing just as hard as we can," Nathan shouted over to Thomas and his crew. "We've got to get to the other side before this swift water sweeps us down to that ship or out to sea. We don't know if that's a warship or which army it belongs to. But we can't afford to be picked up by either one."

The boys continued to row at top speed. There were no more gunshots so they assumed the two musketeers had given up.

Soon Thomas allowed his crew to relax their rowing pace. They were all nearly exhausted, not to mention scared half to death. None of these young lads had envisioned having to dodge gunfire so soon.

In a few minutes Thomas noticed that they were drifting rapidly toward the ship downstream. They were close enough to tell that the ship lay at anchor. It was now getting light in a hurry. They could see the sun rising behind the ship, backlighting it against the open water.

"We'd better row full speed again," Thomas commanded. "We can't get too close to that ship. And the way we're drifting now, we're going to get mighty close if we don't move across the river faster."

"Couldn't we turn our boats slightly upstream and row partially into the current?" Nathan asked Thomas.

"Don't know," answered Thomas. "I'm not familiar with boats. But let's give it a try."

Although neither of them said it, both Thomas and Nathan were beginning to question in their own minds the wisdom of crossing the Cape Fear River at this point. They both wondered if they might not have been better off if they'd kept walking up the south bank of the river. But it was too late now. They were already in the middle of a mile-wide river, and they were drifting toward the ship that could capture them and send them all to their deaths as army deserters, or put them back into the war.

This was quite a predicament for twenty boys who were scared, tired, and becoming confused about life's fairness. None of them had ever crossed a river more than two hundred feet. That's the widest part of Deep River back home, as they could remember it.

The boys kept up the hectic pace of rowing and seemed to get their second wind or a surge of adrenaline as they saw the north shore coming clearly into sight. They soon moved out of the strong currents from the center of the river. The calmer waters nearer the riverbanks allowed them to relax their pace of rowing. They were no longer drifting toward the ship.

As they approached the shore, Thomas visually surveyed the area carefully. He could see no signs of civilization. There was nothing but thick underbrush, mostly live oak saplings and some occasional bulrushes. Soon Thomas had led the group into a small cove where they nosed their boats into the mud and marsh grass. The large cypress trees were now dormant. Large tufts of Spanish moss waved in the morning breeze as though they were motioning to the boys to land their boats here.

The boys quickly tied up their boats. One by one they jumped into the shallow water, wading up through the marshy juniper thickets and onto the shore.

The sun was now rising. Simultaneously the boys all fell onto the grassy banks of the river now being warmed by the morning sun. They were cold, wet, and totally exhausted from the experience and rowing exercise.

For the next half hour no one spoke a word. The combination of escaping, walking all night without sleep, and the strenuous rowing exercise had totally consumed their energy both mentally and physically.

Finally, Nathan broke the silence. "We've got to get out of here soon," he said. "Those men will probably come after their boats. We've got to be gone when they do. Let's move away from the riverbank first. We'll cut the boats loose and that way no one will know the exact spot where we landed.

"As soon as we're on higher ground and have found a

good place to hide, we'll see what we can find to eat. We have a little food that we scavenged from the mess tent. When we've eaten, we will then rest for a while."

Nathan got no argument from anyone on this plan. They would start to look for food, probably fish, later that afternoon when everyone had rested.

Alan had told Thomas about how many good things there were to eat along the river. So they would try to find some of them before they left the river's edge.

After spending most of the day resting and napping, the boys decided to search the riverbanks for food late that afternoon. Luck was with them. Just as Alan had instructed Thomas, there were plenty of fish and a few clams and mussels near the riverbank. Several of the boys made spears from sharp sticks they cut along the bank. Their methods were poor and their technique even worse. But with persistence, they were able to land several small fish they found sunning in the shallow waters of the river's edge.

They dressed the fish and divided up the raw meat. Raw fish was not exactly a delicacy, but they decided it was better than risking being spotted by smoke from a campfire. So they would eat the meat they caught raw for this meal and the rest of the trip home.

When you're really hungry and survival is the uppermost thing on your mind twenty-four hours a day, then raw fish isn't so bad, the entire group agreed.

"I just hope we don't catch an alligator." Herman laughed as he chewed a piece of raw fish and spit out the spiny sharp bones. "I've heard that rattlesnakes and alligators are too tough to eat."

Thomas thought it would be a good idea to experiment with different ways of catching fish while they were here. He had planned to navigate most of the way home by the river. If they could find ways to catch fish, they wouldn't go hungry as they traveled.

Later that evening after the boys had their fill of raw fish, they moved farther back into the woods away from the river. They found a good heavy thicket with plenty of pine needles nearby. They gathered up armloads of pine straw and carried it into the thicket. There they piled it up to form a soft place to bed down for the night. They would get a good night's sleep and then start their long trip home beginning at daybreak. Staying out of sight while traveling would be their big challenge.

As they readied for sleeping on the pine straw beds, the boys had their first chance to conduct a real planning powwow. This was the first time that Nathan had been able to get them all in one group to talk without the worry of being overheard or without being rushed to move on.

"We're in for some tough times ahead," Nathan told the group as they sat in a huddle around him. "There are a lot of obstacles between here and home. I believe we can handle all of them. But everybody absolutely must stick together.

"As you realize, we're all now classed as war deserters. That means that both Confederate and Union armies are against us. We can't run the risk of being captured or shot by either army. Our best chance is to stay out of sight of everyone, not just the army troops.

"And we'll have to find food as we go. We can't afford to risk being spotted by smoke from a campfire, so we'll have to eat any food without cooking it. Finding food isn't going to be easy. No wild plants are bearing food at this time of year. So we'll have to find roots, dried fruits, nuts, wild animals, and fish to eat. We might get lucky along the way and find some leftover grain in some farmer's field. But we'll have to be very careful about taking it.

"There are black walnuts, hickory nuts, and maybe even some haws and persimmons hanging on the trees. If we can find them, we'll be able to eat.

"We can't afford to have anybody hurt or sick on the way home. So let's all be extremely careful and stay dry and out of dangerous places. We have two small pieces of canvas that we brought from the compound. We can make a shelter from the rain when we have to. If we huddle close together we can stay dry under it.

"Everybody remember, if we get scattered we'll use birdcalls to get back together. Even though it's still a little early in the season for these birds to be calling, we'll use the bobwhite call during the day and the whippoorwill call at night."

Then Nathan paused for a few minutes.

"There's one other thing I need to talk about. When we left home a couple of weeks ago, all of you agreed that I should be your escape leader. If anybody has reservations about this now, let me know. Even though I did not solicit this job, I will be happy to do it. But only if all of you want me."

Without hesitation came the reply from David Johnson, "We're with you all the way, Nathan. Just tell us what to do and we'll do it." Then in unison the boys all agreed that Nathan should continue as leader.

"Thank you for the vote of confidence," Nathan said. "I'll do my best to keep us all together and safe.

"We need to organize. Thomas is doing a great job as our escape navigator. He may need help along the way. John, would you and Samuel help him with any details that might come up?

"Steven has agreed to be in charge of finding food. He'll need help, too. Nine of you will help him. Everybody will be on the lookout for food, but this team will do the special things it takes to procure it. Steven and his team will make concentrated searches for nuts, berries, game, fish, and whatever might be out there that we can eat.

"David, you and these three men will be in charge of shelter. You'll need to take care of our canvas so we can set up a tent when rain comes. You'll also need to look out for abandoned barns and buildings that we might use for shelter.

"Now let's all get a good night's sleep and be ready to travel at daybreak."

Everyone rested well that night. Nathan lay awake for a short while wondering if he should post a guard. It didn't take him long to reason that the group faced no immediate danger.

The boys awoke at daybreak and ate the corn cakes they had left from the compound. As light began to wash over the river and through the pines, they made their way out of the thicket.

Thomas led them along the riverbank, walking around the marshy puddles. He hoped to find a path or trail that would parallel the river. Soon he found a little path that widened as it went along the riverbank. Around noontime the trail merged into a wagon trail. It was still running parallel to the river just a few hundred feet away.

At noon the group decided to take a long rest. They had covered a lot of ground and were getting hungry.

Nathan asked if they would be willing to walk a few more hours before they made camp for the evening. They would then go on a food search. They all agreed that this plan made sense. So after a long rest, they resumed their walk.

After about three more hours of walking, the group decided to stop and make camp for the evening. The sun still hung fairly high in the western sky. The boys had traveled a whole day sticking to the river road. They had seen little sign of civilization. Whenever they would see a house or farmstead, they would get off the road and walk in the woods until they had passed it.

They found a steep bank down by the river and erected their two canvas tent halves against it. While David and his helpers were pitching the tent halves, Steven took his crew in search of food. They cut some sharp sticks to use as spears. They began trying to spear fish. But their fish harvest proved to be less bountiful than the day before, maybe because the banks were steeper here.

It was at this point that Herman stepped forward with his big surprise. In his hand he held two small fish hooks and a small coil of fishing line. He had found them under the seat of the boat the first time they had to hunker down as those musket shots were being fired at them. He had carefully rolled up the line around the hooks and brought them along.

Herman and Steven found a large round chunk of pine tree bark and carved floats from it. They cut poles from small saplings on the bank. A couple of the other boys began digging into the rich soil on the riverbank with sharp sticks. They turned up a few large earthworms.

Soon Steven and Herman had fishing rigs ready for testing. Each boy baited his hook with an earthworm and plunged them into the deep water off the riverbank.

Soon Herman's pine-bark cork began bobbing and went under. He quickly yanked out a large catfish. "This baby must weigh five pounds," he shouted.

"Shh, don't get so excited that someone will hear us," Steven told him.

But Herman had trouble containing his excitement. He quickly baited his hook and splashed it back in the water. Almost instantaneously the float began sinking and he tugged fiercely at it. Another catfish hit the bank. This one was bigger than the first one he'd caught. He handed the fish to one of the other boys and quickly baited his hook again. Again he tossed his baited hook into the water and quickly pulled out a large sunfish.

At this point Steven, sitting beside Herman, realized that he'd not even had a nibble on his hook while all Herman had to do was bait his hook and jump back. The fish were attacking Herman's hook and ignoring his.

"Herman, why are you catching fish and I'm catching nothing?" Steven asked.

"Don't know. Maybe you're not holding your mouth right," Herman laughed. "Or maybe some people are born fishermen and others are not. But something must be wrong. Why don't you pull your line up and let's have a look?"

Steven dragged his line from the water and up the edge of the riverbank.

"That's it," Herman laughed. "You're fishing with a skinny little old worm that has no sex appeal. The fish are just laughing at your skinny little old worm as they swim on by to bite mine. My daddy always told me never to fish with a skinny worm. So why don't you get one of those big fat juicy worms like I'm using?"

So Steven quickly put one of those big fat wigglers on his hook and dropped it into the water. With little hesitation he hauled in a big catfish.

In less than an hour the food team was cleaning catfish and sunfish for dinner. They had plenty so each person could eat his fill.

"I never dreamed that raw fish would actually taste good," Nathan said, chewing a strip of catfish and pulling a tiny bone from it. "But then I've never really been this hungry before either."

The others agreed with him as they attacked their raw fish like hungry fish hawks in a feeding frenzy.

"Steady, now," Steven told the group. "There's plenty here for everybody. We're not on rations today. If we eat all we have here, we can send Herman back to catch more. He's such a good fisherman that he has to stand behind a tree to bait his hook. And he never fishes with skinny worms."

Then Steven told the entire group about their experience. All had a good laugh. It was becoming evident that Herman's sense of humor was a valuable asset. It was also obvious that the group was gaining a lot of confidence in their ability to survive and stay out of sight. This could certainly improve their chances of getting back home unhurt.

Nathan felt a strong sense of pride and inner peace knowing that there seemed to be complete harmony within the group. And he also recognized that Herman's stability, which had been a question mark in his mind earlier, was not going to be a problem. From the time of the scene with Skully and Herman's father at the beginning of their capture, Nathan had felt that Herman was the one who needed to be watched.

After gorging themselves on the flesh of raw fish, everyone was ready for a good night's sleep. They all walked to their canvas lean-to and huddled in on top of the pile of oak leaves that had been carried in for their mattress.

"It's been a long hard day," Nathan told the group. "We've put a lot of miles behind us since daylight. Since it's getting cold, we'd better huddle close together for sleeping. With our bellies full of raw fish and a good night's sleep, we should have another good day tomorrow."

A heavy frost covered the ground while the boys slept. When the group awakened the next morning, the boys decided to wait until the sun had shown an hour before they began walking. The beautiful frost crystals covering the dried grass and trees glistened in the sunlight like a million diamonds.

"We're just like the Indians this morning," kidded Herman. "Grandpa said the Keyauwee Indians who lived over near Shepherd Mountain wouldn't travel when there was frost or even dew on the grass. They usually waited until the sun had been up for a couple of hours. They always told any white man who asked them that they had plenty of time to travel after the ground dried. But Grandpa believed they just didn't like walking in wet moccasins."

A couple of hours after dawn, the boys packed their few belongings and started walking. Around noon the sun's warm rays began to disappear. Layers of thin clouds soon gave way to heavier clouds. The skies grew darker. These clouds were blowing in from the coast.

As they walked, the wind grew colder and stronger. Gusts of wind pierced their ears and eyes causing an aching feeling. Some of them wrapped garments around their necks. Some wrapped their blankets around their shoulders.

"If it gets much colder, we could have snow," Thomas told Nathan. "Those clouds are looking heavy and when they sweep in from the southeast that means we could get a lot of snow. Do you think we should stop and try to put up our canvas shelter?"

"Let's wait and see if it does snow first," Nathan replied. "We'll just keep walking and if it does start to snow, we'll find a place and pitch our shelter. If the cold wind becomes unbearable, we may have to stop and take shelter."

By this time all the boys had pulled their collars around their faces. Some were wrapped in every garment they had. They all knew that heavy snow this time of year was not a normal occurrence, but it could happen.

For a couple more hours they trudged on down the road filled with ruts and mud holes. They did their best to dodge the wet places. Soon a few tiny snowflakes fluttered by them. But there were so few of them that Nathan didn't see the need to set up camp just yet.

"Let's keep our eyes open for something that would serve as a good windbreak," Nathan told the group. "If we can find a big rock or a steep bank, we can pitch our tent halves beside it."

As they continued walking, the snow began falling harder. The snowflakes got bigger and bigger. In the distance they could see a large farmhouse and a big barn out back. In a field near the barn, they could see three haystacks.

"Let's head for those haystacks," Nathan commanded. "We may be able to get out of this blizzard there. Let's slip along the edge of the woods and approach the haystacks on the opposite side from the house. No one can see us from the house that way. We need to keep quiet so they won't hear us. Sound carries differently when soft snow is falling."

Nearly twenty minutes later the boys approached the haystacks from the wooded area in back of the barn. Snow was beginning to accumulate rapidly on the soft ground.

The boys all huddled beside the haystacks to shield themselves from the blowing snowflakes. The hay was soft and loosely stacked. Several of the boys snuggled under the hay. This shielded them from the blowing snow and also helped keep them warm. Soon they were all huddled under the loose hay.

Snow continued to fall. But the boys were tucked safely and warmly in their haystacks. They could feel hunger pangs, but the snow kept food off their minds. They hadn't eaten since their feast of raw catfish the previous evening. But they would have to wait until the snowstorm was over before they could find food. For now everyone was snug, warm, and comfortable.

Darkness soon overtook the beautiful snow-covered countryside. The wind had settled now. Large fluffy snowflakes drifted slowly toward the ground. They piled up in fluffy white mounds across the fields and woods. They made for the most serene and beautiful sight the group had ever seen.

Everyone was quiet. They soon drifted off to sleep beneath their hay blankets.

Sometime during the night, the snow stopped falling. But not until it had drifted nearly eight inches deep across the hills, hollows, and woods. In places behind the haystacks, it had drifted up to two feet deep.

As the boys awakened one by one, they looked out to see the serenity of this landscape. They were awestricken by Mother Nature's show of snow-covered terrain. The sight was breathtaking.

Steven's mind went in gear immediately as he brushed back the snow and hay from above him. Lo and behold, food seemed to almost be knocking at his door. There were several sets of animal footprints leading right up to the haystack behind him. Wiggling his way from under the hay, he could see they were rabbit tracks. Steven whispered to Nathan and Thomas, asking them if they could spot any signs of a rabbit anywhere.

"Yeah, he's over behind that last haystack," Nathan said.

"Good, let's about five of us step out and surprise him," Steven suggested. "He can't run very fast in this snow. We'll be sure to catch him if we slip up on him."

In just a couple of minutes, the boys had surrounded and captured the frightened rabbit. Two of the food team began skinning it. They hardly had the rabbit skinned when Steven tracked an opossum and caught him in a nearby clump of snow-covered weeds.

"Looks like we're going to have rabbit and possum for breakfast," he told the group.

It wasn't long until the boys had both animals skinned and cut up into small pieces. They had little trouble eating the rabbit. While it was not gourmet dining, it was sustenance. So nobody complained as they ate the rabbit. They did continue to cut it into smaller and smaller pieces in order to eat it, though.

Soon the rabbit was all gone and they started chewing on the possum pieces. Now that was quite a different story. The more they chewed, the tougher it seemed to get. But most of the boys were so hungry that they were determined to eat it, tough or not.

"I'll chew a while and then let one of you boys chew a while," Herman chided. "Then whoever is chewing at lunchtime gets to swallow it. I put a small piece of possum in my mouth about a half hour ago and started chewing. It's now so big my mouth won't hold it."

"Glad you still have a sense of humor about this," Steven said. "I never once thought I'd be eating raw possum. But I never once dreamed of being in such a predicament as this either. When you're starving, a lot of things taste better than they sound."

The boys were still chewing possum when they noticed someone walking toward the barn from the big farmhouse.

"Everybody behind the haystacks," Nathan said. "Stay quiet and maybe we won't be noticed."

As the person approached the barn, Nathan could see

it was a young girl. She carried a small pail in her right hand. She entered the barn. Nathan assumed she had come to milk the family cow.

"What'll we do if she comes out here?" Thomas asked Nathan.

"Looks like we don't have much choice. We'll have to talk with her. Let's hope she's friendly and not easily scared. The snow is too deep for us to travel today anyway. Maybe we should approach and see if she'll let us stay in this barn until the snow melts."

Nathan stepped closer to the barn and peeked in through a crack in the walls. What he saw was almost breathtaking. He saw sitting on a three-legged milking stool a very beautiful young girl. She appeared to be in her midteens. The look on her face and the glow he saw in her eyes told him that she had to be a friendly sort of person.

He paused for a moment trying to think of a way to approach her without startling her. He finally decided to just step through the barn's front door and speak directly to her. He only hoped his approach wouldn't frighten her enough to cause her to scream for help.

"Don't be frightened," Nathan said to her in a soothing quiet voice as he walked toward where she was seated milking the Jersey cow. "I mean you no harm."

Startled, the young lady jumped up from her perch on the milking stool beside the cow. "Who are you?" she shouted.

Quickly Nathan explained that he and some of his friends had taken refuge from the snowstorm in the haystacks out back. He told her they were traveling together and would be moving on soon. He didn't tell her that they were deserters from the Wilmington Confederate training camp. Then he asked if he and his friends might be allowed to stay in the barn until the snow had melted.

"There are twenty of us and I promise you that no harm will come to you or your family," Nathan explained to her.

Perhaps it was Nathan's sincerity and youth that convinced her that she was in no danger.

"I'll have to go back to the house and ask," she said.

"Should I go with you?" Nathan queried.

"No, I think I should go alone," she replied.

The girl had been gone only a few minutes when Nathan saw the door of the house open. She and her mother stepped out onto the back porch and motioned for Nathan to come to the house. He quickly walked toward them, stopping about twenty feet away. Nathan froze in his tracks when he saw the long black barrel of a musket pointing through the door behind the women. The sights were dead on him. He could see that the man aiming the musket at him was leaning on a cane.

"What do you want from us, young man?" the woman yelled at Nathan. He sensed that the quivering in her voice was caused by fear and not hate.

"My friends and I just want to stay in your barn until the snow melts," Nathan assured her in a calm and confident voice. "We mean you no harm. We took refuge from the blizzard last night in your haystacks. We're grateful for that and we thank you even though we did it without being invited. We hope you'll allow us to stay here today and tonight. Then we'll leave tomorrow as the snow melts."

There was a long period of silence as the woman pondered her next words. "You boys have guns?"

"No," replied Nathan. "We're not soldiers out fighting a war. We're just traveling through."

"You're not a bunch of Yankees, are you? At least you

don't talk like any Yankees I've heard," the woman replied.

"No, ma'am. We're not part of the war and we don't intend to be," Nathan told her.

Then Nathan paused a minute. "If you'll allow us to stay, we'll even help you do some chores around the barn, ma'am. I saw several jobs we can do while we wait."

"Oh, okay," said the woman. "You seem to have an honest face and I guess we couldn't force you to leave even if we wanted to. But, I'm warning you, don't try anything or Cedric might let go with that big black musket he's aiming at you."

"Thank you so much, ma'am," Nathan gratefully acknowledged. "I assure you, we'll not harm anything. With your permission, we'll shuck that pile of corn we saw in the corner of the barn. Do you have other jobs we can do?"

"There's a pile of wood in the woodshed that needs to be split," she said. "If you don't mind working in the snow, you could split that."

"Just show us where to start," Nathan requested.

By noon the boys had shucked the corn, split the pile of wood, cut a couple of trees that had fallen under the weight of the snow into firewood lengths, and forked some of the hay from the stacks into the barn loft.

Nathan went to the house and knocked on the door. When the girl opened the door, he told her that they had completed all the jobs. "Do you have other jobs that we can do for you?" he asked.

As she smiled, Nathan was struck all over again by her striking beauty and the warm glow in her face. Her blue eyes and warm smile reminded him of Sarah Pugh back home.

"Thank you," she said warmly. "Let me apologize for the way we acted toward you this morning. But so many bad things have happened around here lately, everybody is scared. We just didn't want to take any chances. We've had both Yankee and Rebel soldiers here asking for food. And if we don't give them food, they search the place and take whatever they find.

"Mama, Uncle Cedric, and I have talked it over. We believe you when you say you mean us no harm. We trust you. Please don't disappoint us."

Nathan paused. "Don't worry. We won't disappoint you. Now, do you have any other jobs we can do?"

She smiled and said, "You can call me 'Mary.' I am Mary Ferebee. And what is your name?"

"I'm Nathan York," he said. "I'm from back in the Piedmont section of the state and the boys and I are headed home."

"There's a broken wheel on that wagon in the barn," Mary said. "You can fix that. Also the rail fence out behind the barn needs mending, but you may have to wait for the snow to melt before you can fix that."

"We'll fix them," Nathan said. "From the looks of things around here, you must not have had much man-help lately. Isn't your uncle Cedric able to work?"

"No, he was wounded at Yorktown. He can hardly get around, even using a cane. My father and one of my brothers were killed at Gettysburg. My other brother, Fred, has been missing for nearly a year. He left eleven months ago to join the Confederate army and we've not heard from him since.

"Mother and I are doing the best that we can. We've managed to keep part of the farm going with the help of some neighbors. But it hasn't been easy. All the work you boys have done helps us tremendously. We appreciate it very much.

"I know you boys must be getting hungry. What are you doing for food as you travel?"

"This morning we caught a rabbit and an opossum," he said. "We skinned and ate them raw. Most of our food for the past few days has been raw fish."

"We don't have much food," said Mary. "But we'll share some of what we have with you."

"Maybe we can help you with some food, too," Nathan explained. "Do you think your uncle Cedric would let us use his musket to hunt some wild game? We have some expert hunters in our group. This snow will make it easy to track down game. We might find rabbits, squirrels, or maybe even a deer."

In a few minutes Mary returned to the door with not one, but two muskets. She handed them to Nathan along with a horn of powder and a bag of shot.

Steven, Herman, and four other boys took the guns and headed down the snowcovered path behind the barn. They had at least two hours before dark to bag game.

It must definitely have been their lucky day. In less than an hour, they were dragging a six-point buck deer back to the house. They had also shot one rabbit.

Steven and his food committee hanged the deer by his heels on the limb of the old maple tree behind the house. They skinned and quartered the carcass.

"This calls for a celebration," said Mary. She and Mrs. Ferebee agreed to cook corn bread and potatoes if the boys would cook some of the venison over an outdoor fire. Then all the boys would be invited to the house for a feast. Everyone went to work and in about three hours the meal was ready.

Sliced venison, boiled potatoes, baked corn bread, and real butter on the bread was a feast like none of them had eaten in quite some time. Mrs. Ferebee even opened a crock of her special pickles.

Everyone literally gorged him or herself on this feast.

After the meal the table was cleared and the dishes washed. Nathan had posted one of the boys outside to watch for any signs of danger. He alternated guards so that everyone could enjoy the meal.

After the meal the boys hanged the other three quarters of the big deer in the smokehouse.

"We ate just one hind quarter," said Nathan. "The rest should keep nicely in the smokehouse since the weather is so cold."

Up until now Uncle Cedric hadn't done much talking. He finally broke the silence with an invitation for everyone to come into the parlor.

"Why don't you boys bring in a few of those logs you split today and put them on the fireplace?" he suggested. "We could then spend a little time getting to know each other better."

Soon all the boys were seated on the floor of the parlor. This wasn't a large room but it was plenty big enough to seat all of them. A crackling fire in the fireplace and two candles lit the room.

"Tell us who you are and why a group so young as you would be out in this kind of weather on foot," Cedric demanded.

Quiet fell over the room. The pause that followed seemed like several minutes. Finally Nathan broke the silence.

"We promised not to harm you," he said. "And we haven't. Now, can we trust you not to harm us?"

"Son, we don't want to hurt anybody," said Cedric. "I've lost my right leg in this war and many of my friends and kin have been killed or maimed. We've had our fill of killing, looting, and having to hide everything we own. We hope this evil war is about over. So if you're trying to stay out of the war, we're on your side.

"You boys are so different from most who come by here. You came seeking nothing but shelter from a snowstorm. You've already shown us more friendship and kindness than anyone since the war began. You've made no demands. And you've helped us in every way you could. You've brought in the first fresh meat we've tasted in almost a year.

"So, we trust you, son. We want to help you. You seem like a very nice bunch of boys. Tell us what we can do to help."

A sigh of relief settled over the group like a blanket of fog over Deep River in October. Cedric had laid the whole story right out for everyone to see. There was no hostility and no reason to be concerned.

The boys all looked at Nathan, expecting him to respond on behalf of the entire group. So he responded without hesitation.

"Thank you for your kindness," Nathan told him. "We'll level with you. It is not in our hearts to do otherwise. We are all from Randolph County. We range in age from twelve to fifteen years.

"About a month ago we were abducted, roped, tied, and dragged into the Confederate army. None of us wanted to join. Some of us are Quakers and therefore are conscientious objectors. A brutal Confederate recruiter named Skully swore us into the army against our wills. We were then made to walk all the way to Wilmington to a training camp. That two hundred-mile trip took a lot out of us. But we were determined not to fight, so we sneaked out of the camp. We were drafted illegally, so we saw nothing wrong with escaping."

Uncle Cedric continued his questioning for nearly an hour. He seemed satisfied with the answers he got from Nathan. Cedric never agreed or disagreed with the boys' position on the matter, but he told them he sympathized with what they were doing.

There was a pause in the conversation. Mary's mother stood up and walked over to the piano against the north wall of the room. She brushed back some dust with her apron and reached for the large candle on top of the piano. Lighting the candle from the fireplace, she placed it into the candleholder atop the piano and sat on the piano bench.

"Do you boys like music?" she asked.

"Why don't we sing while Mother plays?" Mary suggested.

In a few minutes the boys were all gathered in a semicircle around her, singing familiar songs as Mrs. Ferebee played the slightly out of tune piano.

The songfest lasted nearly an hour. They sang many of the familiar hymns they remembered from school, most of them being Christmas songs.

"It has been years since this much joy graced this house," said Mrs. Ferebee. "Your stopping here has been a real blessing for us. We thank God for sending you. He must have sent the snow just so this could happen."

"We agree with you," Nathan responded. "This bit of fun means a lot to our haggard group of young men standing up for what we believe. And, yes, I believe God sends such blessings to us often when we least expect them. He seems to bless us most when we are doing the best we can to help someone else to a better life.

"I agree with you that sending this snowstorm to make us seek shelter here was one of His miracles; otherwise this time of joy and meaning might never have come into our lives. Many less fortunate people than we go through their entire lives without ever knowing the joy and fulfillment we are experiencing at this moment. I believe if there is a direct opposite of war this is it. We know not what the future holds for any of us, but we know the precious memories of this brief time we've shared will follow us to our dying days regardless of how long or how short that time might be.

"Again, we thank you for your generosity in allowing us to stay," Nathan ended. "We shall pray for your safety and well-being as we go on to whatever life has in store for us."

The boys all thanked their gracious hosts for the evening and the meal. One by one they filed out the door toward the barn. Nathan brought up the rear.

Mary stopped Nathan just inside the door. He could feel her warmth as she stood very close to him. As the flickering candlelight played across her pretty face, he could see her looking directly into his eyes.

"Please pardon the tears," she said, "but that speech you just made gives me a feeling I've never experienced before. I think you have just summed up what Jesus was saying to all Christians in the Bible. No minister could say it any better than you just did.

"You need not be in any hurry. All of you have been so kind to us. We hope you will stay several days. It looks like the snow didn't melt much today. Could you stay at least one more day? There is a lot of venison left in the smokehouse, so you can stay and we may all feast on it again tomorrow."

"We'll have to wait until tomorrow to make that decision," Nathan told her. "But for now, thank you for everything. We're so grateful for your hospitality."

Mary reached out to take Nathan's hand as he turned to walk out the door. "Thank you for all you and your group have done for us. Good night and may God bless you," she told him, looking affectionately into his eyes as he turned and walked away.

Early the next morning everyone was up bright and early, helping with the chores around the barn. When Mary came to milk the cow, she found that the boys had already taken care of all the feeding and cleaning chores.

"Mother's going to have grits, molasses, and butter ready for breakfast in about a half hour," Mary told them.

Soon a bright sun glistened across the farm snowscape. Its warmth promised to melt the remaining snow very soon.

Nathan had already talked with the group and they had agreed to stay one more day here in this friendly territory. This would give them time to get rested and allow some of the blisters on their feet to heal. It would also ensure another good meal of cooked fresh meat under their belts.

The boys spent the entire day working around the farmstead. They repaired the roof on the house, split fence rails, cut more firewood, picked up black walnuts in the woods, and did all the little odd jobs Mary and her mother asked them to do.

Mary came out of the house several times during the course of the day to tell Nathan additional jobs that needed doing. It was obvious to everyone that she could accomplish this without making so many trips out to talk with him. It was also obvious that she was enjoying every minute of her little chats with him.

The snow melted rapidly throughout the afternoon. By nightfall it had almost disappeared except in the shady spots near the trees.

By dark every one of the boys had again worked up a man-sized appetite. Mary and her mother, with the help of Uncle Cedric, had prepared an even more elaborate meal from the venison than they had eaten the previous evening.

They shared conversation, thoughts, and pleasantries

more freely than they had at the previous feast. Several of the boys requested another songfest following dinner.

Then Uncle Cedric began telling war stories while everyone sat speechless on the floor of the parlor. He kept the boys spellbound for nearly two hours spinning yarns about his experiences and his close calls in combat and training.

He talked about how he and the other soldiers would load their weapons and on command fire at the opposing line. Some would fall dead. Some would advance and others would retreat. Many fell wounded. Any soldier who had a limb injured would be left to die or carried off to the nearest medical facility for treatment. Sometimes there would be an ambulance, which was usually a team of horses and a wagon, to transport the wounded to the nearest makeshift hospital.

Cedric had been wounded in a battle and hauled off in such a manner. He had been hit in the foot; the bones in his lower leg were shattered. The hospital was an old house with a kitchen table serving as the surgery table. The floors were littered with straw and sawdust to absorb the blood.

All the wounded would be brought to the front door of the house. A surgeon would take a quick look at the wound and advise a private helping him on how to slow or stop the bleeding. A strong dose of whisky and quinine water would be given to help dull the pain.

The surgeon would then have one wounded man after another brought to the table where he would amputate the limb that was damaged. He always removed the limb well above the wound. His attendant would then tie a tourniquet around the bleeding limb and take the patient to another room, hopefully to recover. Another attendant would then remove the severed limb and scrape the blood and tissue off the table as best he could.

Cedric told of how a large pile of arms and legs would accumulate outside the house where the attendants tossed them through the window of the operating room. When a wagonload of them accumulated, they would be hauled off and buried. The stench was almost unbearable and Cedric still had memories of that big pile, which contained his own shattered right leg.

"My leg was just one of dozens helping build that large pile of limbs outside the surgery room window," he said with a crack in his voice. "I still wake up at night with a vivid picture in my mind of those legs and arms piled almost up to the windowsill. Sometimes I have to get out of bed and throw up."

After a long pause Cedric continued, "I suppose I'm one of the lucky ones, though. I lived to tell about it. Most of those with me didn't. War is hell and nobody ever wins. May the Lord help us to someday rise above the human urge to kill and maim in wars."

A long silence followed. A thousand thoughts whipped through the brain of each person in the group. Nothing more needed to be said.

All this time Mary sat close to Nathan, almost touching him. He could feel a magnetism between them that may have been more than his youth could interpret. But there was little question that she had feelings for him that were stronger than just an ordinary relationship.

When Uncle Cedric finished his storytelling, the group again thanked their gracious hosts and began heading back to the barn.

As they were leaving, Mary again stopped Nathan, taking him by the hand. "Wait," she said. "I want to talk with you."

"I'll be there in a few minutes," Nathan yelled to the boys as they walked toward the barn.

"When do you plan to leave?" she asked.

"Now that the snow has melted, we must go on," Nathan explained. "There may be a search party tailing us."

"What will you do when you get back home?" she asked. "Won't the Confederates have someone out looking for you by the time you arrive?"

"Well, I suppose they will," Nathan responded. "It'll no doubt be Skully and his men. We haven't done much thinking about that yet. I suppose we'll all have to hide out and try to steer clear of Skully and his henchmen. They will certainly be searching every house looking for us."

"What will Skully do if he catches you?" Mary asked. "Aren't you afraid he'll hurt you, maybe even try to kill you?"

After a long pause Nathan answered, "Well, he promised before we left that if any of us escaped he'd catch us and hang us for being war deserters."

"Oh, Nathan," Mary cried flinging her arms around him. "Don't go. Stay here and hide out. We can find places for all of you to hide. Our neighbors will help you. Please don't go back to where this Skully can catch you. He'll probably never give up until he's caught every one of you. This war can't last much longer. Can't you stay here until it ends?"

There was a very long pause. Mary wiped back tears with her apron as she held on to Nathan.

"I'll have to talk it over with the others," Nathan told her.

"We need you and we want to help you," she said. "We'll do whatever it takes to make this work out for you."

As Mary looked piercingly into his eyes, Nathan could feel a big lump in his throat.

"In just two days I've learned to like you a lot," she told

him. "It seems as if I've known you all my life. If you leave tomorrow, it will take a long time to get over having had you stay here this short time. Oh, please, can't you stay? Won't you, please?"

Nathan could only answer, "I'll talk it over with the boys."

Tears welled up in his eyes as he walked slowly toward the barn. He felt a sadness gnawing at his insides as he left Mary's side. It was something that he really couldn't explain. He certainly couldn't let this feeling be part of the decision on whether they stayed or left.

Leaving Mary with her feelings for him would not be easy. He also felt a sadness at the thought of leaving the relative comfort of such hospitality that this fractured family had shown them.

But something else was also bothering him as he slowly walked back to the barn. All those questions that Mary had asked about the fate of this group of boys once they reappeared at their homes in Randolph County were troubling him also. He just hadn't had the chance to seriously think through the possibilities of being hunted down by Skully and his men the way a band of hunters might pursue a fox to his certain death. For the first time it really began to sink into his mind that his little band of underage marchers was stepping headlong into a death trap. They were going to be treated like war criminals. The course seemed clear; facing Skully could be a lot like the battles that Cedric had just described in graphic detail.

As Nathan settled onto his mound of hay for the night, he was quite restless. He tossed and turned for several hours as question after question kept popping into his young mind: Had the folks back home heard about their escape? Would Skully try to capture them when they returned? Just how far would Skully go in his quest to capture them? Would it be humanly possible to hide out from Skully for the rest of the war? Where would twenty boys hide? Just how long could they hide? Was there a way to prevent Skully from pestering them?

After a few hours of sleeplessly pondering these questions, Nathan had almost concluded that his little band of boys would be better off staying here where they had been offered at least some friendly refuge. Or they might go some other place far away from Skully. Somewhere over in the Uwharrie Mountains might be easier to hide out in than trying to elude Skully back home.

He also had heard of a large cave somewhere over on Shepherd Mountain that might be a good place for a group of twenty to hide. He remembered his father once talked about such a cave. He had told about John Lawson, Surveyor General for North Carolina, mentioning a cave in his diary. Lawson had described the cave he discovered back in 1701 as being large enough to accommodate over a hundred Keyauwee Indians. Since Shepherd Mountain was only about thirty miles away, it might be a good place to hide out. But would there be people living in that area whom they could trust the way they could Mary and her neighbors?

Weighing all the alternatives against Mary's offer to stay left him both confused and frustrated. *If we stay too close to the training camp from which we escaped, they may find us,* he thought. *But will we be any better off when the word gets out that we're back home and Skully is hunting us?*

Nathan tried to keep his feelings for Mary from entering into the decision. He felt a warmth for her that he'd not ever felt for any other human being. He hadn't even felt this way toward Sarah Pugh back home.

Deep down, though, Nathan knew that his final decision had to be based on what was best for the entire group of boys. And the decision was not totally his to make. He had to let democracy take its course and give the entire group a chance to decide what to do. The wee hours of the morning arrived before Nathan dropped off to sleep.

Early the next morning, the boys all bounced out of their warm beds of hay ready to resume their homeward trek. Nathan asked them to remain inside the barn for a little talk before they started.

He first explained the conversation that he had with Mary the night before. He then described the fears that had arisen in his own mind. He described the possibilities that might cause Skully to go on a real manhunt for them. He explained the consequences if they were caught, and he told them of Mary's offer to stay and hide out here.

Silence fell over the group. Their plight was now sinking in like a stone in water. They were fugitives from the law back home. Or worse yet, they were victims of a lawless society. And a dictator named Skully would not rest until he nailed their hides to the shed.

After a few minutes of deliberation, the group agreed to accept Mary's offer to stay here temporarily. They needed a little time to sort out the pieces of this puzzle.

Soon Mary walked out to the barn and invited the group to come to the house. "Mother and I have cooked salt pork and grits," she said. "We even made pork gravy."

Nathan thanked Mary and they all began strolling silently toward the house.

"Why is everyone so gloomy?" she asked. "It's a beautiful morning. We should all be happy."

"We have all fully realized for the first time what it really means to be fugitives from the law," Nathan told her. "We know that we'll be treated like criminals wherever we go. Perhaps we should have stayed back at the training camp."

"Have you made a decision yet on whether to stay here with us?" she asked.

"Yes, we will stay for a short while. We need more time to decide what strategy is best for all of us."

"Oh, Nathan, I'm so glad you're staying," she said as she walked even closer to his side.

All through breakfast there was very little talking. Mary and her mother both tried to make pleasant conversation, but they got only a limited response.

For the rest of the day the boys chopped wood, split shingles to patch the barn roof, and repaired the rail fences. But they did their chores with much less enthusiasm than they'd shown the previous two days.

In midafternoon, Nathan called the entire group together for a council session. He sensed that something must be done to break the tension and gloom.

"Let's consider our alternatives," he suggested.

"First, we're probably wanted back home as war deserters already. Surely the word of our escape has reached there by now. Skully will delight in hunting us down if we go back to our homes. We know we have legal rights because of our ages, but the law obviously means nothing to Skully."

"Yeah, the law won't stop Skully from hanging one or more of us," said Thomas. "The law means nothing if he decides to hang us. It's not likely that anyone in the community can stop him if he really decides to come after us. That's one disadvantage in being peace-loving Quakers. You can't really force someone to do something and make it stick in a case like this."

"Maybe the war will be over soon and we'll be safe from Skully," mused Steven.

"Do you think we can find places to hide where Skully can't find us?" Nathan asked. "Are there places that even

Skully and his men can't penetrate?"

"There are still some men hiding from him," said Steven. "He hasn't caught Joseph Teague. He stays in a barrel down by the river part of the day. At night he slips back to his house. He has hidden out ever since the war began without being caught."

"I think we could all hide out on Purgatory Mountain," said Thomas. "There are rocky ledges, small caves, mountain laurel thickets, and big trees up there. I once hunted up there with my father. It is so rough that Skully and his men would have to come after us on foot. A horse can't travel in that rough country very well."

"I disagree," said Steven. "There are plenty of good hiding places up on Purgatory Mountain alright, but Skully will probably stop at nothing to catch us. I think we should either stay here or move on to some of the Uwharrie Mountains to the west of Randolph County."

Both Thomas and Steven had a firmness in their voices as they spoke. It was obvious they differed strongly on this issue.

"If we stay here, there could be trouble, too," Thomas argued. "A patrol from Wilmington might catch us. It looks like we're trapped whichever route we take. Looks like we should move on. I'd feel much safer hiding out on Purgatory Mountain than in this area where we don't know the territory."

Nathan could see this disagreement needed mediation.

"Why don't we think about it a little longer?" Nathan suggested. "Let's wait until tomorrow morning and take a vote."

Everyone agreed to the plan and they all promised to abide by the decision of the majority. For the rest of the day, there was much buzzing and discussion about alternatives.

It was obvious that the group was divided on this question.

Nathan was, of course, a little concerned over the differences in opinion because up to now there had been total harmony and agreement on everything. *Is the group coming apart on this issue?* he kept asking himself. *Is the group losing its sense of purpose? Does my relationship with Mary enter into the rift in any way?*

Nathan dropped off to sleep that night still pondering these and many other questions. He still had to decide how he would cast his own vote.

Chapter 7
Trouble on the Home Front

The boys had now begun to spend a lot of time worrying about their own future safety. But they also expended a lot of mental energy in concern for what might be happening to the folks back home.

"I feel a little guilty at times," Calvin told his brother Nathan, "thinking about our own troubles when I know Mother and Rebecca are having a tough time trying to keep everything together back home. They must be fending off Skully and his men, as well as having to deal with the neighbors over what has happened."

The big question was whether the news of their Wilmington escape had reached their homes yet. The boys at this time didn't know it, but the news had hit home. And it was causing almost as much turmoil in their community as when the war first broke out more than three years before.

All the talk at the meeting house and the mill was no longer about the war. It had now turned to the escape of those twenty brave young Randolph County men from the Confederate army down at Wilmington. And there was no end to the public speculation about where they were and what they were doing.

Skully received the news only a few days after it happened. He quickly spread the word throughout the community. He swore he'd catch the last one of these draft-dodging, war-deserting, young whippersnappers. And he was furious. He made no bones about it. He intended to bring swift justice and sure revenge.

"Just wait until I get my hands on them," he often repeated. "They'll regret the day they busted down the walls and walked out of the army."

Almost every day Skully or one of his men made the rounds to the homes of all the boys who'd escaped. They constantly made threats and harassed the women and children. They were so overbearing as to make themselves quite obnoxious. They warned the families each day about helping the boys hide if they came home. "You'll be harboring a criminal if you do," Skully would tell them. "And harboring criminals is also breaking the law. You, too, will be guilty of a war crime if you harbor a fugitive. And you can be hanged for it."

Skully told Nathan and Calvin's mother, "A patrol is after your boys and they'll probably catch them before they get very far. But if those brats do get this far, I'll get them. They'll be sorry they ever did such a thing."

On another of his visits to the farm, Skully told Mrs. York, "I believe that oldest boy of yours is the troublemaker. I'll take personal pleasure in catching him if he shows up here. And I'll see that he gets his punishment."

"You have no legal right to harm any of the boys," Mrs. York warned Skully. "I've had someone check on it. You broke the law when you captured them and sent them off to Wilmington. They're all under the legal draft age."

"Law or no law," Skully boomed out at her, "they're in the army now. They escaped training camp in wartime and that makes them deserters. They'll be treated like any other war deserter when we catch them."

These daily encounters with Skully seemed to be giving Mrs. York her strength back. Her will to fight was growing stronger each day. Without doubt she was mentally preparing herself to help the boys fight Skully. She definitely would not be cowed by this obnoxious miscreant.

At the same time though, the burden of waiting, worrying, and not knowing where the boys were weighed heavily on her spirits. Each passing day, she and Rebecca grew more apprehensive. It was like having an open sore; the hurt was always there. They could only wait and wonder.

Mrs. York knew she was legally right, yet she felt helpless to stop Skully. Enforcement of the law was weak or almost nonexistent at this point in the war. The Confederacy was floundering and obviously could not exist much longer. Surrender had to come soon. That was her major source of hope. But for now a state of lawlessness existed and Skully knew it. Regardless of what the law might say, he would go to any length for revenge; and it seemed that no one could or would stop him.

The question that haunted Mrs. York most was this: When the war ended, would all old scores be automatically settled? Or would the state of lawlessness continue? Would Skully go on back to Moore County and let bygones be bygones? Or would he stay here and get revenge?

Mrs. York felt that Skully's grudges were personal. He probably would not be satisfied to forgive and forget. His vendetta was strong; he would probably delight in staying around and settling old scores even after the war ended.

She was right. Inside, Skully was seething. He never accepted defeat gracefully. If these boys returned home and went free, he considered it a personal defeat.

Without doubt, Skully's contempt for the boys was growing. If they returned, he'd leave no stone unturned in his search to find them.

Mrs. York believed that Skully might go so far as to make good on his threat to execute one or more of the boys if he caught them. This way he could easily get the others to turn themselves in if he promised them their lives, if not their freedom.

Mrs. York asked herself many times, *Is there any way Skully can be stopped?* She had even asked some of her neighbors the same question. No one had an answer.

"I wish we could find some way to get word to Nathan and Calvin, wherever they are," Mrs. York told Rebecca. "If we could only warn them to hide out somewhere far away from here until the war is over, they'd be better off. They're hardly more than babies, yet here they are being treated like criminals and war deserters. And people like Skully are hunting them like they were wild animals."

"Oh, Mother, I'm afraid for the boys," said Rebecca. "They are in a lot of danger, aren't they? I'm afraid for us, too. Those bluecoats who came through here last week took our last ham, so we're getting low on food. It's getting almost impossible to hide food, because those soldiers have learned to search every possible place we can conceal it.

"It's going to be time to plant soon. Without Nathan and Calvin, I don't know how we can do it."

"With God's help we'll survive somehow," her mother consoled her. "We'll just keep praying that this nasty old war will end soon. And we'll hope that Nathan, Calvin, and James will return to us unharmed.

"Our lives won't ever be the same again. But we'll make new lives when the war's over."

"Something else scares me," Rebecca confided. "I'm afraid of Skully and his men. That tall one with a beard frightens me. Some of the girls at Sunday meeting say they have been threatened by the two men who ride with Skully. Gloria Wright said the man with the beard sort of had his way with her."

"How could he sort of have his way with her?" Mrs. York questioned.

"He told her that since her brother Charles was in the group of escaped boys, he'd probably catch him when he returns home. He said that if she'd be intimate with him, he would see to it that Charles was not harmed if he was caught. Gloria finally consented but not until after she'd argued with him for several days. And now he's threatening her again.

"I'm afraid that he or the other men might threaten me the same way," Rebecca told her mother. "Not many of the boys in that group have older sisters. And since I have two brothers in the group, I may be their next target."

There was a long pause. Rebecca's mother stared out the window for several minutes as she searched for an answer to her daughter's question.

"Let's not cross that bridge just yet," she told her with motherly compassion. "Maybe it won't happen.

"First of all, Gloria is quite different from you. I doubt that she put up much resistance. This bearded soldier is not the first man she's been intimate with. If she had really wanted to keep him off her, she probably could have.

"If one of them seriously threatens you, I think you can be forceful with him. Try hard to resist. But your best strategy is to try to keep yourself out of situations where you're alone. It's not likely that one of them will try anything unless he catches you alone."

"Oh, Mother, I'm scared and confused," Rebecca cried, embracing her tightly. With tears rolling down her young, beautiful face, she sobbed, "Mother, I have these feelings from time to time that I can't explain. I sometimes feel like I want to have a man. I feel like I could make love to him and give him everything the way you did with Father. Then I realize that might never be. I realize this war might take us all without my ever knowing the joy of loving a man and having children of my own.

"And, Mother, I sometimes cry for you. You have lost the happiness of having Father. Not having him here to share your joys and fears has to bother you very much. I miss him as a father. But you miss him in such a different way. Mother, you have been given such a heavy burden that I don't know how you can bear it."

By this time her mother had begun to sob with her. They held each other for several minutes in silence.

"I miss your father more than you can possibly know. I suppose I'll never fill the hollow place in my life that his death has left for me. Even if the war ends tomorrow, getting over your father's death will take a long time. This is what is so brutal about war. Many of those who die were never hit by enemy bullets, yet their loss is even more painful than the death of a soldier."

After another long pause, Rebecca's mother spoke softly as she stroked Rebecca's long, flowing brown hair. "Rebecca, you're a beautiful young lady. You have all the feelings a young lady your age should have. Cherish them. They're what makes you the beautiful person that you are.

"Just pray that someday this war will end and you'll know love the way I have. Have hope. After the war, you and the right young man will find each other. Then you can share with him all the love that you have inside.

"In the meantime, your virtue and love are worth fighting for. If Skully's men threaten you the way they did Gloria, we'll fight them off with our last ounce of energy. Let's hope we're not forced to do something drastic. Remember, since I'm now a widow, they may try to attack me, too. I may even be more of a target for their sexual advances than you.

"Keep your chin up, Rebecca. When this war ends, we'll somehow find the strength to build our lives over again. We will live and love in ways that are different than they were before. And if God wills it, you and I will both love again."

They went to sleep that night somewhat consoled, with renewed courage and a sense of joy at having shared these inner feelings as only a mother and daughter can.

As the days rolled on, Skully and his men became more unbearable. Their obstinacy toward the families of the boys who had escaped was almost overwhelming.

Skully or one of his men rode out to the York farm almost every day. None of them made sexual advances toward Rebecca or her mother, though.

Skully didn't realize it but his verbal terror campaign against the escaped boys was uniting the entire community, maybe even the whole county, against him. To most of the community folks, he represented a direct link to the Confederacy, and his actions were actually uniting them against it. Most of them now considered the Confederacy a lost cause and the source of most of their mental anguish. It was obvious that if the boys came back to this community to hide, they would have the full support of everyone. Everyone except Skully and his men, that is.

Mrs. York maintained her composure each time Skully or his men threatened her. She just stood silently and listened, rarely answering them.

Rebecca could see her mother's strength was growing. She was proud that Mrs. York could stand up to them and not get upset. So Skully's threats were serving a useful purpose in this respect. In fact, for the first time since her father died last spring, Rebecca could see her mother starting to show that old fighting spirit again. The will to live with strength and enthusiasm seemed to be returning.

Rebecca felt a closeness with her mother growing stronger with every passing day. She and her mother had always been close, but this seemed to be something very special that only a mother and daughter fully attuned to each other's inner lives can know. The common cause of standing to fight for her brothers' lives drew them closer as well. She now believed that standing shoulder to shoulder together, the two of them could win against Skully.

Both Rebecca and her mother felt they were prepared to handle Skully's threats and could help with some kind of plan to hide Calvin and Nathan from Skully—if they returned.

But the same questions nagged them day after day and night after night: Where are the boys? Have they been recaptured? Would they come back here to hide? Would they hide somewhere else?

Deep down they both had a gut feeling the boys were somewhere out there fending for themselves. They believed the boys were on their way home and would be smart enough to avoid Skully and his henchmen at all costs. They felt that somehow these hardy young men were leading the other boys and helping them to survive the hardship.

"God provides and I'm sure that in His own way, He's taking care of our boys," Mother consoled Rebecca.

Chapter 8
On the Road to Purgatory

The boys had no way of knowing the kind of treatment Skully and his men were handing out to their folks back home. But somehow they had an uneasy feeling each time thoughts of home came to their minds. Deep down they felt that something bad was happening and that their families were being mistreated. They discussed such possibilities during their deliberations about whether or not they should stay and hide out on the farm. But they knew that anything they might say was purely speculation.

When morning came, Nathan still wasn't sure how the vote would go. During the discussions the night before, it seemed that the group was split about half-and-half on whether to return home or stay.

A good night's sleep had helped Nathan decide how to cast his vote. He had mentally weighed all the possibilities and really didn't want to leave the safe refuge that had been offered here. And he would like to stay with Mary as long as he could. He had grown quite fond of this beautiful young lady and to just walk away from her wouldn't be easy.

But thoughts of Skully harassing his family back home would race through his mind. He felt that he and all the boys in his group were needed at home. So, Nathan's vote would be cast in favor of the continuation of the trip homeward.

After breakfast, Nathan asked the boys to gather in the

barn. They discussed the matter briefly and then voted. Fifteen favored traveling home. Following the vote, Nathan questioned those who voted to stay.

"Do you wish to stay behind and let the rest of us go on without you?" he asked.

The five who voted to stay quickly agreed that they should remain together as a group. They would all leave right away and would stay together whatever happened.

They agreed to leave by noon. There would still be time to get several miles behind them before daylight ran out. The warm sun was now putting an irresistible sparkle into the air. This was enough to make everyone feel good, and they were itching to travel. This uplifting experience along with plenty of rest and relaxation had given them a renewed spirit of hope to deal with whatever might lie ahead. They could now see things in a different light. They had recharged their batteries and replenished their energy to deal with the uncertainties which lay ahead.

The boys began to scurry around packing their few belongings for the trip. Nathan walked toward the house. What he had to do now wasn't going to be pleasant or easy. He knew that telling Mary, her mother, and Uncle Cedric was going to take courage.

Mary stood waiting just inside the door. Nathan could tell by her forlorn look that she already knew. He sensed that she was reading his mind, yet there was anxiety in her voice.

"What have you decided?" she asked. "Please say that you've decided to stay."

Nathan gently took both her hands in his. "Mary, it saddens me greatly, but we must go today. The group voted to go and I must abide by their decision."

There was a long pause as Mary stared deeply into

Nathan's eyes. Tears welled up in her own eyes as she bowed her head slightly.

"You've added so much to my life in these few short days," she told him. "And now you're taking all this happiness away. Things will never be the same for me again. I don't know how I'll ever fill the void your leaving will create in my life. Do you think we'll ever be together again?"

Another long pause followed.

"The way we both feel now, we must meet again," Nathan said. "We must find a way to meet after the war is over. I will mark this place well in my mind. I promise to do everything within my power to find you after the war.

"But you must remember that I am a hunted man," Nathan warned. "I may not survive the ordeal that lies ahead for me. But the memory of having spent this time with you will help me through it. I will never forget you. And if I survive, I give you my promise that I will try to find you after the war."

"We're both young, but I hope this feeling we have for each other never goes away," Mary said. "I'll be praying every night for your safe return back to me after the war."

Mrs. Ferebee and Uncle Cedric had overheard everything from inside the kitchen door. Since she shared her daughter's desire to have Nathan return, Mary's mother decided it was time to speak.

"Nathan, we want you and the boys to know how much you've meant to us these past few days. We appreciate all you've done for us. And we thank you for the mannerly and gentlemanly way you have handled yourselves here.

"You're certainly welcome to stay here. We would do everything possible to help you. But we understand your reasons for leaving and desperately hope to see you again.

But if we don't you'll always live in our hearts.

"To show our appreciation, we'll fix you a bag of food and supplies to help make your trip a little easier. These should last a few days. We'll also give you one of Uncle Cedric's muskets. You can return it after the war is over. Think that might increase our chances of seeing you again?

"We'll serve you lunch before you leave. It may be your last hot meal for a while. It'll be ready by noon. We'll call you in a little while as soon as you've finished getting ready to travel."

Speechless with gratitude and sadness at leaving, Nathan turned and walked briskly back to the barn.

"What did Mary and Mrs. Ferebee say about our leaving?" asked Steven.

Nathan explained his conversation to the group. They were delighted at having one more hot meal before they left and elated at having a bag of food to take along.

The boys enjoyed their hot meal. Then Uncle Cedric explained local directions and gave them several travel hints. He told the best routes to travel to avoid being detected.

"You'll have to cross back over the river soon," Cedric told them. "When you come to where the Haw and Deep Rivers run together, you'll be following the Haw if you don't cross over. I'd suggest that you not cross the Cape Fear, though. If you wait until you come to the Haw, there's less chance of your being detected. And besides, the Haw isn't nearly as wide as the Cape Fear.

"When you get to the Haw River, there's a mill and bridge about two miles upstream from where it leaves the Cape Fear. It'll be a little extra walking, but this will be your best bet for crossing back to the Deep River side."

The boys departed with little fanfare. Nathan thanked Mary, her mother, and Uncle Cedric on behalf of the group.

He and Mary had already said their good-byes, so leaving was now a formality.

"Promise you won't ever forget," Mary said to Nathan as he walked away.

"I give you my word," Nathan responded.

Then the group of twenty boys disappeared down the country path behind the barn.

Nathan felt a large lump in his throat as he walked away from Mary. He was unsure of his feelings at this point. He only knew that whatever he felt for Mary, leaving her was now the most painful thing that had happened to him since his father's death. Nathan only hoped that he would live to see this young lady, who had given him this ecstatic feeling, after the war.

Things went well for the rest of that day. The boys trudged along the river road, which was a very pretty area with its scenic vistas just as Cedric had described. They had gone several miles by the time darkness overtook them. They found a good place to sleep in a grove of large loblolly pines. There was plenty of pine straw for bedding.

The boys slept well that night and arose at daylight to continue their hike upstream toward home. They had been walking only about two hours when they found what could be trouble. Nathan believed it needed to be checked out.

A few hundred feet from the trail, near the river a small curl of smoke was twisting its way skyward. Thomas and Nathan walked cautiously over to examine it and could see that it was the remains of a campfire. The fire had been doused with wet river sand, but it was still smoldering.

Nathan quickly examined the surrounding area and found that a group of twenty-five or thirty people had spent the night there. The residue and tracks proved they had horses and wagons. Deep wheel tracks in the moist soil told him that the wagons were hauling heavy loads.

The tracks led in the same direction the boys were traveling. Nathan returned to the group and reported what he and Thomas had found.

"We'd better wait here a while," he explained to them. "Whoever it is can't be more than an hour or two ahead of us. We can't afford to get too close. I don't know if this might be a group of farmers hauling produce to market at Fayetteville or if it's a bunch of soldiers. It could even be a search party looking for us. Either way, we can't afford to take chances. We'd best let them get a little more distance before we head up the trail again."

"I've got an idea, Nathan," said Thomas. "I'll be a good scout and find out what's up there ahead. My daddy always sent me up the tallest tree to get my bearings when we were hunting in the woods and got lost. If some of you boys will give me a lift to that lower branch, I'll climb that big oak over by the river and see what's out there. This is flat country, so I can see a long distance."

"Okay," replied Nathan, "but be careful. Don't let anybody see you. And, for God's sake, don't fall out of that tree."

"Don't worry about my climbing," Thomas said. "My father always said I could climb better than a tomcat any day. And I'll take it easy so I won't attract any attention if anyone is in seeing distance of us."

In a few minutes Thomas began slowly and deliberately climbing the big tree limb by limb. He was soon at a height of around eighty feet when he came to an abrupt halt. Thomas froze in place, staring off toward the north. His attention was focused on something. The rest of the group was eager to know what it was.

Then Steven yelled up at Thomas, "What is it? What do you see out there?"

"Shhh!" Thomas hissed, motioning for everyone to keep quiet.

A few more minutes passed and Thomas inched quietly higher in the tree. He gazed silently off into the distance. A serious and almost pained look came over his face. The suspense was gripping the boys below like a poison ivy vine clinging to a sapling.

Ten minutes had passed and Thomas signaled to the boys that he was coming down. Then he began to slip slowly down the trunk of the giant tree. When he finally planted his feet back on the ground below, Thomas was nearly breathless. His pale face told the group that he'd seen something scary.

"What's wrong, Thomas?" Nathan asked intently. "You look as though you saw a ghost. What is it? What's out there?"

"My God, we're almost in a war," he said gasping for breath. "It looks as if a battle might start up ahead of us. That group traveling in front of us in a band of graycoats. There can't be more than fifty of them. Back down the river behind us is another bunch of Confederate soldiers. There may be as many as a hundred of them. They're headed straight this way and could be here in less than an hour.

"Now the worst part of it all is that less than five miles up the river off to the north there's a big bunch of bluecoats. They're headed straight down the trail toward the Confederate troops. There must be several hundred of them.

"We could be in the middle of a battle if we stay here," Thomas said excitedly. "If all the soldiers keep going the way they're now marching, they could engage in a battle only a couple of miles from here.

"We gotta get out of here," Thomas said. "We'd be much better off if we could cross the river. But I see no way to get there without being sighted in the open water by some of those soldiers. I saw a town on the other side of the river. It must be Fayetteville, but I don't see how we can get there now.

"Our best bet is to hide in the thicket down by the river while those Confederate troops behind us go by. We might even have to get down into the edge of the water behind the riverbanks to keep out of sight."

At Nathan's command, the boys quickly made their way down to the thicket on the riverbank and all found places to hide. The thick bramble briars, saw grass, and honeysuckle made their hideout quite uncomfortable, to say the least.

They crouched low in the underbrush for over an hour before they heard the rumble of wagons and hoofbeats of horses. Nathan motioned for everyone to lay low and stay out of sight until all of them had passed. Thomas did peek out from his special vantage point behind a big birch tree to assess the situation.

In about ten minutes the convoy of supply wagons, foot soldiers, and mounted officers were out of sight. Thomas estimated their numbers to be less than a hundred men. They were a ragtag and weary-looking bunch, he observed. They didn't appear to be terribly fit for fighting the large Union army that was approaching.

Thomas had the urge to run out and warn them. He felt that if they only knew they were about to walk into a death trap, they would turn around and head back east. They and the group of their own kind just up ahead would be no match for the Union army marching toward them. But Thomas knew for their own safety that he and the boys must lay low and stay out of sight.

When about a half hour had passed, Thomas raised up from his hiding place and stepped out toward the road to be sure the group had passed. Then he gave the all-clear signal.

The boys all climbed out of the thicket and up the riverbank. Some of them had wet feet from standing in the mud along the river's edge. They stayed clear of the road and watched cautiously to see if any stragglers might be behind the main group of soldiers.

Nathan knew that regardless of what happened next, much danger lay ahead. Even though the Confederate soldiers had passed, if a battle ensued they might retreat. And they'd probably come right back this way. The Union troops would probably be in hot pursuit. This could put his group right smack in the middle of a battle.

Nathan, Thomas, and Steven quickly started fishing for alternatives. Somehow they had to get across that river. It offered the best natural buffer zone from the battle. But how? When? And at what risk? They could retreat back down the river. But did that offer any better protection than where they were?

They decided to just stay put a little longer and nibble from their food bag while they waited. Mary's mother had given them a bag of potatoes. Each boy ate a raw potato. They still had plenty for later meals.

As Thomas had predicted, in about two hours the first shot rang out. Soon a volley of shots followed. A second and third volley of musket shots then a steady roar of shooting could be heard.

The gunfire slowed and then stopped. All was quiet on the battlefield now. Nearly a half hour went by.

Thomas whispered to Nathan. "What're we going to do now? We can't stay here. And we don't know which way to go from here to stay out of the battle."

"We'd better try to find out what's happening," Nathan decided. So he and Thomas instructed the boys to move back close to their thicket hideout. They could dart into these thickets in short order if the need arose.

Then Thomas started to climb the big oak again. This time Nathan climbed up behind him. Both boys ascended the giant tree with extreme caution as they stepped up limb by limb. They hoped to get some idea of who was moving in which direction. Then they could decide what to do next.

When they had climbed about two-thirds of the way to the top of the tree, Thomas stopped. He motioned for Nathan to move up close behind him. They could see a lot of activity about two miles to the north. Together the two boys continued to climb cautiously and slowly up the tree. They were careful not to shake the branches, staying on the farside of the tree trunk from the activity.

The activity on the battlefield was brisk. They could see several bluecoat soldiers picking up bodies and attending to their wounded buddies. Most of the graycoats must have made a run for it to the west. They could see a small band of men and horses in the distance.

Nathan and Thomas climbed higher. They were close to the top when they spotted what was obviously the band of Confederate troops that had passed them a couple of hours earlier. These ragtag Confederate soldiers were getting ready to launch an attack on the flank of the Union army. Cannons were being hauled into place and men with muskets were taking up positions along the edge of a big field. It scared the boys. Everything was shaping up just the way Cedric had described the battles he'd fought in.

In a few minutes a cannon roared and lobbed its deadly load toward the blue-coated soldiers. They began firing their rifles back. Soon gunshots were splitting the air from two directions. The two armies had squared off in a head-to-head attack. They were marching toward each other, firing their muskets as they came.

Soldiers would raise their muskets and fire. Men would fall dead and wounded on the ground. Soldiers would reload their muskets and fire again. More men would fall.

Nathan and Thomas peeped out from behind the trunk of the big tree. They didn't want to risk stopping a stray bullet, even though they were probably out of range of the musket shots.

For almost a half hour, Thomas and Nathan watched. It seemed like an eternity. Both boys were afraid to move as they watched this display of mankind in its ugliest moment. They were scared. They wanted to throw up.

They watched men intentionally cause the lifeblood to flow from their fellowmen and their horses. The clearing, which only minutes before had been a quiet wheat field, now lay strewn with dead and dying bodies of men and horses. And both Nathan and Thomas thought to themselves, *Why does such shame have to be? Why does God allow this? If God built man in His own image, why would He let men do this to other men?*

Then the shooting stopped. What was left of the band of Confederates, which had passed only a couple of hours ago, was now a small company in full retreat. They quickly disappeared into the tall pine trees to the east. The blue-coats gave chase, but only for a few minutes.

Right before their eyes, Nathan and Thomas had witnessed a bloody skirmish that would be etched into their memories forever. They did not know exactly where they were at the time, but they could see a small, nearby village. Nathan thought he remembered hearing Cedric call this little village Averysborough or Averasboro, he wasn't sure which. It lay just a few miles from the Cape Fear River and didn't appear to be of major value to either army. These may have been troops from both armies heading for the big battle that General Johnston had promised General Sherman if he came back to central North Carolina. The boys would perhaps never know the details of this skirmish, but they would lie awake many nights seeing the scene replayed in their minds.

Both boys felt weak. They knew that many of the bodies lying dead and maimed in those bloody gray coats were young, unprepared boys their age. Had they not escaped the training camp at Wilmington, some of those bodies could have been their own. Both boys sat limp and motionless for a few minutes.

"I've never seen anything so awesome or sickening," Nathan told Thomas. "Let's wait a few minutes before we climb down."

"We can't wait long," Thomas said. "Those men in retreat are headed this way, so we must get out of their sight. We must get across the river if at all possible."

They climbed slowly down the tree and quickly called the other boys together to explain what they'd seen from their treetop perch. They also explained their plan for crossing the Cape Fear River.

"We saw a bridge a mile or so upstream," Nathan said. "It'll soon be getting dark, but we can make it to the bridge by then if we rush. We'll have to dodge the retreating company of Confederate soldiers, though. So everybody stay close together and keep quiet. When we meet them, we'll have to hide until they pass."

They all hit the road walking at a very brisk pace. They made it to a thicket beside the bridge before the retreating soldiers did. Since the boys didn't meet the soldiers,

Nathan surmised that the Confederate company must have made camp close by. This could further complicate their plans.

A road intersected with the river road near the bridge. It seemed to be a more heavily traveled thoroughfare than the river road.

Across the river two houses were visible. They could be part of the small village they were seeing.

This seemed to be a fairly well-traveled bridge. Just how Nathan and his boys were going to cross it, even after dark, was at this point a mystery and a big challenge.

Thomas and Nathan stepped away from the thicket to check out the bridge. They could see that many local people used it. Each time a wagon, rider, or cart approached the bridge, it stopped before crossing. Nathan and Thomas decided to move closer to find out why. As they neared the bridge, they saw a guard posted on their end of it. They couldn't tell if he wore a uniform. But either way, the chances of getting twenty boys past him without trouble were nonexistent, they believed.

So Nathan and Thomas decided they must formulate some other plan for crossing. They carefully studied the situation and found a small log raft tied up to the bank. There was one hitch, though. It was tied to the far bank.

The two talked over several possibilities for crossing. They would certainly make a night crossing on the raft. It might take two or three trips, but the group could land safely on the other side—if they could only get to the raft on the far bank of the river.

The water was too deep to wade and the river too wide to swim at this point. They looked for a log on their side. If they could find such a log, one might float across the river on it. He could maneuver it over to the raft and confiscate the vessel for the crossing. But no log was available.

Soon a farmer with a small wagon pulled by a team of horses crossed the bridge.

"That's it," said Thomas. "If one of us can hitch a ride across with some local farmer, we could get the raft."

Both boys pondered the question. The farmer might not be friendly. He might turn them in. They could capture a farmer, tie him up, and take his team and wagon; but that had its risks also.

It was getting dark now. They didn't have a lot more time to ponder. Maybe they could slip up on the guard and overpower him after dark.

Just then they heard the rumble of a cart coming. An elderly farmer with a two-wheel cart pulled by a team of oxen came into view.

"That's it," Thomas said quietly to Nathan. "You go bring the boys to the riverbank."

Before Nathan could respond, Thomas had run off toward the bridge. He hid in a small clump of tall, dead weeds beside the road until the cart came by him. Then he bolted in front of the team and grabbed onto the tongue of the cart between them. He swung onto the bottom of the hitch beam between the two oxen.

The oxen jumped a little, but then settled back down and paid him no attention. Thomas knew this would be important when the guard stopped the farmer at the bridge. He could stay out of the guard's sight by hanging onto the wagon hitch beneath the two beasts.

Thomas hung onto the oxcart rigging, holding on for dear life. Fortunately the guard's only source of light was a small lantern. He let the farmer pass. As the big metal-wheel rims began churning across the rickety boards on the bridge, it took all the strength Thomas could muster just to maintain his grip. It seemed like this bridge would go on forever.

Once the team stepped off the bridge on the other side of the river, Thomas began trying to figure out how he'd get loose from his upside-down mount. He had to worry about letting go without being trampled by the oxen or being run over by the big wheels of the oxcart. He decided the best way to do this would be to roll off the right side in front of the lead ox. This might spook it a little, but Thomas could make a clean break and run. The farmer would not be able to see him in the dark.

As Thomas began to move forward under the tongue of the cart, the team of beasts began to quicken their pace. If he jumped now, he'd surely be trampled. Thomas saw no other way to escape than to stop the team. These critters were obviously spooked by his movement and he would only be able to deal with them by brute force. He rolled over onto the top of the tongue of the cart. This really excited the two big critters. They quickly changed their fast-paced walk to a dead run. Thomas realized that now he really had trouble.

The driver of the oxcart, who had been unaware of Thomas's presence up to now, finally figured out what was going on. He was frantically trying to slow his team down. But these brutes had minds of their own and nothing seemed to work. *That's why they call these animals bullheaded,* Thomas thought quickly as he dealt with his predicament. Thomas knew his best chance to stop the big animals was to grab their halters.

It was all Thomas could do to hang on as the animals ran faster and faster. Finally he managed to get his hand on the nose strap of the lead ox. He tugged at the strap, but the beast just kept running. After several tries, Thomas got his hand under the nose strap of the other ox. He tugged with all his strength. Finally the two big brutes slowed down and stopped on the edge of the road.

Thomas didn't say a word to the farmer. He quickly bounded over the back of the lead ox onto the side of the road and ran down the bank into the weeds. The farmer yelled but Thomas just kept running.

As Thomas approached the river, he stopped to listen. He didn't know what happened to the farmer. Was he going to give chase? Thomas sat on a log for a few minutes. Then he heard the farmer command his ox team to move on. Soon Thomas heard the rumble of the cart and knew he was safe for now.

Now all Thomas had to do was find his way down to the riverbank, locate the raft, and cross back over the river. He moved cautiously back toward the riverbank, pausing often to listen to see if anyone might be following him. The night was so dark that finding the boat was going to be a chore.

Just locating the riverbank was going to be dangerous. In this pitch-darkness, he could fall into the muddy water if he lost his footing and slipped. He even considered abandoning the whole idea of a raft-crossing. Maybe he could walk back and get the boys to walk across the bridge during wee small hours of the morning. Maybe the guard would fall asleep and they could just walk past him.

Thomas sat down on a rock to think things over. As he sat there, he heard another wagon crossing the bridge above him. The wagon master had a small lantern attached to his wagon. A weak glow from the light bounced off the water between where Thomas was sitting and the bridge. And he could see the river's edge.

Once Thomas located the riverbank, he still had to find the raft. He thrashed around in the bushes for almost an hour before locating a small clearing. He waited a few minutes in the clearing, then searched the edges that led to the riverbank. There he found the raft, partially lodged in the mud, tied to a small tree near the edge of the water. He looked all around the bank before he found both oars. He knew that it would take two boys rowing all the time to make the river crossing.

Thomas untied the raft and tugged desperately to get it out of the mud. Then he took one oar in his right hand, quietly shoved the raft from the bank, and began paddling. He rowed slowly, making sure the oars did not touch the sides of the raft. He couldn't afford to make any noise. He had already caused enough excitement for one evening, and he didn't want to attract the attention of that guard up there on the bridge. He also had to be concerned about the raft's owner. He was only borrowing it, but he didn't have time to explain.

Thomas had been rowing for about fifteen minutes when the far riverbank could be seen. Finding a suitable place to land the raft wasn't easy since the bank was very steep. So he rowed upstream until he finally found a small clearing with a shallow bank.

Docking his launch beside a big rock that jutted out into the river, he stepped onto the bank. He tied the raft to an overhanging tree and started walking.

Once on the bank Thomas knew he had another big task ahead of him. He had to find Nathan and the boys. He'd now been gone for several hours and had no idea where the group might be. He stopped and listened for any human sounds. He knew he dared not call them or the guard might hear. And if he went searching in this darkness, he might stumble and fall back into the river. He considered waiting until daylight to look for the other boys.

Then Thomas remembered that the group had

pledged to use birdcalls to assemble if anyone got lost. Even though it was a little early in the season for a whippoorwill to be issuing his mating call, he'd risk it. Maybe the guard would be a city boy or a Yankee who didn't know the sexual habits of whippoorwills.

So Thomas began to whistle *whip-oor-will, whip-oor-will, whip-oor-will*. He whistled softly at first, knowing this would be less likely to catch the guard's attention. Then he paused. He waited but heard no answer. Then he repeated the call, louder this time. He paused again. In a few minutes he could hear a faint *whip-oor-will* whistle in the distance.

Thomas was elated. The boys had now found each other. All they had to do now was to whistle each other up like a mating pair of birds finding each other at nesting time in the spring.

Thomas just kept whistling the whippoorwill call. He knew that in time the boys would come to his beacon. And Nathan soon figured out that answering his calls would not be necessary. It would not help for that guard to hear the calls getting closer to each other. It took only about a half hour of birdcalls for the boys to find Thomas. When they all arrived, he explained the whole ordeal to them.

Thomas asked some of the boys to board the raft and found that half of them would fit comfortably. Nathan accompanied the first group across the river. Steven stayed behind for the second crossing.

Soon Thomas had ferried both raftloads of boys across the river. He tied the raft back where he had found it. Then he walked the group up the path that led from the river to the road. Soon they were walking on the road.

They decided to travel a few miles before they found a place to bed down. Soon they located a large grove of loblolly pines with plenty of soft pine straw. They were out of sight of the road and well hidden from the river.

At daybreak Nathan was awakened by what sounded like the neighing of a restless horse. He raised up, rubbing sleep from his weary eyes and looked around, but could see no one except his sleeping group of boys huddled together beneath their warm blankets.

It was still too early to make out the details of the surrounding landscape. The chill in the early morning air did not invite him to leave his warm nest just yet, so he lay back down.

Nathan was dozing off again when through his half-sleep he again heard a noise. This time he was sure it was a horse. The noise was coming from just over the ridge, so he sat up again to get some idea of what a horse might be doing in their camp. He wondered if maybe they had set up camp in a horse pasture.

Nathan quietly stood up and looked into the direction from which the noise had come. It was back toward the bridge. He looked in that direction for several minutes but saw no signs of movement nor did he hear any more noises. Dawn was shedding more light on the entire landscape. Soon Nathan could see the silhouette of a horse against the eastern sky. The horse was saddled and bridled.

"Psst! Thomas, wake up," Nathan whispered. "Don't say anything but just look. We may have trouble."

Thomas sat up beside Nathan and gazed toward the horse.

"We should probably wait a few more minutes until it gets lighter to see what this is all about," Nathan said quietly. "Let's wake everybody but tell them to be very quiet. Then we'll go check out the situation. We may have to make a run for it, depending on who or what is nearby."

Daylight spread across the landscape in a hurry. The sheer beauty of the sunrise brought quick mental awareness of the surroundings as they surveyed the situation. Nathan and Thomas could see that everyone was awake and ready to move out quickly if it became necessary.

They could see just one horse and that was the good news. But they could see no rider.

"Let's slip over toward the horse quietly," Nathan told Thomas. "But we don't want to take any chances."

Crouching in the weeds, the two of them made their way toward the horse. They could not see a rider, but there were bloodstains on the saddle, which told them whoever was riding this horse must have been hurt. Still no sign of the wounded rider.

Nathan and Thomas called the other boys over.

"Let's fan out and see if we can find the rider," Nathan instructed them. "Stay quiet and be careful, though. We don't know what or who might be here."

In just a few minutes Steven and Calvin, who had been walking together through the wooded area, called to the group. "We've found him. He's over here," they called out quietly.

Lying at the foot of a big sweet gum tree, they found a young man wearing a Confederate uniform. The gray coat was heavily bloodstained and the man was unconscious. His labored breathing told them that he was seriously injured. The dried stains on his coat showed that he'd been bleeding for quite some time.

"He must have been shot in that battle we saw yesterday," said Nathan as he leaned over to unbutton the soldier's uniform. "Let's get some water from his canteen, clean him up, and see if we can help him. He seems to be hurt very badly."

Steven and Nathan worked with the wounded soldier for almost an hour. They could see him starting to respond a little. He moved one arm slightly and then he turned his head and tried to talk. In a few minutes the bleeding young soldier opened his eyes. He was slowly regaining consciousness. He tried to sit up, but Nathan insisted that he lie down and rest.

"Where am I? Who are you?" he mumbled weakly.

"Just take it easy," Steven insisted. "You've lost a lot of blood and you need to be still. We've almost stopped the bleeding. You don't want to get started bleeding again."

Steven gave the young soldier a drink of water from the canteen in his saddlebag. He had a fever and was very thirsty.

"Let me look closer at your wound," said Steven. "You have a serious gunshot wound in the side. What happened to you anyway?"

In a very weak voice the young man explained to Steven how he had been riding with the group of Confederate soldiers that attacked the Union army yesterday.

"I'd never been in battle before," the young soldier explained. "In fact, I have not been in the army very long. I'm only fifteen years old. A recruiter came and got me from my home and made me go to Wilmington for a few days of training. I never wanted to fight, but the recruiter forced me to join the army anyway.

"I had just finished a few days training at that camp in Wilmington and they gave me this new uniform and put me and several of those in training with me into this company. Our company was headed up to join General Johnston's army somewhere near Raleigh, I think. We were going to try and head off General Sherman's army.

"None of us wanted to fight. But they gave us uniforms and muskets and sent us out to fight anyway. There were some boys who came in the week after we did who busted out and got away. We should have done that, too.

"When all that shooting started yesterday, I was scared

to death. I pointed my gun at the enemy and shot once. I saw a man fall. While I was reloading, I saw the man beside me get shot off his horse. He was some kind of an officer, I think.

"I'm not sure of everything that happened after that. I grabbed his horse, mounted, turned it around, and headed in the opposite direction from the fighting. We ran like scared rabbits.

"I heard the captain behind the line yell at me to stop. I just dug my heels into the horse's flanks and rode right past him at full speed ahead. I heard a lot more yelling as I rode by some other soldiers. Then I felt a bullet pierce my left side. But I just kept riding."

"It had to have been a Confederate officer who shot you," said Steven, "because you've been shot from the front side."

"Yes, I saw him raise his gun to shoot," said the young soldier.

"I don't know how I got here," he continued. "I rode off into the woods and passed out. I can remember the horse walking across that bridge sometime during the night. I was so scared and hurting so badly that I don't remember what all happened."

"You just relax now," Steven told the boy. "We're going to try to dress and wrap that wound for you. Then we'll make some broth for you if we can."

Steven and two other boys busied themselves tending to the young soldier. Some of the other boys cooked corn mush and salt pork in a tin Mary had given them. They fanned the smoke from their open fire so it would not rise and be seen by passersby on the road.

"We'd better look around and get our bearings," said Nathan. "We came here in the middle of the night and we don't know anything about our surroundings."

Thomas walked a couple hundred yards down the path leading away from the road. He found a tall tree with plenty of branches. He climbed high enough to see the surrounding territory, and looked in all directions to get his bearings. In a few minutes he was back on the ground talking with Nathan.

"We are a good distance away from any houses," he said. "There's a rather prominent trail a few hundred yards back near the river that will take us toward home. I think we should take it and head upstream as soon as we can travel."

"What're we going to do about the wounded soldier?" Thomas asked Steven.

"He'll slow us down if we try to take him with us," said Nathan. "And we can't stay here for very long. We're too close to the bridge for comfort. But we can't leave him here to die, either."

Thomas and Nathan went back to join the other boys who had prepared breakfast and were feeding salt pork broth to the wounded soldier. Steven finished cleaning and dressing the wound as best he could, considering what he had to work with.

Nathan called Steven aside to talk with him about the wounded soldier. "How is he?" Nathan asked.

"Not good at all," Steven related to Nathan. "He's lost a lot of blood and is quite weak. I really don't see how he lived to get here."

"Will he be able to travel?" Nathan asked. "We could put him on his horse and lead the horse as we travel."

"He's so weak that I don't believe he can make it very long. He told me he's from Chatham County. We may be fairly near his home. Maybe we could take him to some farm family near here and ask them to take him home. His name is Norman Farrell."

"Maybe we can move him a little farther into the woods and stay here with him for another day," Nathan suggested. "That would give him time to regain some of his strength. We'll let him rest here for a little while longer before we try to move him though."

Chapter 9
Traveling Troubles

It was midafternoon by the time Nathan and Steven decided to move Private Farrell farther back into the woods. They felt he'd be better off away from the road where there would be less chance of being detected.

"He doesn't appear to be any stronger," said Steven, "but it'll be getting dark soon. If we're going to move him, we'd better do it now before darkness comes. He's burning up with fever and part of the time he's not even conscious. But I believe we'll have to take a chance and move him."

They stretched the limp body of the young soldier onto a blanket. Six of the boys grabbed hold of the edges of the blanket and carried Private Farrell. He became unconscious as soon as they lifted him. They carried him several hundred feet farther back into the wooded area.

When they placed him on the bed of oak leaves and pine straw, he still did not regain consciousness. Steven fanned him and rubbed his body with cold water for a long time. His overwhelming fever continued.

After a half hour or so of working with him, it became obvious that Private Farrell was not going to make it. Steven felt his face. His temperature seemed to be dropping. Steven felt for his pulse. There was none. Private Norman Farrell was dead. He was now a victim of a war he never wanted. He had been mortally wounded in a battle he feared and despised. He had been killed by his own battle officer who would, if he only knew, say that Norman died a coward. But the twenty boys who now stood with their heads bowed over this lifeless body saw him differently. There on the blanket before them, but for the grace of God and the decision to escape the shamefulness of war, could lie any one of them.

Everyone stood in silence beside the still body of their departed friend of only a few hours.

"We did everything we could," Steven spoke, his voice quivering. "God knows we tried to save him.

"Norman was one of us. He was drafted against his will. He was too young to be drafted. He wanted no part of this cruel war but wasn't given a choice. His own officer shot him as he tried to escape the sure death of enemy bullets. He was a victim of a war that neither he nor any of us want or believe in."

Again silence fell over the group. The sorrow of losing a fellow human being was part of the cause. But mostly it was because of the thoughts racing through their own young minds.

Private Farrell's death was one more reminder of the seriousness of this war and it reinforced the predicament in which they now found themselves. At an age almost too young to understand such things, they felt and knew the true ugliness of war as only those who fight in it can ever comprehend.

Finally Nathan broke the silence. "We should probably bury him here. That's about the only thing we can do now. I believe we should do it as soon as possible."

The boys found a clearing in the soft soil of the river bottom and they began digging there with the only tools they had—sharp sticks and their bare hands. After nearly two hours of digging, they had excavated an opening in the moist earth deep enough to serve as a decent grave.

"The least we can do is give him a funeral," Nathan said.

So the boys gathered around the grave and bowed their heads. As is the Quaker custom, they prayed silently. Nathan broke the silent prayer. "O God, forgive Norman for any and all his wrongdoings. Even though he turned and ran in the heat of battle, he was no coward. He chose death himself rather than take the life of another human being. We know You must have a place in Your heaven for one with such innocent and pure intentions. Amen."

Then Nathan instructed the boys to lower Norman's body into the grave. Slowly and quietly they raked all the moist brown soil into the grave to cover his body. They saved the buttons and insignia from his uniform. They would give them to Norman's kin if they could find them after the war.

Some of the boys made a crude cross out of poles they found in the woods. They erected it over the mound of soil covering his body while several others gathered stones and piled them up at the head of Norman's grave. Darkness enveloped the area as the boys finished covering the grave.

"We'll have to make camp nearby," said Nathan. So they put up their tent halves and spread their blankets for a bed near Norman's grave.

Early the next morning, the group awoke to a brisk chill in the air. It was, however, tempered by warm beams of early morning sun. They quickly ate breakfast and broke camp.

In the activities of the previous day, none of the group had observed what happened to the horse Norman had ridden. He must have strolled off into the woods or walked off down the dusty road. They could only assume that someone living nearby might claim and care for him. He was certainly a fine-looking animal.

"We've got to cover as much ground as possible today," Nathan told them as they hit the road.

A warm sun and soft breeze made walking very pleasant that day. By nightfall they had put quite a few miles behind them.

Three more days of good weather made walking very enjoyable. It also took them past where the Haw and Deep Rivers join to form the Cape Fear. They were now following Deep River upstream. They were in Chatham County and delighting in the knowledge that the next county over was Randolph.

Everything was as Thomas described in his daily directions. He was proving to be an excellent navigator just as Nathan had predicted. Thomas was a bit of a daredevil at times, though. Living and walking on the edge of danger seemed to be his specialty.

The terrain was now becoming more hilly as they walked deeper into Chatham County. The country was beginning to look more like home.

As midafternoon approached, they could see a small rain shower forming off in the distance. So the boys stopped early. They quickly pitched their tent halves and huddled under them. After the shower passed, they made camp for the evening nearby.

The next morning they woke to see the skies hanging heavy with threatening gray clouds. The boys quickly packed their gear and started walking. The humid air they were breathing told them that a heavy drenching could be in the offing soon. They walked faster, hoping to find some kind of roof or building for protection. Their tent halves weren't big enough to keep twenty boys dry if a real frog-strangling, gully-washer rain came.

Thomas soon spotted a small country church in the distance. He led the group quickly but cautiously toward it.

It was located in a small clearing with no houses in sight.

Light rain started falling as they approached the church. They walked faster. The rain fell faster. Then the bottom fell out as the boys broke into a dead run toward the lonesome little church.

"I hope we can get in," Nathan told Thomas as he gasped for breath. "This rain is really coming down and it looks like the kind of storm that might stay around for a while."

Lady Luck was with them. The door was unlocked and there was no one in sight. So the pack of wet and somewhat smelly boys barged in and began taking off their soaked boots.

In the middle of the room was a small stove and a stack of firewood. Thomas began searching and soon found some matches. He built a fire in the little stove while everyone huddled around. Soon they began taking off their clothes and drying them by the fire.

Evening came and everyone was now dried out and warm. Rain was still pouring outside as darkness closed in over the small brown building and engulfed the surrounding countryside. The boys settled in for a good night's sleep.

Rain was still falling as daylight finally made its way through the heavy gray clouds. The boys gathered by a small window overlooking the soaked landscape.

"Doesn't look like good traveling weather today," said Nathan. "We'd be soaked to the skin in no time flat out in this rain. Looks like a real flood."

Herman, being the comic that he was, couldn't resist this one. "Guess we're kind of like Noah in his ark. I'm just glad we're on the inside looking out and not the other way around."

"We can't afford to be caught here," said Steven. "What

will we do if someone comes? Would we be better off wet or caught?"

"We'd better take our chances and stay here, at least for a little while," answered Nathan. "It's not likely that anyone would be out traveling in this kind of weather. But we can keep somebody on watch at the window. If someone approaches, we can all slip out the back door."

Thomas and some of the boys found more dry firewood stacked beneath the church outside the back door. They cooked a pot of dried beans and salt pork on the stove. Everyone enjoyed a good hot meal for a change.

Rain continued to pour down in torrents. All that day the boys stood and watched through the window as the little potbellied stove kept the room toasty warm.

"It's been a long boring day," said Nathan, "but at least we've been warm and dry. Let's hope the rain stops soon. We need to get out of here before someone discovers us."

The last glimmer of light was fading across the western sky when the two boys standing guard at the windows caught a glimpse of something moving outside. The movement was coming from across the little clearing where the church stood.

Nathan quickly whispered, "Everybody down. Stay quiet."

Then the door opened with a thud against the wall. Two gray-coated soldiers walked in and slammed the door behind them. They were thoroughly soaked and chilled to the bone.

The boys remained motionless. The soldiers appeared startled as Nathan stood up to confront them.

"Who are you?" one of the soldiers bellowed in a deep voice. He was reaching for his musket stuck in the wet saddle he held in his left hand.

"We've just come here to get out of the rain," Nathan explained. "Looks like you've done the same. We've been here all day. You're welcome to share the quarters with us, though."

The soldier stuck his musket back into the saddle holster and dropped the saddle to the floor. The other boys slowly raised up from beneath the pews where they'd been crouched for several minutes. Only then did the soldiers realize that Nathan was not alone.

"You boys in the army or just live around here?" the big corporal asked Nathan.

"Just passing through," he responded. "This church looked like a good place to stay dry in this downpour. We'll be moving on as soon as it quits or lets up a little."

"It's still raining hard," the corporal said. "It may be a while before it stops."

"We've built a fire in the stove and have a pot of beans and salt pork on it," said Nathan. "You're welcome to share."

"Thanks," the corporal replied. "Don't mind if we do."

The soldiers stripped off their wet clothes and placed them in front of the stove to dry. Then they helped themselves to the beans.

When they finished eating, introductions were made.

"I'm Corporal Brown and this here is Private Tyson. And who are you?"

"My name's Nathan. This is Thomas, Steven and . . ." Nathan went around the room introducing each boy.

Soon the stench of wet, dirty clothing, wet boots, and wet saddles filled the room. That coupled with the fact that twenty-two hungry young men had just had their fill of dried beans made breathing an ordeal, to say the least. Nathan opened the window partway.

The boys and their two newly acquired roommates

paid little attention to the smell. The boys cleaned the bowls they had used and washed out the bean pot with water dropping from the roof.

Soon the two soldiers were stretched out on a couple of pews near the stove. They were tired and dropped off to sleep. In a few minutes, they were sleeping as soundly as newborn babes.

"Should we slip out of here while they're asleep?" Thomas asked. "If they found out who we really are, they may give us trouble."

Nathan thought about it for a few minutes. "It's still raining pretty hard out there," he responded. "And even if we did leave, they could catch us soon unless we take their horses. Maybe we should just stay here and take our chances."

Soon all the boys had bedded down for the night. Nathan got up several times during the night to chuck more wood on the fire. He also wanted to be sure that everything was still in order.

The two soldiers were already up and dressed by the time dawn broke. Nathan and the boys awoke to find the rain had stopped during the night but the skies were still overcast.

"You boys going very far?" Corporal Brown asked Nathan as they both stepped toward the church window.

"Not too far," Nathan replied sheepishly.

"Just what are you boys up to, anyway?" the corporal asked. "You seem to be troubled by something. And besides, it seems a little strange that twenty boys your age would be out here in the middle of nowhere caught in a rainstorm. Are you in some kind of trouble?"

"We've been off on a trip," Nathan replied. "We're just heading back home. We need to get back to our homes to help take care of things around our farms."

"I believe you're in some kind of trouble. I want to know what it is."

There was a long pause. An uneasiness filled the air.

"Private Tyson and I have come here from over at Averasboro. We were in a little battle there a few days ago.

"We heard from a captain there that a bunch of new recruits broke out of the Wilmington training camp a few weeks ago and scattered out across the countryside. Some went north and some went west. You wouldn't happen to be some of them, would you?"

Again there was a long period of silence.

"If you are part of that bunch of deserters, we'll have to take you with us," Corporal Brown said. "We have standing orders to bring any war deserters we find back to Wilmington."

There was another long pause.

Nathan and Steven glanced at each other but maintained their silence. The rest of the boys all tilted their heads forward, glancing quickly at each other and then at Nathan. What was he going to say next? How would he get them out of this situation? He was not one to tell an outright lie.

At least a dozen thoughts raced through Nathan's mind at once as questions flew through in rapid-fire succession: *Should I lie to them? Should I give the command for everyone to spring forward and out the door? Should we try to overpower these two? Will one of the boys panic and get everyone in trouble?*

Out of the corner of his eye Nathan could see the two saddles and saddlebags lying over by the front door. He could see that the two soldiers were unarmed. He also noticed that both he and Steven were several steps closer to the saddles and muskets than the soldiers were.

Nathan began to stammer as he stepped sideways toward the center aisle leading toward the door. He was nudging Steven ahead of him. As Nathan and Steven stepped into the aisle, they made a quick dash to the saddles. They picked up the two muskets and a pistol from the bags. Nathan motioned to Thomas. He picked up the musket that Mary had given them.

In unison the boys pointed the guns at the two startled soldiers. "Both of you put your hands against the wall. Keep them up in the air," Nathan commanded.

Without hesitation, the surprised young soldiers did as commanded.

"We're sorry to have to do this," said Nathan to the soldiers. "But we don't have a choice.

"Thomas, Steven, could you and a couple of boys get some ropes from their saddlebags?

"We're going to tie you up and leave you here. Corporal, would you step back away from Private Tyson?"

Quickly the boys tied the hands of each soldier behind his back.

"Now, set them down beside the altar rail and tie them to it," Nathan ordered. "Tie their feet together, too."

Then Nathan stepped over to the two prisoners and apologetically explained that the boys meant them no harm. But they would be leaving them tied at the church altar.

"This is Saturday," Nathan said. "That means the people who go to church will find you tomorrow and release you. We hope no harm comes to you."

"You boys are just getting in deeper trouble doing this," Corporal Brown said. "Now you're not just war deserters, you're resisting authority and refusing to obey a command. That means you're increasing your chances of being hanged when you are caught."

Nathan paused a moment and pondered the statement but didn't respond. Then he commanded his boys to pack up and get ready to move out.

As they left the church, Thomas questioned, "Should we take their supplies and horses? It might help slow them down if they get free of those ropes anytime soon."

"No," answered Nathan. "But we will hide their guns and supplies under the church. Let's hide them in different places so it will take them a long time to gather up everything. We'll hide their horses in the woods but not too far away. Thomas, you and Calvin take their horses and tie them to trees. Put enough distance between them so it will take time to find them. All this will slow the soldiers down considerably if they decide to try to follow us.

"Now let's hit the road. We'll stay off the main road until we're well away from the church. We'll walk on the dead leaves in the woods for a while. That way they can't see our footprints in the mud and won't know which way we went."

The boys walked out through the soggy wooded area and into a field. They walked almost a mile before they stepped back onto the road.

"We can travel faster on the road," Nathan said. "And we need to get as much distance as we can between us and that church."

They walked until noon with only one brief rest stop. That afternoon they came to a creek that had to be forded. Normally this would have been no problem. But the previous two days of rains had swollen this stream well out of its banks. The roar of muddy floodwaters crashing against the rocks and trees told them they'd have to detour.

"What'll we do now?" Nathan asked Thomas. "We certainly can't ford the creek with water this high. And we don't have time to wait for the floodwaters to recede."

"Looks to me like we need to head upstream until the

creek narrows down to where we can cross it," Thomas suggested.

They walked upstream for about half a mile where they came to a wooded area at the foot of a small hill. The rocky hill formed a gorge with banks high enough to contain the gushing flood waters.

Thomas stepped over to examine the situation. He could see it was too wide to jump and too deep to wade. And swimming in this swift water was out of the question.

"Let's check the depth of the water," Thomas said. He found a stick about twelve feet long and thrust it into the rolling floodwaters. It plunged completely out of sight in the dingy water as Thomas almost tipped into it. "So much for wading. I guess we'll have to move farther upstream."

Just then Thomas spied a large possum grapevine hanging from a big sycamore tree growing on the creek bank.

"That vine may be our answer," Thomas said with excitement in his voice. "If we cut it off about two feet from the ground, we may be able to use it to swing across the creek."

They cut the vine and Thomas began tugging at it, testing to see how firmly it was attached to the sycamore branches. He bounced up and down on it a couple of times while clinging to the vine.

"I believe it's strong enough to hold us if we swing one at a time," said Thomas. "It appears to be long enough to allow us to swing all the way across and drop off on the other side.

"Who wants to be first?" he asked. "If you fall in the water, you will have to swim out. So we need someone who's a good swimmer."

Steven volunteered to be first. He took a running start and swung in a big arc out over the rumbling waters. But he didn't let go on the other side. Instead he swung back and dropped off on the side where he started.

"It's going to take more force to get all the way across," he told Thomas. "Maybe if someone gave me a hard push I could make it."

So Steven again took the vine in hand and two of the boys gave him a big shove. He landed on the other side well clear of the stream.

The vine swung back and then one by one the boys took turns swinging across the swollen stream on the possum grapevine. That is, all except Nathan and Thomas.

"How are we going to manage this?" Nathan asked. "The last man won't have anybody to push. Steven says you can't make it without a push."

"You go ahead and I'll take my chances," Thomas said. "There's a small bush upstream from where everyone else landed. I'll angle toward it and grab it when I drop off."

So Nathan took the vine and Thomas shoved him to the other side. The vine swung back and Thomas grabbed it. He studied the situation for a few minutes. He calculated the angle and how he would make the close connection.

He backed up as far as the vine would go. Then he made a hard run with the vine in his hand. As he cleared the water on the other side, he let go of the vine and grabbed the small oak bush he'd seen. But as he took the trunk of the little tree in his hand, he could feel its roots giving way from the wet soil.

Both Nathan and Steven tried desperately to reach Thomas. But he was too far down the bank by this time. Into the rolling water he plunged. The big splash was hardly noticeable as the tumbling waters rolled on. Thomas disappeared under the water. The force of the flood swept him swiftly downstream.

Thomas was fighting frantically to stay afloat. Nathan

and Steven saw him surface again about seventy-five feet downstream from where he fell in.

"Quick, get our rope out of the pack," Nathan yelled to anyone who might hear him. "We've got to throw a rope to him."

One of the boys handed Nathan the rope and he ran downstream as fast as he could, trying to stay ahead of Thomas as he bobbed up and down in the raging waters. Nathan flung one end of the rope as hard as he could throw it in the direction of Thomas's movement.

Nathan missed. The rope sank to the bottom. He quickly pulled the rope back in as he continued to run downstream. He threw it back to Thomas and this time it hit him.

"Catch hold of the rope and we'll pull you in," Nathan shouted.

Thomas grabbed the rope with both hands. Several of the boys pulled him to the edge of the stream.

"Hold tight to the rope while we pull you up the bank," Nathan told him.

"I'm not sure I can hold tight enough to get up the bank," Thomas said. "My hands are almost numb."

"Here, tie the other end of that rope around my waist," shouted Steven to the other boys. "It'll take several of you to do it, but lower me down to where Thomas is."

The boys did as Steven had commanded. He reached out for Thomas to take his hand. But Thomas could hardly move. Hypothermia had almost overcome him in the cold water.

"Let me down into the water beside him," Steven commanded the boys. Then he grabbed Thomas around the waist and yelled, "Pull us up."

When they reached the top of the bank, Steven let go

of Thomas as some of the boys took him. He was too cold to stand.

"Get our blankets and tent halves out of the pack," Nathan ordered. "Let's get these wet clothes off him and wrap him in a couple of blankets. He's about to freeze to death.

"You'd better take your wet clothes off and wrap in a warm blanket, too," Nathan said to Steven.

The other boys soon had Thomas and Steven wrapped in blankets. They hung the wet clothes up to dry on a tree. A warm sun helped with the task.

In a couple of hours Thomas and Steven had recovered and were both asking each other, "Why didn't we think of that rope before the last man jumped?"

"I guess we've been on the run so long that even our brains are getting tired," Thomas said, laughing. "But maybe we'll know better next time."

The sun's warm rays soon faded in the western sky. Nathan had the boys set up camp in a small grove of cedar trees near a honeysuckle thicket. He knew they would be out of sight there if those two soldiers they left tied up back at the church tried to follow them. His group had a hard time finding dry leaves for bedding, because the rains had totally soaked everything on the ground in the woods. After a long search, they found a large field of dried broomsedge, which they harvested to make a soft cushion for their beds.

Chapter 10
Up the River

After a good night's sleep, the boys packed up and hit the road. Nathan posted front and rear guards as they made their way back to the road near the river.

Overnight the floodwaters had receded. The river was now contained within its banks. But the gushing waters roared fiercely as they crashed over rocks and trees that had fallen into the stream during the flood.

The front guard set a swift pace. The boys put a lot of distance behind them that day. When night came, they found a good thicket only a few yards from the road and bedded down. Most of the boys were physically exhausted. They ate more raw potatoes and cornmeal soaked in river water. Then most of them quickly dozed off.

Nathan, Steven, and Thomas sat and talked quietly.

"Do you think our two friends are still tied up back at that church?" asked Nathan.

"Maybe they got loose and just don't believe it's important to hunt for us," replied Steven. "I feel a burden of sorts. I hope we didn't leave them there to die."

"Surely somebody has come to that church by now," said Thomas. "And besides there's nothing we can do. What's done is done. My father always says, 'Don't look back unless you plan to go that way.' We'll never know whether we did right or wrong. So let's forget it."

"You're right," said Nathan. "We must stay focused on the future. You said we can't be more than one or two days away from home. There's even a chance we could arrive late tomorrow evening. That means we're already getting close to Skully's territory. We'd better make every move with extreme caution. We don't know if he's going to be waiting with his hounds, horses, and henchmen to get us or not. But we can't take any chances. We'd better have a planning session with everybody before we leave in the morning."

The three boys settled themselves for a good night's sleep.

Dawn broke through a misty morning haze. Sunshine splashed through the trees, which were sprouting their first buds of spring. Birds warbled their daybreak serenades loudly from nearly every treetop. It was the kind of morning that made you grateful to be alive. These twenty young boys were truly grateful.

When the boys had eaten their corn mush and salt pork, Nathan called them together for a council meeting.

"We've weathered some tough times," Nathan began. "It's amazing that we've come through so much without anybody being seriously hurt or getting sick. I'm proud of all of you.

"But we've not yet met our real test of cunning and courage. Thomas has done a great job of navigating. We've not been lost anywhere along the way. He estimates that we have one or two more days of walking until we get back to our homes.

"It's important that we stay hidden when we get back. We'll first find a temporary hiding place and then each night one or two of us will slip into our homes to see our families and find out what is happening. Then we can plan our strategy.

"I believe the best place for us to hide will be over at that big honeysuckle and briar thicket near where Panther

Creek comes off Purgatory Mountain. There is a big rock where we can hide.

"I believe I should be the one to go home to see what is going on in our community the first night. The rest of you can stay hidden until I report back. I think it would be too risky for all of us to try to slip back to our homes at the same time."

The boys walked slower along the path down by Deep River than they'd walked the previous day. They were more deliberate and very cautious.

Shortly after midday, they passed Cox's Mill. They were careful to stay out of sight of the mill and the road leading to it. Now they could see Little Pilot Mountain. This became their navigation beacon. It was the next mountain over from Purgatory Mountain, and the sight of it gave them a very pleasant association with home.

Under Thomas's able navigation, they took the trail that led near the Holly Spring meeting house. By nightfall they had found Panther Creek. They made their way up to the thicket at the place called "Buzzard Rock."

"Let's bed down here and stay quiet," said Nathan. "Then when it gets dark, I'll take Calvin and slip down the trail to our house. We'll find out what's going on and be back before daylight. We both know this country even in the dark, so we shouldn't get lost.

"This thicket is to be our headquarters for now. No one is to leave until we all decide to leave together.

"If anything happens to me, Thomas will take over and tell you what to do next. If we get scattered for any reason, remember we'll use our birdcalls to get back together."

Soon everyone was settled in for the evening. Nathan and Calvin began their trek down the hill toward home soon after darkness fell. They took every step with extreme caution, trying to be quiet enough that no one would hear them.

As the two boys approached the York farmstead for the first time in many weeks, they heard a familiar sound. It was Old Blue barking. Both lads felt a touch of homesickness, a feeling that hadn't bothered them since the week they left.

"Come on, Blue, don't you recognize us?" Calvin whispered. The excited bluetick hound just kept coming down the drive. He was now running full speed ahead toward the familiar voices he'd just heard. His barking stopped as he approached Calvin and Nathan. "Here boy," Calvin and Nathan repeated in unison.

There was no doubt, Old Blue recognized them. He made a flying leap into Calvin's arms and started licking and nudging him as though he were a newborn pup. His master had returned and Blue was the perfect welcoming committee of one.

Nathan and Calvin were overwhelmed by Blue's reception. They sat down on the edge of the dark road welcoming the chance to savor a few minutes with their long lost friend.

Nathan and Calvin also needed some time to calculate how they would approach their house without frightening their mother and Rebecca. After hearing Old Blue sound the alarm, they were surely armed for intruders by now. The two boys reasoned that they could cause unnecessary problems if they startled their mother and sister with their approach.

They decided on the direct approach. They believed their mother and Rebecca would suspect that Blue's response would indicate it was them instead of some intruder. So they decided to walk up near the house and shout. Hopefully neither Skully nor his men would be anywhere near.

The two boys stopped behind the big red oak tree

about two hundred feet from their house.

"Mother, Rebecca," Nathan called from behind the tree in their front yard. Old Blue walked onto the front porch and wagged his tail as if to say, "This is a friendly voice. Let him in."

Nathan called again. There was still silence.

Then Calvin called. But still no answer.

For the fourth time Nathan called out, "Mother, Rebecca. It's Nathan and Calvin. We're coming to the front door."

The two boys hesitated for a couple of minutes. Then they walked cautiously to the front porch.

"It's us, Calvin and Nathan," said Nathan again as they stepped in front of the door.

The door opened only slightly as a lamp was thrust through the crack. Then the door flung open widely. Mother rushed out the door gathering both boys into her frail arms at once. She stood quietly hugging them for a couple of minutes. Rebecca joined them in the big hugging huddle. Tears streamed down all four faces.

"By the grace of God, you're still alive," their mother sobbed, nudging them both into the house.

"It seems like a year since you left," Mother said as they walked into the kitchen and lit a candle. "Are you alright?"

Nathan told her that everyone had survived and that no one in the group had been injured or even gotten sick.

"But we want to know how you and Rebecca have been doing with us gone," Nathan told her. "How have you managed with just the two of you here?"

"We have managed but it hasn't been easy," she said. "We'll tell you about it. But first, are you hungry?" Mother asked.

Of course they were famished.

"We ate raw potatoes and ground corn a little while ago," Nathan explained. "But we are hungry. Do you have any fresh milk?"

"Yes, we have a crock of milk down at the springhouse."

"Calvin and I will take the lantern and go to the springhouse for it," Rebecca insisted.

In a few minutes they were back. The boys began guzzling fresh milk as though each swallow would be their last.

"Tell us what's been happening," Nathan requested. "Have you had any trouble from any soldiers or from Skully and his men?"

So Mother's story began.

"Everything was quiet for about two weeks after you left. The parents and kinfolks of the boys who were captured got quite upset, of course. But Skully and his men stayed out of sight. We didn't see much of them.

"Your being captured and dragged off to Wilmington was about the only topic of conversation down at the mill and at the meeting house for several weeks. In fact, you boys are still the only thing anybody talks about around here. Many rumors are circulating about you. We've heard so much about the things you and the group have done that I know they can't all be true. I can hardly wait to hear what you have to tell us."

"First, could you tell us some of the things you've heard about us?" Nathan requested. "Then we can tell you what has happened to us."

"I hardly know where to begin," said Mother.

"Just start from the time when we were first abducted," said Nathan.

"Well, we heard from the very first day that you were beaten and mistreated," Mother began. "We heard that one of the boys had been shot on the way to Wilmington. We weren't told which one.

"After you'd been gone a little over two weeks, we heard that all of you tried to escape the training camp. Our report said that some of you were shot trying to get away.

"Then Skully came out here and told us that you had escaped and that he believed you were headed toward home. He said that he and his men were looking for you. Skully says he and his men plan to catch you and will treat you as war deserters when they get their hands on you. He told us that he would send you right back to Wilmington. Or he might do even worse things than that to you.

"Skully and his men ride out to the homes of every one of the boys several times a week. They make threats. And they have been unduly harassing all of us who are related to any of the group.

"Skully says he wants to catch everybody in the group. But he particularly wants you, Nathan. He seems to hold a personal grudge against you. He says he'll personally punish either one of you if he catches you."

A long pause followed.

"Are you the group's leader?" Mother asked.

"Yes, and I have to decide right away what we're going to do," Nathan replied.

Then for the next two hours Nathan and Calvin explained the details of their trip. Mother and Rebecca sat spellbound, interrupting often to ask questions.

"Tell us in more detail how Skully and his henchmen have been treating the two of you," Nathan requested.

"They tried to make our lives miserable for the first few weeks after we heard of your escape," Mother said. "One of them visited us every day for two or three weeks. Skully personally visited most of those times. He seemed to enjoy threats that make us miserable. He has now cut his visits down to just two or three times a week, though."

Just then the clock struck four times. The night had slipped away so quickly that they hardly noticed the time.

"It's only a couple of hours until daylight," said Mother. "You'll have to find a place to hide. We can't take any chances. If Skully finds you here, he'll take you away again and make all our lives as miserable as possible.

"Skully is spending most of his time rounding up deserters now. He claims there were over two hundred men hiding out in his territory when he first came. He says he's now caught over half of them. I heard down at the meeting house Sunday that he plans to hang one boy he just caught over at Buffaloe Ford. He's also planning to bring several men to trial over at the courthouse for refusing to report for military duty."

"But he can't bring us to trial even if he catches us," said Nathan. "We're too young to be legally drafted anyway."

"That's just what worries me," replied Mother. "There's not much law and order left in the Confederate states, I understand. Stealing, killing, raping, and looting are running rampant. Skully knows that as long as the war is on he has a free hand to do as he pleases. He seems to think wearing that gray uniform puts him above the law.

"That's why I believe he'll delight in punishing and torturing you if he catches you. So your best hope is to stay out of his sight. Just don't let him get his bloodthirsty hands on you."

"I wish I knew what we should do next," Nathan confided in Mother. "I know there's risk in whatever we do. Trying to outsmart that rascal isn't going to be easy.

"We must go now, though. Calvin and I promised we'd return to the group as soon as we learned what was happening in the community. We must go back and tell the group what we've learned. We'll come back tomorrow and try to figure out our next move. In the meantime, don't tell anyone we're here."

"Let me suggest that you talk with a knowledgeable person before you decide what to do next," Mother said. "Yancy Pugh is a wise God-fearing man and knows the country around here like the back of his hand."

"That's a good idea," Nathan responded. "Could you ask him to come over here tomorrow night and talk with us?"

Mother agreed as the two boys slipped out the door, down the long driveway, and disappeared into the darkness. Old Blue stayed on the front porch at Mother's insistence.

Nathan and Calvin made it back to their hideout just as dawn broke over the eastern horizon. Tiny glimmers of dew sparkled in the grass and twigs, and caught Nathan's eye as he watched the morning sun rise. The other boys were waking as the two of them crawled back into the big thicket where they were hiding.

The night had slipped away so swiftly. Yet to Nathan it seemed more like a week since the group had arrived here on this familiar ground. It was hard to believe they had arrived only yesterday.

The waking boys left little doubt of their interest in what Nathan and Calvin had learned at home. They began firing questions like soldiers marching forward into combat.

"First, let me tell you that just as we suspected we've got plenty of troubles waiting for us," Nathan began. "It's true that Skully and his men are out to get us. They obviously don't know we're back yet or they'd be out searching for us now. But indeed, they may be.

"We have a lot of plans to make if we expect to survive

Skully's hunting expeditions. Tonight I will slip back to talk with Yancy Pugh and seek his advice on what we should do. Calvin and I will take Thomas back with us. Between him and Yancy, we can probably find places to hide where we'll be safe. Yancy knows where many men are now hiding.

"As soon as we all get in our more permanent hide-outs, we can take turns going back to our homes at night. Skully and his men probably won't try to find us in the dark. But for today I think everyone should lay low in this thicket."

As the sun rose higher in the eastern sky, Nathan and Calvin decided to catch up on the sleep they lost last night. They both curled up in a pile of leaves under a dogwood tree, which had fought its way out through the honeysuckle thicket. It was beginning to bloom and sprout young leaves in the warm spring sun.

The other eighteen boys sat and talked quietly about their trip. They recalled some of the close brushes they'd encountered on the way back from Wilmington. A few new juicy details were already being added to some of the stories.

Some of the boys began to get restless in midafternoon. Nathan and Calvin woke up to find some of them thrashing around in the woods beside the thicket. Nathan quickly realized he'd have to put an end to the noise or run the risk of being detected.

"We've got to stay quiet and out of sight of Skully and his men," Nathan warned. "They might already be searching the county over for us. They plan to send us back to Wilmington if they catch us. Or they may do worse than that. They may even make a public spectacle of us and do something more drastic than that to one or more of us."

"Like what?" questioned Herman in a belligerent tone of voice.

"Like putting us in the Asheboro jail or maybe even hanging us," Nathan shot back at him.

"You don't really think Skully would hang us, do you?" asked Herman. "He knows the law is on our side because we're too young to be drafted. And besides, the people here wouldn't stand for such a thing. I think some of the non-Quaker people here would hang him if he tried to hang one of us."

"Don't be too sure of that," responded Nathan. "Mother told us that he and his men have been doing many dastardly things lately and getting away with them. She said they've been bothering the women and girls and even raped one of them. They have rounded up several deserters and hanged two men over at Franklinville. They have also caught a man hiding in a cave on the banks of Deep River and sent him off to Virginia to fight. There are even some people living nearby who side with him and think of us as war deserters. There has been speculation that they might even side with Skully and help make a public spectacle of capturing and hanging us."

"We just can't let Skully get away with such things," Herman scolded. "I'm tired of hiding and sneaking through the thickets like a rabbit hiding from a fox. I think we should either kill Skully or face him down soon.

"I'm going home tonight. I've had about all of this I can take. I know my father will protect me at home. So I'm through playing cat and mouse. I'll be leaving when you and Calvin go home tonight."

"Can't you wait just one more day?" Nathan pleaded. "After we talk with Yancy Pugh tonight, we should have a plan for hiding out until the war is over."

"Even if the war ends tomorrow, Skully would probably keep after us just to settle the score," Herman insisted. "We may never be safe as long as he's alive."

"Herman, if your father couldn't stop Skully from taking you away, how can he protect you now? It saddens me to hear you talk of taking the life of another human being. We have little chance of surviving if Skully gets his hands on us. We'll be much safer keeping out of his reach until the war's over. Then maybe he'll be sent back home to Moore County. We'll just have to hope that happens.

"Can't you just wait until tomorrow to decide what you'll do next?" Nathan begged Herman.

"Nope! I've had all of this kind of life I can take," he insisted. "I'm going home as soon as it gets dark. Does anybody else want to join me?"

No one spoke. Nathan held his breath in fear that others might catch Herman's case of homesickness and join him.

At first everyone just stared at the ground. Then the other boys all turned their eyes directly on Nathan as though they expected him to restrain Herman from leaving.

Finally Thomas spoke. "Is there nothing we can say or do to change your mind, Herman? I think you should take Nathan's advice and wait until tomorrow to make a move. By then we'll know what kind of plan we can work out to hide from Skully."

But it was no use. Herman's mind was made up. It was obvious that nothing the group could do or say would change it.

"I believe the rest of you are cowards or you'd go on home, too," Herman said. "Are we just going to let this scoundrel bully us around the rest of our lives?"

"No, we've just got more sense than to stick our necks into Skully's noose," replied Nathan. "This is no ordinary human being we're dealing with. He's already hanged several people and seems to enjoy seeing people suffer. I just feel much safer out of his sight.

"Okay, Herman, go if you must," Nathan relented. "But for God's sake, don't tell anything about the rest of us. Don't give Skully or anybody else any information that might help capture us. Tell only your family and warn them not to tell anybody anything about our escape or our return trip."

Things were very quiet for the rest of the day. Nathan kept his fingers crossed, though, hoping Herman would realize that he was a loner in his decision. Maybe the fact that no one had agreed to join him in deserting the group would change his mind.

When evening came, Nathan, Calvin, and Thomas all prepared to leave to talk with Yancy Pugh. Herman still hadn't changed his mind.

As they left, Nathan suggested that Herman walk along with the three of them for a while since they were all headed in the same general direction. As they walked, Nathan didn't try to talk Herman out of his decision. Instead he talked about the bullwhip incident between Herman's father and Skully when they were leaving for Wilmington.

Nathan could tell that Herman was quite sensitive on this subject. He realized that concern for his father may have prompted Herman's decision to go home. Herman's father was a bit of a hothead himself, which may account for his son's unwillingness to conform to the group's plans.

Soon they came to the fork in the road where Herman was supposed to leave the group to go toward his home. Nathan suggested that they all sit down for a short rest. They talked for a few minutes about conditions in general, but no one tried to pressure Herman into changing his mind.

Nathan and Thomas tried to impress the importance of secrecy on Herman and encouraged him to get his father to help him find a hiding place somewhere on his farm. He would do the group a tremendous favor if Skully and his men never knew anything about Herman's being back home, Thomas stressed.

Then they sat quietly for what seemed like five minutes.

"Why don't you come on to our house and we'll all talk with Yancy Pugh," Nathan suggested to Herman. "You can hear what he suggests and then if you still want to go home, that's okay. You'll have plenty of time before daylight to get there."

After a brief hesitation, Herman agreed to come with them.

As the four boys approached the York family farmstead, Old Blue came running out with his usual welcoming song. His high-pitched bark filled the air with familiar notes for half a mile around. Nathan could see Mother and Rebecca were standing on the front porch with Yancy Pugh and his wife, Ruth, as the four boys approached with caution.

Chapter 11
Advice on Hiding

Everyone embraced and exchanged greetings on the front porch.

"How are your children?" Nathan asked, not wanting to single out the Pughs' daughter Sarah for special inquiry.

Mrs. Pugh explained that Sarah would have loved to come this evening but since this was not to be a social gathering her father thought it best that she stay home with her sisters.

Then the group quickly moved into the house. There was an uneasy air of caution about the gathering. It was almost like they were holding a war strategy session and everyone feared the enemy was lurking in the bushes nearby.

Nathan quickly began explaining the predicament in which he and his group now found themselves. He briefly covered all the highlights of their capture, the trip to Wilmington, their escape, and the trip home.

He carefully avoided mentioning Mary back at the farm where they had taken shelter from the snowstorm. Nathan reasoned that Yancy might tell his daughter Sarah and that could accomplish little in Nathan's relationship with her.

Yancy listened to Nathan's story intently, interrupting occasionally to ask questions. After hearing Nathan out, he began to speak.

"What Skully and his men have done to thee and thy

group is wrong. It is certainly a miscarriage of justice. But what thee has done is also wrong in the eyes of the law. Thee did not agree to join the army, yet thee was forced into it. Deserting the army in time of war is a very serious offense. Skully knows that and he'll, no doubt, use it against thee."

With that Yancy paused. "I feel that God will forgive thee for what thee has done. When faced with a threatening situation, thee did what a God-fearing person must do. And thee did only what most any other right-minded persons would do.

"I'm a God-fearing man and do not condone wrongdoings such as either Skully or thy group has done," Yancy went on. "But I suppose in this case thee must make the best of the situation. It's the lesser of two wrongs with which we must deal.

"I do not believe that thee should be forced to serve in an army at thy age. Nor do I believe that thee should under any circumstances take up arms for the purpose of killing thy fellowman. Therefore, I will do everything within my power to help thee defend thy right to refrain from bearing arms."

Yancy sat in silence for several minutes. Everyone in the room stared, waiting to hear his next words. He was not a man of hasty or ill-conceived decisions.

"First, I think thee would be foolish to turn thyselves in to Skully," he advised. "He would certainly take it upon himself to punish thee. And he's already stated that he would send thee back to Wilmington or off to serve in a fighting brigade somewhere. Either way, thy group would all be forced right into the thick of battle soon."

Another long pause followed.

"I think thee should hide out and pray that this cruel war ends soon," Yancy continued. "But hiding twenty people is not going to be easy. Skully is furious, so thy group will have to hide well in some place where he cannot easily search for thee.

"Skully has already said that he will take great pleasure in finding and punishing thee. He'd like to make an example out of one of more of thee if he can catch thy group. He would especially like to get his hands on thee, Nathan. He already knows that thee are the leader of the group. That means he would probably make an example by hanging thee as a war deserter.

"Skully is no ordinary human being. He is in some ways almost like a wounded animal on matters such as this. He has no compassion for anyone and I'm afraid that he would delight in hanging one or more of thee.

"Skully will be searching all over, once he learns that thy group is back from Wilmington," Yancy said. "Hiding from him will not be easy. He has already gained quite a reputation for finding people who hide out. He claims to be the toughest recruiter in the Confederacy. It is said that he came here because it is generally known that Randolph County has more deserters, draft dodgers, and conscientious objectors than any county in the South. It is believed that more than a hundred men are still hiding out in this county."

"So where do you suggest we hide?" Nathan asked.

"Most of those now hiding are in caves along Deep River or up on Little Pilot Mountain or Shepherd Mountain, according to people I've talked with over at the county seat," Yancy replied.

"I believe thy best chance would be to scatter out and find places to hide up on Purgatory Mountain. It is one of the most rugged parts of the county and is close enough to thy homes for thee to slip back at night for food and clothing. There are many rocky overhangs and ledges that can furnish shelter. Also the underbrush, briars, and honey-suckle vines are so thick that horses and hounds can't eas-ily go there. And I do not think anyone else is hiding there.

"Purgatory Mountain is so rugged and the briars, brambles, thorns, and vines are so thick that thy best bet for getting there is to wade up Richland Creek until Pan-ther Creek branches off from it. Skully and his men and hounds would probably not go up that way to find thee."

Nathan thought about the idea for a few minutes. "Hiding out on Purgatory Mountain would probably be our best chance of keeping out of Skully's reach," he agreed.

"Let me give thee some more advice," Yancy told Nathan. "Try to spread out so that only two or three boys stay at each place. There are plenty of rocky ledges and overhangs where all of thee can stay out of the weather. A few of thee at a time can slip back to thy homes at night for food and supplies. Don't make any fires and keep the noise down."

With this Yancy Pugh and his wife bid the group farewell.

"Good luck, my boy," he told Nathan, placing a strong muscular hand on his shoulder. "Thee had to face man-hood years earlier than most boys do. And thee is obvious-ly handling it well. That means God has singled thee out for this task and has handed thee a special place in His scheme of things, my boy. So whatever situation thee might face, do not forget that God commands, 'Thou shalt not kill.' "

The Pughs boarded their wagon and drove the team down the dirt road. Everyone stood silently and watched them disappear into the darkness.

Yancy had spoken with much authority in his voice. He left little doubt in the minds of the four young lads, who

now stood silently watching him ride away. He had paint-
ed a picture that seemed more grim than either Thomas,
Calvin, Herman, or Nathan had realized.

Nathan finally broke the silence. "Do you still want to
go home?" he asked Herman in a low, quiet voice.

"Yancy Pugh certainly makes our predicament sound
serious, doesn't he?" Herman replied. "I'm afraid it would
be a mistake to let Skully find me or learn where I am. Now
I'm not sure I should go home. I'm scared, Nathan."

"Why don't you go on to your home tonight?" Nathan
suggested. "You have plenty of time before daylight. You
can see what is happening and find out how your father is
doing. Then you can return to our hideout before dawn."

Herman agreed and quickly departed. Nathan still
had doubts that Herman would return to the group.

Nathan, Calvin, and Thomas visited for another hour
with Mrs. York and Rebecca. Nathan and Calvin gathered
up supplies and enough food to last them several days.

"I'll sure be glad to get some different clothes," Calvin
noted. "I feel that I've grown into these. I've worn them for
so long they've become like an outer skin to me."

While Nathan and Calvin were gathering up their belongings, Thomas took the opportunity to visit with Rebecca.

"Thomas, I'm so glad to see you," said Rebecca in a
low whisper as they sat on the tattered leather couch in the
corner of the parlor. "I was so happy to see Nathan and
Calvin last night and to learn that all of you were safe and
well, that I didn't sleep at all after they left.

"I have really missed them," she said. She paused,
glancing timidly in Thomas's direction. "And I've missed
you almost as much as I missed them. I've laid awake many
nights worrying about all of you. Hour upon hour I've pic-
tured in my mind some of the many horrible things that

could be happening to you. I have visualized you in battles and have imagined that all of you were shot or captured. And I've dreamed that you were mistreated by army guards."

"All that worry was for naught," Thomas said as he gently laid his right hand on top of her soft, warm, clasped hands. "What matters is that we're here and we're safe—at least for now."

He hesitated as they both looked at each other, briefly.

"Now that you're going to hide out from Skully, I'll worry even more," she whispered. "Everyone around here is more afraid of Skully and his men than of the war. All of you will have to be extra careful to keep away from him. He's a mean man and he doesn't give up easily, especially when he's being driven by revenge."

"Try not to worry," Thomas said. "We've all become accustomed to hiding. For several weeks now, our every thought and every move has been tempered with the fear of being found by the wrong people. We've become quite good at staying out of sight. We're all like a bunch of deer that have learned to hide by day and move at night. Hiding is second nature to all of us now. We'll be very careful."

Thomas stood up as Nathan and Calvin moved near the door.

"Promise me that you'll come back one night when Nathan and Calvin come home," she pleaded, touching Thomas's hand as they walked across the parlor. "I never knew how much I really cared for you until you'd gone. I'll miss you even more and pray every day for your safety."

Thomas looked deeply into Rebecca's brown eyes as they strolled slowly to the front door. She sensed his feelings for her even though he spoke not a word.

All three boys bid Mrs. York and Rebecca farewell at the front door. Their parting was a bittersweet occasion.

Their lives were in great danger but at least they felt more in control of their own destiny than when they had been forced out of their homes by Skully several weeks earlier.

The boys' forms faded quickly into the darkness. Mother and Rebecca stepped back inside the closed the door.

"Mother, do you remember that you told me I'd know when the young man who's right for me comes along?" Rebecca asked. "You didn't tell me how I'd know if he's the right one. Seeing Thomas tonight made me think he's the right one. How can I be sure?"

"You just take plenty of time," she answered. "If Thomas is the right one, you'll both know it in due time. In the meantime, pray that he escapes Skully and the war. You're both very young yet. When the war is over, you'll have plenty of opportunity to get to know each other better. If you truly love him and he loves you, everything will work out. If he's not the right one, you'll know that in due time also."

Many thoughts raced through Nathan's mind as the group walked back toward their hideout. His dominant thought was how to tell the group waiting back at the hideout about their plans. But he also wondered if Herman would come back to the group or if homesickness would get the better of him once he returned to his parents.

The three boys discussed what Yancy Pugh had told them as they walked along the road, stepping from rut to rut. They discussed the merits of trying to survive up on Purgatory Mountain and of keeping out of Skully's sight.

By the time they arrived back at the hideout, a plan was clear in Nathan's mind. He would ask the group to follow him up Richland Creek to where Panther Creek branches off from it. Then they would walk up to the top of Purgatory Mountain and find individual places to hide.

They would set special meeting times and arrange to have gatherings of the group.

Nathan knew that each boy must be totally in favor of the idea if it was to work. He knew he must put forth his best effort in trying to convince them.

When they arrived back at the hideout, the other boys were still awake waiting to hear the report. Nathan briefly explained the highlights of their conversation with Yancy Pugh and how he had suggested hiding on Purgatory Mountain.

"We're all sure of one thing," Nathan explained. "Skully is out to get us and he's not likely to give up easily. All of you know the predicament we're in, so let's sleep on it and tomorrow morning we'll decide what we should do next."

The boys all nestled in for the night—what there was left of it—and were soon fast asleep; that is, everyone except Nathan. He found himself tossing and turning, wondering about what lay ahead for him and his group.

Nathan did finally drop off to sleep, but with so much on his mind it was only half-sleep. In his state of semi-slumber, he woke up thinking about whether the group would stay together or would dissolve. He also listened, hoping to hear Herman return to the hideout before dawn.

Daylight came and there was still no sign of Herman. Nathan continued to hope against hope that he would show up soon.

The boys prepared and ate breakfast of salt pork and grits, which Nathan and Calvin had brought from home. They even had blackberry jam to go with their corn cakes. Then they quickly cleared their campsite and gathered around Nathan, waiting to hear his complete report and plan.

Nathan began with a question. "Well, you all know the situation and you've had the night to think about it. Do we hide out on Purgatory Mountain or not?"

Almost in unison the boys all said, "Let's do it."

"I'm glad you agree," Nathan said. "Is there anyone who doesn't want to hide out there?"

No one answered.

"Then we'd better plan a strategy. We can't just go find a thicket and crawl in it. The mountain is treacherous. I've even heard there are panthers and bobcats on Purgatory Mountain, and we'll have to watch for rattlesnakes and copperheads on warm spring days."

For the next hour Nathan explained in detail some of the things Yancy Pugh had told him about the mountain. "It's not a big mountain. It's not even a thousand feet above sea level. But it is very rough and rugged.

"Mr. Pugh said it was important that we spread out among the rocky ledges and thickets," Nathan repeated. "And we will need a system to warn each other if danger approaches. Let's use the hawk call during the day and a hoot owl call at night. But try to be quick with the calls so that we won't be mistaken for the real live birds.

"I asked Yancy Pugh to get word to all your folks that we're back. He will tell your families to expect you to come for night visits only. It's just too risky to travel during daylight hours. We'll set up a schedule so that a few of us can slip quietly back home and pick up food and supplies each night."

After Nathan had finished explaining his plan to hide out on Purgatory Mountain, he asked if anyone had questions or reservations about it. There were none.

"There's just one more thing," Nathan said. "We've come through a lot together these past few weeks. We've been very lucky and God has favored us through good times and bad. We've survived mainly because we stuck together and helped each other.

"For our continued survival, we'll still need to stick together and help each other in every way we can. Perhaps we should pledge our loyalty to each other. If one of us gets into danger, the rest will need to help out. If Skully catches one or more of us, we should agree to tell him nothing that would help him find the rest of us.

"Is everyone willing to honor such a commitment?"

Everyone nodded yes in unison. But then Nathan decided to poll the members of the group individually. He went around the circle and each boy answered in the affirmative when his name was called. It was unanimous.

When Nathan had finished, Thomas asked the inevitable question. "What about Herman? Since he hasn't returned, do we assume he's abandoned the group?"

"He knows the situation," said Nathan. "He heard our entire conversation with Yancy Pugh last night, and he knows that he doesn't have much chance of survival unless he hides from Skully. Let's just hope he stays out of Skully's grasp."

All the time he was talking, Nathan was still hoping that by some miracle Herman would come back to the group. He knew that Herman had a poor sense of direction. Nathan felt there was better than a fifty-fifty chance that Herman had tried to find his way back to the group and had gotten lost.

"We should try to find our way up to Purgatory Mountain late this afternoon," Nathan suggested. "We may have to travel part of the way after dark. Then early tomorrow morning, we can find individual hideouts. We'll need daylight to locate the best places to hide, but we must be cautious.

"We'll divide the food we have left before we separate. This should be enough to keep us for at least a week. By the time the week is over, each one of us should have had a chance to go back to his home and get more food and fresh clothing.

"Let's plan to get together every Monday night at the headwaters of Panther Creek. That's not hard to find. We can use our whippoorwill calls and meet about an hour after dark. We can swap stories and keep up with what is happening."

Shortly after sunset, the boys gathered up their belongings and prepared to leave for Purgatory Mountain. There was little conversation. It was a sad occasion because the boys realized that the close comradeship they'd enjoyed for the past few weeks was about to end. From here on they would be more concerned about individual survival.

Darkness began to settle over the landscape. Thomas led the group down the path from their hideout and onto the road. He'd traveled this road many times at night and could navigate well under such conditions. His night experience hunting raccoons and possum was about to pay off.

"Let's stay close together until we get to Richland Creek," Thomas suggested. "Then we'll spread and walk single file up the creek to where Panther Creek branches off from it.

"This is pretty rugged country from Richland Creek on up to Panther Creek. Panther Creek is fairly short. Its headwaters are on Purgatory Mountain. When we get there, we'll wait until daylight. Then we can spread out and look for individual hiding places.

"There are plenty of rocky ledges on both sides of Panther Creek. We can all find good hiding places among them. The water is very clear in Panther Creek so we can drink and bathe without fear of disease. Devil's Rock up at Panther Creek headwaters is almost like a cave. There will be room for several of us to stay there."

Just as the group started to move out, Nathan gave the command to stop.

"Listen," he commanded. "I thought I heard something."

In a minute they could hear the faint distant whippoorwill whistle.

"Let's wait here for a few minutes," Nathan said. Then he answered the whippoorwill call.

The group stood quietly waiting for an answer. Soon the answer came back.

"That could be Herman," Nathan said. "Thomas, why don't you keep answering and see if the whippoorwill call gets closer? If it's Herman, he will move closer to us."

For the next fifteen minutes Thomas did whippoorwill calls. Each call was answered. His suitor was drawing closer. Was it Herman or was Thomas mimicking the mating call so well that a male bird was moving in on him, expecting to make love to his fair lady bird?

As expected, it was Herman. He joined the group and started explaining how he had tried to return to the hideout the previous night. And as expected, he'd gotten himself lost in the thick woods down near the creek. He had spent most of the day hunting for the hideout.

Nathan breathed a sign of relief and told Herman, "Come on and I'll explain our plans as we walk along."

Before Nathan could begin, Herman broke in. "God knows I'm scared. Hearing Yancy Pugh talk last night was frightening enough. But it wasn't until I talked with my mother and father that I realized what a real mess we're in.

"This man Skully is an animal. He's terrorizing the whole county. He has no regard for the law and seems to be getting away with about anything he wants to do. He's stealing everything in sight.

"Rounding up draft dodgers and deserters seems to be

an obsession with him. He's being pressured, he says, by the Confederacy to round up every possible male, regardless of age, and send him off to fight. My father says that's because Randolph County has more men hiding out from the war than any county in the whole Confederacy.

"The worst part is that our group has now become his major target. He figures if he catches one of us, he'll get all twenty of us. That'll make him look good, and so he's going to be devoting much of his time to finding us.

"Father says it goes deeper than just getting twenty of us back into the war. Skully is personally offended because he recruited all of us and we escaped. So he won't rest until he catches us. It's as if he has a personal score to settle with us. And Nathan, he wants you worst of all. He knows you're the leader, and he'll try to make an example of you if he catches you.

"We're like a bunch of animals being hunted by a pack of dogs. He hates us. He's labeled us as common criminals, and most folks in the community despise him for it. The people in the community would like to stop him, but they're afraid of him. So no one is going to step forward and do anything to stop him from hunting us down like wild animals."

Nathan continued to walk beside Herman in silence.

"Herman," Nathan finally answered in a low voice so the others couldn't hear, "I hope God will help me stand up under the pressure. Just a few months ago, I was a scared boy hoping to survive the war. Now, I feel like the fox in a giant hunt being chased by dogs and men with guns."

"Look on the bright side," Herman said in jest, "more than half the time the fox outsmarts the dogs and men and escapes."

Coming from Herman, who was the natural comedian, this was encouraging. Only two days ago, he wasn't so positive. This same Herman questioned Nathan's judgment; now he was a source of real encouragement.

They walked in silence for several minutes.

"We're going to win," Nathan stated positively to Herman. There was a touch of jubilance in his voice as he continued. "We know this country better than Skully or his men. The people who live around here will help us and they won't help him. And furthermore, I believe God is on our side. It appears that Skully has offended so many people around here that one of them might just kill him and end our having to hide. Or the war may end and all will be forgiven and forgotten."

The group walked on in silence. A new thought was now speeding through Nathan's mind. This whole matter of survival was going to be more than the equivalent of a fox hunt. It was going to be a kind of war within a war, and Nathan knew the opposing side had the big guns. The thought of being in a war for survival was frightening. *I don't like the odds*, Nathan thought to himself. *He has men on horses with guns and dogs. We have ourselves just trying to stay alive. I think I really do know how a wild animal feels trying to escape from a predator. But that is the nature of things in the animal world, and humans shouldn't have to live this way.*

His sense of responsibility to the group was now weighing heavier upon his shoulders with each passing day. He realized, though, that the immediate goal was to find hideouts for each person as quickly as possible. This thought would totally occupy his mind for the next few hours.

Chapter 12
Ascending to Purgatory

Shortly after morning broke, Thomas led the shabby group through the wooded area into the heavy underbrush. They crept gingerly along the leaf-covered path, ducking under branches and vines. Steven brought up the rear.

The fear of being caught had now moved to the top of their minds. Most of the boys were as nervous as a baby rabbit leaving his nest for the first time. They made their way up a winding trail, which looked much like a cow path. No one talked. Only the sounds of chirping crickets and the singing of spring robins stirred the silence.

Dogtooth violets and the golden blossoms of dandelions could be seen occasionally from the path. Leaf buds were beginning to swell on most of the trees as dogwoods and maples displayed their delicate blossoms in all their spring splendor.

Nathan and Herman walked together and talked quietly, marveling at the beauty of the sights they were viewing.

"Look at that beautiful redbud tree," Herman pointed out. "I've heard that it's also called a Judas tree. My father said there's a legend about Judas hanging himself from a tree that looked very much like this one shortly after he betrayed Jesus."

"That's just a legend, isn't it?" asked Nathan.

"Yes," Herman said. "But after so long, legends become fact; or we all get to believing there is truth in them, then they become fact."

"Are you saying that something becomes fact just because a lot of people believe it, Herman?"

"Well, it almost seems that way," he answered. "To show what I mean, take the case of those witches in Salem, Massachusetts. Because a lot of people believed those women were witches, the townspeople accepted it as fact. They even killed some of these women, because the fact had been established in the minds of the people: They were witches."

"Do you believe they were witches?" Nathan asked.

"No, and most of the other people in this country don't either," Herman answered.

"Then it's a fact that they're not witches, right?" Nathan replied.

"Come on, Nathan," Herman pleaded, "we're twisting things around a lot and proving nothing."

"I suppose you're right, Herman," he said. "But there is a point in all this. My papa always said that only a few people get in trouble over what they don't know. But a lot of people get in trouble over what they know to be a fact when it just ain't so.

"But most legends are harmless and they entertain a lot of folks. So why not have them and pass them along to future generations?" Nathan chuckled.

"Okay," said Herman, "how about another legend? There's one about the dogwood. The story goes that Jesus was forced to carry the heaviest wood available for his cross. At that time the dogwood was a large tree with dense, heavy wood. Since his cross was made from the wood of this tree, God promised to punish the dogwood and make sure that it never again grew large enough to make a huge cross. God also caused the blossom of the dogwood to form a cross like that used for Jesus's crucifixion. All four ends of petals, which form the cross, have red stains indicating where his hands, feet, and head bled while Jesus was hanging. The middle portion looks like his body withering on the cross."

They stopped and examined a dogwood flower.

"It really does fit the description," Nathan said. "That's an interesting legend. It sort of reminds you of our situation. Jesus knew people were out to kill him. He knew he was doomed to death as he struggled to carry that heavy cross up the mountainside where he was to be hanged upon it. And here we, too, find ourselves struggling up a mountainside knowing that we're likely to be put to death if we get caught by Skully. But if he does catch us and kill us, will anybody remember us a hundred or even ten years from now? Will it ever be written anywhere that we died for a particular cause? Will we maybe even be remembered as cowards who refused to fight in a war to defend our homeland? Will the fact that twenty young men were born, lived less than sixteen years, and then died because they refused to take the life of another human being in battle mean anything to generations of people not yet even born?"

A long pause ensued.

Finally Nathan broke the silence. "You surely know a lot about trees, Herman. What other tree stories do you know?"

"See the white blossoms that are now wilting on those small trees up on the side of the mountain?" Herman asked. "They're called serviceberry trees. They are the first tree to bloom in the spring and their blossoms are a sure sign that winter is ending. Settlers living farther north named them serviceberries for this reason. When people died during the winter, the ground was frozen so hard they couldn't dig a grave. So they preserved their bodies and waited until spring to bury them. When the first little white blossoms burst forth from these trees on the mountainside, the settlers knew it was time to hold burial services for all the people who'd died during the winter. Thus, they called this harbinger of spring the serviceberry.

"There's another story about copycat trees," Herman continued. "Those giant trees you see up on the mountain are chestnut. They are the second largest trees in the country. Only the giant redwood trees out West are bigger. They get so big you can even drive a horse and wagon through them. Several trees try to mock the redwoods by growing similar leaves and bark, but they just don't grow that big. Likewise, back East there are several trees that try to look like our giant native chestnut trees. They're called chestnut oaks. They look like the chestnut tree, but they only grow half the size of this mighty giant. And they have acorns instead of nuts.

"Purgatory Mountain has hundreds of the chestnut oak trees. But they grow kind of scraggly compared to real native American chestnut trees.

"My father told me that at the rate people are cutting down trees, this country may someday have no more of those mighty trees left. What a shame it would be if we no longer had the redwoods in the West and the chestnuts in the East.

"I know a very sad story about another tree. My father told me last night that Skully rounded up and hanged a man for deserting his company in Virginia. This young man had come home to be with his young wife during the birth of their first baby. He planned to return after the birthing. But Skully caught him and refused to accept the fact that he was on leave from his unit. He had him hanged from a large white oak tree over near Buffaloe Ford. Then he left the dead soldier's body dangling from the tree limb until his pregnant young wife could be brought to the scene.

"The tree began to die within days after the hanging and nobody understood why. There seemed to be no damage to the tree, yet this mighty oak died soon after the hanging. People over at Buffaloe Ford say the tree died from shame."

Herman paused for a few minutes. "What a disgrace to a majestic creation like the mighty white oak," he mused. "God, no doubt, saw this dastardly deed as humanity at its very worst. For someone to disgrace a stately tree with such a despicable act must be like slapping God right in the face.

"In the eyes of God, this must be the most embarrassing war His people ever fought. There are so many brothers against brothers, fathers against sons, and sons against fathers fighting for a cause they can't understand or justify.

"And here we are caught in the middle of our own war. The shame and disgrace of it all is almost unbearable. But we have little choice. We must run and hide just to survive. Will mankind ever live down the shame of organized war?" he asked.

Herman finished talking and no one responded. There was nothing to be said which could bring comfort to these twenty weary young boys who had been victimized by a nation with a severe life-threatening illness. They had been born at a bad time in history and their spirits were tiring from the turmoil.

The boys just dropped their heads and walked in silence for several minutes. They could but contemplate what Herman had said. One so young yet so wise to the world and the humanity inhabiting it had to be admired.

Herman often covered his fears with humor. But his serious moments were sometimes prophetic.

Thomas said to no one in particular, after what seemed like an hour of silence, "I'm glad the leaves are coming on the trees now. That'll help us hide from Skully."

Soon the deer path they'd been traveling on faded into heavily timbered forest. The boys were now walking uphill through a dense growth of tall pines and chestnut oaks. They topped a ridge and spotted Richland Creek in the valley below.

Thomas led the group down to the creek. They stopped to have a cool drink and sit upon the rocks for a brief respite. Some even took off their boots to bathe their tired, smelly feet. Most of the boys splashed refreshing cool mountain water over their faces and feet.

After their rest break, Nathan directed the group upstream along the exposed rocks. The water level was below normal, allowing them to step from stone to stone and onto the sandy banks. They walked past several overhanging clumps of brush, vines, and briars as they made their way upstream.

"It would be impossible to ride a horse up this creek," said Thomas with a touch of glee in his voice. "If Skully comes after us, he'll have to do it on foot. That'll at least give us a chance to outrun him."

After about an hour of trudging upstream, Nathan came to where a smaller stream connected to Richland Creek.

"This is Panther Creek," Nathan said. "It's one of the shortest creeks in the county. I've been here hunting with my father several times. My uncle brought me coon hunting up here last year.

"From here on the briars and underbrush make the

going rather tough. My uncle joked that even the snakes and possums have a hard time crawling through this brush during summer."

"How much farther to Purgatory Mountain?" asked Steven. "I've been there only once before."

"We're already on Purgatory," said Nathan.

"Why is it called Purgatory Mountain?" asked Herman.

"I've heard several stories about it," said Thomas. "Some of the early settlers who first came here traveled south from Pennsylvania through the Shenandoah Valley of Virginia. They stayed for a while in a big Indian clearing at the lower end of the valley near Roanoke. A small mountain there which had been a bountiful Indian hunting ground was named Purgatory. This mountain looked like that one so those early settlers named it Purgatory Mountain, also.

"Another story has it that lightning is particularly bad here. It strikes out and sets fire to the mountain often. The place becomes a burning hell. Legend has it that the Indians told the first settlers the evil spirits, which they interpreted as the devil, lit the fires. So no one ever bothered to put them out. They just burned until they ran out of fuel.

"The early settlers said when this happened, it reminded them of somewhere between heaven and hell. And they felt it was closer to hell. So, they called it Purgatory Mountain."

The boys walked up Panther Creek and soon came to where it became a small stream fed by a clear pristine spring.

"This is the Panther Creek headwaters," said Nathan. "It's easy to find, and we should plan to meet here every Monday night if at all possible. We can make our way here at around dusk.

"We can slip back to our homes down the creek the

way we came up here. Just try to leave no trail or any markings that might let anyone else know where we are.

"This is Thursday, so we'll be meeting back here in four days. In the meantime, some of you can slip out to your homes and get food and clothes. Let's use our whippoorwill calls to assemble.

"Now we can fan out and find rocky overhangs, caves, and thickets to hide in. We can visit back and forth, but we should not congregate in large bunches. Three or four at a time should be plenty at any one place."

With this, the group of twenty haggard-looking young men spread out and began their search for rocky ledges, overhangs, small caves, and earth indentations. Soon everyone was situated.

Late in the afternoon, Nathan felt that he should probably check on the younger boys to see if they'd each found an appropriate hideout. But then he thought better of the idea. *They really don't need to be mothered*, he thought. *Everyone here is fully capable of looking out for himself*. The last few weeks had made all of them quite responsible individuals, especially for their young age. He felt that each of the boys had reached manhood in his own way. Therefore, he would not question their ability to find and maintain their own hideout.

The first full day of hiding found most of the boys catching up on some much-needed sleep. They'd completed a hard journey and this long rest was very welcome. Some of the boys slipped down to Panther Creek and washed their dirty clothes. The odors these garments generated were more than they could stand.

The second day most of the boys looked for ways to keep themselves occupied. Several of them whittled ingenious devices such as slingshot prongs and sticks to make bird traps.

Soon they were trapping quail and an occasional song-bird. Even doves and robins fell prey to their snares. And they ate what they caught—raw, of course. But they soon learned that a juicy raw quail was not so bad compared to some of the food they'd had to endure on their journey home from Wilmington.

"Young quail is a lot easier to chew than that tough possum we caught in that haystack a few weeks back," Herman said, laughing.

The boys took turns traveling home at night. They each came back with many weird, strange, and bizarre tales of what was happening in their homes and communities.

During the day, they gathered in small groups and talked over their findings. They discovered many ingenious ways to relieve the boredom of just hiding under their rocks. Several of them brought needles and thread from home to mend their tattered, worn-out clothing. Five hundred miles of walking, hiding, running, and hiding again had taken a toll on their outer garments.

Their favorite pastime, though, was gathering in small groups and swapping stories. Nathan, Thomas, and Steven made it a point to circulate among the different groups so that they would know everyone was doing okay. They relayed stories among the small groups.

Some of the boys became quite good at embellishing stories. They loved to put their own spin on some of those same yarns they'd heard from their parents and families. Herman was most in demand as a storyteller, because he was loaded with good ones his father and grandfather had told him. And he could add humor and intrigue at just the right places.

Herman particularly liked to tell the story of a man from up North who had visited Herman's Quaker uncle ten years earlier over near the Holly Spring community. It seems that this man came to the community looking for a farm to buy. He planned to relocate his family from somewhere up North to Randolph County. He never told his host exactly where home was. The incident happened around 1849 or 1850.

Being the good Quaker gentleman that he was, Herman's uncle took this man in as his houseguest, as was the custom. The Northern gentleman ate his meals and spent the nights with this Quaker family. Then during the day he'd ride out into the countryside looking for land to buy.

Each evening he told his host about his adventures. After about a week, the visiting Northern gentleman said he'd found a place that might fit his family's needs, but he just needed to check out some details.

The next morning when he joined the host Quaker family for breakfast, the Northern gentleman had a troubled look on his face.

"What's the matter with thee, friend?" Herman's uncle asked.

"I had a strange dream. It was so vivid in detail that it bothers me. I dreamed I was looking at a farm and I came upon a giant oak tree with gnarled branches. It was such a unique tree that I was drawn to it like a magnet. I went over and walked around the tree. I even kicked the tree, and much to my surprise I heard the rattle of metal from inside it. But it was just a dream," he confided and went on about his day's activities.

The following morning the visitor again came to breakfast with more details about his dream. He had again dreamed of this same gnarled oak tree and again he'd examined it carefully. This time he saw things in much greater detail. This huge tree was filled with silver, and it would jingle whenever he kicked it. But again he and his host went their separate ways for their day's activities.

The third morning, the Northern visitor came down and awakened Herman's uncle before daybreak. "This dream has hit me again like a bolt of lightning. It was so real that I must go immediately to find the tree. In my dream I even saw the path leading to where that giant oak is standing. Would you accompany me to it?"

His skeptical host, Herman's uncle, decided that since this dream was so real to his guest, perhaps he should at least humor the man and go with him to search for the silver tree.

The two men set out on horseback soon after daylight. Within an hour the Northern gentleman halted his horse and shouted, "That's it. There is the tree I saw in my dream. Its every detail is clear to me now.

"In my dream the tree was filled with shiny metal objects," the man insisted. "I kicked it and I could hear the sound of metal. I shall not be able to rest until my curiosity about this tree is satisfied. I must know."

Both men galloped their horses over to the site of the giant oak. They examined the tree carefully. Then, at the suggestion of the Northern gentleman, they grabbed an axe from the saddlebag and hit it against the base of the tree. It did indeed make a jingling sound. So the two men began chopping into the trunk of this big white oak. In about five minutes, they cut into a hollow spot in the tree and sure enough there were three silver dollars. They continued to chop and soon coins came rolling out by the hundreds.

The two excited men gathered up all the shiny disks and loaded their saddlebags. Together they had nearly six thousand of these coins. They talked over their find and what should be done with the money. Herman's uncle, being a man of high Quaker principles, insisted that they keep the coins for a while and see if anyone in the community claimed them. If not, they'd keep them for themselves.

A week went by and the visitor told his Quaker host that he must return to the North to sell his property. Then he could relocate his family and buy the farm he had found. He decided to take his half of the money with him to help buy food and supplies for his family to make the trip south.

He explained to Herman's uncle that his three thousand silver dollars were too heavy to make such a long trip in his saddlebags. So much extra weight in his saddlebags would wear out his frail horse, he feared. Then he suggested that if he could exchange his silver dollars for paper money the trip would be much easier on his horse. So Herman's uncle solved his problem by trading him paper money for his half of the coins.

The man left with his saddlebags full of paper money. Herman's uncle now had all six thousand coins. A month went by. One day Herman's uncle asked a knowledgeable friend to look at his rare cache of coins. The result: They were all pewter of very little value.

So they both rode over to the giant hollow oak where the coins had been found. They examined the tree and found that a limb had been removed up high on the trunk. A hole had been cut into the hollow part of the tree and the counterfeit pewter coins had then been dumped into the hollow of the big oak. It was a first-class scam and Herman's kind and trusting uncle had been taken in by one of the biggest con games the community had ever known.

Herman could keep a group spellbound for hours with his stories. Another he told was about the two Scottish brothers who had come to this country to seek their fortunes. They had searched for gold and found it in several places. They had been searching for gold on Purgatory Mountain and on Little Pilot Mountain nearby when they suddenly had to leave. No one knows why they left or where they went. But many people who had worked for them knew they had a large iron pot full of gold nuggets and gold dust. When they left, they buried it. To this day no one knows whether they buried this big iron wash pot filled with gold on Purgatory Mountain or Little Pilot Mountain.

"The Scottish brothers never returned and their wash pot full of gold is still hidden on one of these mountains," Herman said each time he told this story. "The brothers believed there was a lot of gold to be found in several of these Uwharrie Mountains in Randolph County. They may come back after the war and dig for gold in these mountains."

One hazard appeared to the boys on Purgatory Mountain that they'd failed to calculate. Steven was lying lazily in the front of his hideout one morning, and he kept hearing a rustling in the dry leaves behind the rock. He carefully peered over the rock to see a huge timber rattler charming a chipmunk. Bang, the snake struck the unsuspecting little ground squirrel. Life was over for the little furry creature and the snake had his first meal since coming out of winter hibernation.

But Steven had a problem. What do you do when a critter as dangerous and hungry as this rattlesnake sets up living quarters just a few dozen feet from your own home? He knew the big rattler had to go. He also knew the snake was quite vulnerable while he was swallowing his prey.

So Steven called one of the other boys over and together they speared the snake with a sharp stick. They first thought of catching and relocating the reptile. But later they decided the fewer live rattlers they had on this mountaintop the better.

Rattlesnake have good meat, Steven had heard, but raw snake meat is a little tough and stringy. So Steven skinned his snake and discarded the carcass. He hung the hide out to dry and would later make a beautiful belt from it.

During a midafternoon chat, Nathan, Thomas, and Steven sat lazily watching a group of ants build a mound nearby. Only a few feet away was another group building its own mound.

The boys noticed a couple of the ants from the first mound wandering over to the other. Quickly these ants were confronted by a group from the second mound. Several of their own colony came up from behind to join in the fracas.

In a few minutes a full-scale ant confrontation was taking place. Ants from each colony began to reinforce their kind. They formed lines and the front tiers would engage in battle, then fall back and reinforcements would move up to take their places. It was all-out war the way humans fight. The ants were organizing and fighting much like Cedric had described Civil War battles.

The three boys sat quietly watching the ant war. They had watched these little creatures work many times before, but never had any of them taken time to observe all-out war between colonies.

"I've heard that ants are the only other creature besides humans that fight organized wars," said Steven. "I once read that they do battle much the same way people fight. They organize front lines and then bring up new lines of ants from the rear to try and control territory. Sometimes they even use crude weapons. That seems to be what we're watching now."

"I've seen other animals fighting," said Thomas. "I've seen dogs, cats, buck deer, raccoons, and even possums fight."

"Yes, but they are fighting for individual rights to control space, procure a mate, or get food," Steven answered. "Only ants organize to engage in mass killing of their own kind through such confrontation."

"Surely ants don't fight wars?" asked Nathan. "We may be arguing about something we can't prove either way. It appears to me that nearly all animals are both aggressive and defensive. And they may be more harsh in dealing with their own kind than they are with other kinds of animals. Cardinals fight other cardinals and blue jays fight other blue jays to keep the numbers of their own kind at the right level in our yard. That's nature's way of controlling the population. It's possible that humans are more aggressive toward their own kind than any other animal on Earth."

"I don't know if this is something we can prove or disprove," Steven answered. "Maybe someday people will study animals and find answers to such questions. Who knows, maybe sometime people will collect animals from all over the world, like Noah did before the flood, and put them in one place so they can study them. Maybe they can learn from them why war is necessary for animals or people in order to settle their differences. Maybe somewhere, like right here on this mountain, they'll set aside a place to gather animals and study them."

The boys watched the ants do battle for a long while. They had little else to occupy their time and attention as they hid from Skully and marked time waiting out a war.

On Monday the group gathered for its first council meeting at the Panther Creek headwaters. Everyone seemed eager to tell his story. Most of the boys had sneaked back to their homes at least once and had many interesting and curious stories to tell. Nearly every story included strange happenings between Skully and his men and the local people. No one was yet sure if Skully knew of the group's return to the area.

Discussions at the council meeting kept leading in a direction that troubled Nathan. Several of the boys wanted to hunt Skully down and kill him. To make matters worse, two of the boys had even brought guns back from their homes to their hideouts.

Nathan, Thomas, and Steven, who were all Quakers, tried to quell any and all talk of killing. They believed the situation could work itself out peacefully if they'd just give it time. But several of the boys didn't buy that argument. They believed that the war wouldn't be over for them as long as Skully was alive.

Chapter 13
Moonlit Nights and Trouble

Nathan managed to calm the group. He convinced the hot-heads among them there was no need to push their luck with Skully. There was a better than average chance that he didn't even know they were back in the area yet. If they tried to hunt him down and failed, this could just mean extra trouble for everyone.

"Why are you Quakers so set against killing Skully?" Herman asked. "It seems that sooner or later it's going to be him or us. How can you justify sitting idly by while someone is plotting to kill you? You know that it's going to be you or him."

No one answered him. Everyone sat quietly waiting for Nathan, Thomas, or Steven to answer. They didn't.

Nathan ended the meeting with the promise that everyone would keep a cool head and stay in hiding. No one was to try and take matters into his own hands. They agreed to meet back there on Thursday evening because Nathan felt that waiting a whole week might give too much time for tensions to build. Of course, he didn't bother to explain this to the group.

The next morning Nathan called Thomas and Steven over to his hideout, which was a large overhanging rock with a big cavity under one side of it. He felt they needed to discuss the pressure that seemed to be growing from within the group.

"We're all members of the Society of Friends," Nathan

reminded them, "and there are five others in the group. Some of Herman's relatives are members, so he should already know answers to the questions he's raising. So far we've managed to keep the group away from the killings in this war. But now it looks like things may get out of control. Do you think we can talk some sense into these hotheads?"

"We've been taught at the meetings that violation of the commandment saying 'Thou shalt not kill' is an unpardonable sin," said Thomas. He paused for several minutes. "But I think about it often when I'm alone. Can we really live by this teaching we've learned when our lives and the lives of our friends are so threatened?

"We'll always know in our hearts that killing people is wrong. But sometimes our choices of the moment test our religion almost to the breaking point. I hope we don't reach that breaking point."

"This whole war is so terribly wrong," Nathan answered with a note of disgust in his voice. "It is such a shame that men march against each other with the intent of taking their lives. Sometimes it's brother against brother or son against father.

"Just the way wars are fought is a disgrace. A mounted officer pushes his men to form lines and march forward. They stop and lift their guns at his command. They take aim at a man they've never seen before. They each pull the trigger and the man in their peep sight falls while his lifeblood seeps slowly into the ground in front of him. Then they reload and march and shoot again. The ones who stand and shoot are called brave. The ones who turn and run are called cowards and are often shot by their own officers, as Private Farrell was.

"This must be the greatest disgrace that God ever witnessed in the humanity He created. Surely He feels shame for the reckless way in which mankind squanders the greatest gift He ever gave the world—the gift of human life. The hatred that men harbor in time of war must be almost unbearable to God Himself."

There was a long period of silence as the three bewildered young lads stared at the ground in true Quaker fashion.

"Nathan, do you fully understand what this war is about?" Steven asked.

There was a long pause while Nathan composed his thoughts.

"I've read about wars taking place all over the world," Nathan said. "At any given time there are many wars taking place somewhere in the world. It's almost as though war is part of human society and men must vent their aggressions against each other by killing their enemies in an organized way.

"Some of the people who write about such things say that war is inevitable. They think that every society must go to war with some other society about once every generation; otherwise the people get restless and begin killing their own friends and relatives.

"Most wars are fought over who will control territory or who will control other people. The unfortunate part is the fact that most wars are fought in the name of religion. And in most wars each side usually delights in claiming they're fighting a holy war. Each side usually claims that they expect to win because God is on their side.

"The Bible we study at Friends' meetings is filled with such stories. It is quite difficult for young folks like us to understand that the Bible, in which we're supposed to believe so strongly, tells us these two opposing stories. First, it says, 'Thou shalt not kill,' and then follows it a few pages later with a story of a small army of just a few hundred killing a hundred thousand men. The story usually says the small army was triumphant because God was on its side or because they were God's chosen people. I have a hard time comprehending this.

"Folks so young as we can come to but one conclusion: Wars are inevitable and as long as there are people there will be wars. And both sides in every war will always believe they are right. When men had only sticks and stones to kill each other, they waged war with them. When they invented spears and knives, they became more efficient at killing and thus war became more dreadful. Now they have guns, swords, and cannons; and the degree of killing in each battle becomes more awesome.

"Wouldn't it be shameful if someday mankind invented a weapon that could kill thousands at one time? If this ever happens, man might either completely wipe all life from the Earth or be forced to change his whole approach to war. Mankind could possibly make all-out wars so dangerous that he'd be afraid to keep fighting them.

"As for this war, I think it's being fought over property rights. The South is in control of the country's major food and fiber production. The North dominates industry. President Lincoln says we must fight to preserve the Union. But it appears that this war is about more than any of these causes.

"I think it's about the value of human life. Whatever reasons that might be given, the war is really about whether some human beings should be the property of others. As you know, the slavery issue has long troubled us Friends. Many of our people have moved to states like Ohio and Indiana to escape slavery in the South. We have done what we believed to be right because most Friends never owned slaves. Nearly all of the ones who did freed them years ago.

"Our people have gone the extra mile to help slaves

gain their freedom. Randolph County had almost three hundred black people living free even before the war started. And our people did more than just free the slaves, they gave them livestock and land and showed them how to farm.

"Ours is not the first country to practice slavery. The Bible is full of stories about slavery. Throughout biblical times, tribes conquered other tribes and made slaves of other people. They even castrated the male slaves to prevent them from fathering babies from their own women. If a person got so deeply in debt that he couldn't pay, he became the slave of his creditor until he paid off his loan. In fact, one of the best-known stories in the Bible tells about how Moses delivered his people out of Egyptian slavery.

"But we were perhaps the first country in the world to practice slavery on such a grand scale. We were one of the few countries to pick a race of people and make them the property of another. We bought and sold slaves like they were animals. They became commodities like workhorses or oxen.

"Sometimes the slaves were sold away from their families; and once they were sold, most never saw their relatives again. Quakers have been known to buy many slaves at auction and set them free, like my father and uncle did for George and his family. But even after they were set free, many of these black people were recaptured and sold back into slavery. That's why my father shipped George and his family to free territory in Indiana instead of just setting him free here.

"The part Friends played in the Underground Railroad will someday make us proud, because I believe history books will be kind to the Friends on this issue. Unfortunately no records were kept, so only word-of-mouth stories about the Underground Railroad will ever be recorded in history books. It may even be a century or more before black folks are truly liberated and the importance of the Underground Railroad will be recognized.

"I'm proud of the Coffin family and all of those other good people who helped smuggle black people to freedom. Hundreds of slaves from Georgia, Alabama, and South Carolina came through here on their way to freedom in the North. They were often smuggled from one Quaker home to another. Our families were part of the Underground Railroad, and I'm proud of them for it.

"Our county was never as strongly for slavery or this war as many. North Carolina was the last state to secede from the union. And Randolph County wasn't in favor of seceding.

"When the war broke out a lot of our neighbors joined the army. Our county had over three thousand men to join the army in 1861. That was a lot of men considering that there were only about fifteen thousand people in the whole county."

When Nathan finished speaking his piece, a long pause ensued.

Then Thomas asked, "Do you think killing other human beings who want to keep slaves in bondage is ever justified?"

"I can never condone intentional killing," Nathan said. "But perhaps this cause is more justified than some. Throughout history there have been wars where men killed each other to take their land, wealth, and women.

"The inborn aggression that man has for his own kind can be controlled. We Quakers have proved that over and over. I believe that someday man will realize this and will look for ways to control this urge to kill. If Quakers have found ways to control our aggressions and resist the urge to kill, why can't all mankind do it?"

The three boys sat quietly for a long time pondering these many thoughts and questions. Nathan had been able to state what they really believed without criticism from anyone. Just verbalizing their beliefs about war, killing, and slavery helped to crystalize their thinking. Their understanding and grasp of humankind certainly reached far beyond their age.

They now mentally confirmed that their beliefs were worth standing up for. What their parents and friends had taught them had not been in vain. They only wanted to live their time on Earth as peacefully as possible.

Their resolve had now been firmed up. They must surely oppose any plan the other boys might have that would involve killing. Even as despicable as Skully was, they could never condone taking his life.

Meanwhile back on Purgatory Mountain, several of the other boys had gotten together in small groups. They, too, were discussing the horrors of war and killing.

A warm early April sun broke through the budding trees as the fragrance of spring flowers permeated the air. Birds chirped and flitted through the overhead branches while nature flourished on Purgatory Mountain as if to say, "No matter what hardships humankind might place upon itself, the natural world goes on. God's world and His great creation quietly move ahead totally synchronized in their own time and rhythm."

Several of the boys planned to travel to their homes that night for food and clean clothing. Up to now Calvin had always gone with Nathan when he went home. The boys often traveled in pairs because they could more easily make the trip that way.

After Steven and Thomas had left Nathan's hideout, Calvin came over and asked if it would be okay for him to go with Herman that night. They would both take the same path most of the way. Then they would split up at the fork of the road near Bachelor Creek and each go to his own home.

Nathan knew that Herman was a poor navigator and prone to getting lost, yet he reluctantly agreed to the plan. But he felt a sort of fatherly obligation to warn Calvin of the dangers he might encounter along the way. He also felt that he should talk with Calvin about the Quaker beliefs, which Herman had questioned the night before. Nathan discussed the biblical teachings regarding killing and reminded Calvin that Friends could not justify killing, even in the case of a tyrant like Skully.

Nathan felt a little apprehensive about Calvin's leaving with Herman as they prepared to walk down Purgatory Mountain that evening. He prayed that they would play it safe and not take foolish chances.

It was a beautiful spring night as warm breezes rustled through the bushes and stars dotted the skies. Moonlight washed over the mountain, lighting the way for Calvin and Herman. Nathan lay awake hoping and praying they would not get lost as he questioned his decision several times. Yet he knew he could not totally control Calvin. The decision to go with Herman was really Calvin's and not his to make.

The two young men walked along the moonlit trails and then onto the rutted wagon road. They talked quietly as they stepped briskly down the trail. Soon they came to the fork in the road where Herman was to branch off toward his house. They sat down for a short rest before parting company.

The two boys agreed to meet back at this spot as near midnight as possible. They would leave their homes in time to get back at the appointed hour.

When Calvin arrived back home he had a hard time

explaining to his mother and Rebecca that nothing had happened to Nathan. "He's alright. He just let me come home with Herman to keep him from getting lost."

Then Mother explained the reason for her concern. "One of Skully's men was here this afternoon. I think Skully knows you boys are back. He was asking a lot of questions about you. That's why I was afraid something might have happened to Nathan. I believe Skully is already searching for you boys in the wooded areas around here. So tell Nathan that everybody must be extremely careful."

Calvin gathered up food and clean clothes. Not long before midnight, he left to join Herman back at the fork in the road. As Calvin approached the fork in the road, he could see Herman standing there in the dim moonlight. The two boys met and started up the main road. Before they could take even a hundred steps, a tall, slender, bearded man jumped onto the road in front of them. He was holding a pistol in his hand pointed at them.

"Don't move," the booming voice thundered. "I've got you and if you try to run you're dead. This pistol's loaded and Skully told me to use it if I had to."

The two scared young men froze in their tracks. They knew that Skully's henchman had them. They knew they were in trouble.

"I've been waiting for you," he said. "I was resting in that wooded area over by the side of the road when you came by here earlier. I heard you say you'd meet back here at midnight, so I knew all I had to do was wait and you'd be my prisoners. Skully will be proud of me. Now tell me your names."

Both Calvin and Herman refused to talk. The group had discussed this possibility earlier and had agreed not to give Skully and his men any information at all if any one of them was caught.

"That's okay," the man said with a diabolical chuckle as he instructed Herman and Calvin to light a pine-knot torch to illuminate the road ahead of them. "I'll take you to Skully. He knows how to make lads like you talk. He'll be back tomorrow, and then you'll tell him everything you know or wish you had."

With this the man made the two frightened boys stand against a tree with their hands high up on the trunk. Then he tied their hands behind their backs.

"How lucky can I get?" he said. "I've been out here all day looking in these woods trying to find where you boys might be hiding. Then I go to sleep beside the road and you two come by. Now, all you have to do is tell us where the rest of the boys are hiding.

"Early tomorrow morning I'll take you over to Skully's place where you two stubborn little squirts will be the guests of honor for a while until you decide to tell him where the others are hiding."

Then he saddled his horse, which had been tied in a patch of woods off the road. He tied a rope around each of the boys and forced them to walk behind while he rode toward Skully's house.

Nathan waited up for Calvin to return. It was already past midnight and he hadn't returned. Nathan began to develop an uneasy but strong internal feeling that something had gone wrong.

Morning came and Nathan could find no trace of Calvin or Herman. By now he knew that something had definitely happened to this young pair. He woke Thomas to tell him the two boys were missing.

Thomas tried to console him. "Herman probably got lost again and Calvin is out looking for him."

"No. I have a strange feeling inside," Nathan replied. "I believe something has happened, so let's go wake Steven and talk about it. We have to do something. We at least have to find out what went wrong. Maybe we can send someone out to see."

They walked over to Steven's hideout and explained the situation.

After a couple hours of discussion, they agreed that Thomas would go on a search for the two boys. He knew the countryside in detail; and he also had a knack for moving around without being seen, even in daylight.

Nathan and Steven would stay on Purgatory Mountain with the group and try to keep them calm. They knew that things could become volatile as soon as the news spread.

Thomas left Purgatory Mountain in early afternoon. He told Nathan that he would try to return before morning with a report if he learned anything. However, he warned that the group shouldn't get upset if he wasn't back by the next morning.

Nathan and Steven could feel a state of unrest and tension building as the boys talked among themselves. Nathan tried to talk one-on-one with as many of them as possible to tell them that Thomas was checking things out and would have a report. In the meantime, each of them must stay calm.

The next morning came and Thomas still hadn't returned. Nathan took him at his word, though, and awaited his return, staying as calm as possible under the circumstances. By now he had concluded that Calvin and Herman didn't get lost trying to find their way back. If they had, Thomas would have found them and brought them back by now.

In late afternoon, Thomas returned. As he approached, Nathan knew from the worried look on his face that his report was not good.

"The worst has happened," Thomas quickly told his two companions. "Skully has them and is bragging that he'll bring the rest of us in anytime now. He's telling the entire community that one of his men captured the two of them on the road to their hideout. He says he'll make an example of them if that's what it takes to bring us out of hiding. He says he'll do whatever is necessary."

"Did he say how he'd make an example of them?" Nathan asked.

"Yes; hanging, if necessary," replied Thomas. "I sneaked into the mill to talk with Raymond Kemp. He told me a lot of things. He believes that if we don't turn ourselves in, Skully will hang Calvin and Herman."

"What can we do?" Nathan asked the other two. "It seems we have but two choices: We must either stop Skully or turn ourselves in."

"Yes, but I don't think this group of mad young men is going to turn itself in," said Steven. "In fact, most of the group wants to see Skully dead. They think that's our only chance of surviving."

"I have a plan," said Thomas. "This is Thursday and the group is supposed to get together tonight over at the Panther Creek headwaters. Maybe we can sell them on the plan."

"Let's hear your plan," begged Nathan.

"Raymond Kemp told me where Skully lives. Raymond believes he has Calvin and Herman tied up at his house or in his barn. The scary part is that his cabin is located near Richland Creek below where we've all been entering the creekbed in our travels to our homes. I slipped over to his place just at daylight and studied the layout. Skully lives in a wooded area and there are no houses nearby. We could go in at daybreak and capture him. Then we could rescue Calvin and Herman. We could tie him up and leave him. That would give us a chance to leave this part of the country. We could then go west either to Shepherd Mountain or Caraway Mountain and hide."

"What about Skully's henchmen?" asked Nathan. "Won't they give us trouble?"

"He has only one left," said Thomas. "That tall, thin one with a beard is still helping him. But Raymond thinks that if anything happens to Skully, he'll turn tail and run. He knows this community hates both of them and would welcome a chance to hang them."

"How do we catch Skully?" Nathan asked.

"I watched him at daybreak this morning from the top of the hill behind his house. He has fish baskets set in Richland Creek. He went down there to gather his catch this morning. He probably does that every morning.

"The creek has a steep hill on each side of it at that point. If the three of us waited on the side of one of those hills, we could get the drop on him. There is plenty of thick underbrush to hide us and the moon is almost full, so we can see how to move into place before daylight. We could move in on him and capture him. He didn't have a long gun with him this morning, but he may keep a pistol in his belt for protection."

"If just the three of us went, we could capture him and tie him up," Nathan said. "If we allow some of the others to go, they might get trigger-happy and shoot him just because they could do it."

"Do you think we can pull off such a mission?" Steven asked.

"Yes, and I brought three muskets to do it," Thomas said. "I went to my home and got three guns that were kept upstairs. I hid them in a honeysuckle thicket over on Richland Creek. We can go by there and pick them up on the way over to Skully's house tonight."

"Can the three of us in good conscience point muskets at a man and threaten to kill him?" asked Nathan. "Suppose he resists, leaving us no choice but to shoot?"

"We'll just have to risk that," said Thomas. "Skully plans to hang your brother and Herman if we fail. We'll just have to pray that we can pull this off without killing him. I think it's a risk we're forced to take."

Reluctantly Nathan agreed. He would try to sell the idea to the group that night at the council meeting. He knew this was going to take some real clever convincing on his part to get the other boys to go along with such a plan. But he felt he could do it, especially since Herman, the one who usually led the opposition, was not in the group any longer.

If they agreed, Nathan, Thomas, and Steven would go directly from the meeting and carry out their plan at daylight. If successful, they'd let the boys know to move out toward the west just as soon as they rescued Calvin and Herman.

Chapter 14
Decision Time on Purgatory

The atmosphere was so thick you could cut it with a knife as the tattered group of young men gathered that Thursday evening near the Panther Creek headwaters on Purgatory Mountain. Hardly anyone made a sound. An air of fear, hate, and uncertainty seemed to have settled over them like smoke from a wood fire on a cloudy day.

Nathan quickly commanded the group's attention. He wasted no time and minced no words as he told the boys what Thomas had relayed to him from his overnight reconnaissance trip. With a certain boldness in his voice, he also explained their plan for capturing Skully and releasing Calvin and Herman.

A total but uneasy silence gripped the boys as they listened. There was little doubt in anyone's mind about the seriousness of the situation they now faced. No one argued with Nathan's plan. Any feelings of aggression they may have held toward Skully had now been replaced with fear for their own lives. Survival was now their prime goal in life, although Nathan feared that revenge might also be weighing heavily on the minds of some of his young companions.

The atmosphere also seemed to be one of desperation at this point. With little discussion of the pros and cons of the plan, it was agreed that Nathan, Steven, and Thomas would carry out the rescue operation. The rest of the group reluctantly agreed to wait in their hideouts for their next instructions. They would all gather their meager belongings and be ready to move out just as soon as this three-man rescue team returned with Calvin and Herman.

The meeting ended while the evening was still young, and Nathan, Thomas, and Steven started down the winding, narrow mountain path. A full moon rising over Purgatory Mountain lit their way in the semidarkness as they began walking along the creekbed. A warm breeze made this a pleasant evening yet the boys took little comfort, knowing what they were about to face.

"This is the first time I've ever been on Purgatory when there was a full moon," whispered Nathan. "Something about this moon over Purgatory tonight gives me a strange, eerie feeling. Maybe it's what we're doing, but everything seems different this evening. It's as though we're being watched. It feels as if . . . maybe God Himself has His full attention focused on us tonight."

Thomas and Steven agreed that things had a strange feel about them. Their consensus, though, was that the seriousness of the situation probably caused this feeling. The inherent danger in this mission, along with the high drama which was now playing out in the moonlight on Purgatory Mountain, left no doubt: This was not an ordinary evening.

"I hope none of the boys in our group will try to take matters into their own hands," said Nathan. "Some of them have guns with them. They all know they may have to defend themselves before this hiding ordeal is over. Let's hope none of them try to follow us and play the hero by doing something foolish."

Soon Thomas had led this small band of mercenaries to the thicket where he had hidden the three muskets earlier that day. He quickly retrieved the weapons from beneath the briars and looked them over in the bright moonlight.

Then the three boys sat down beside the road and proceeded to load the guns.

"I already feel a certain kind of guilt loading this musket," said Steven. "I feel as though just in the act of pouring powder and shots down the barrels of these muskets we're committing a sin."

A long pause followed as the boys continued to fumble with the powder horn and lead shot.

"Do you think we should load these guns heavy?" asked Thomas. "We don't plan to use them; but if we are forced to shoot, can we really afford not to have them heavily loaded?"

Without further conversation, the three proceeded to place a double load of powder and shot in each of the three long-barrel muskets.

Then Thomas led his small band off down the trail. He knew this deer path would wind its way back to Richland Creek. After a couple of hours of nimble-footed walking, they cautiously made their way up the cove to the hill above a small clearing that formed a partial circle around Skully's house.

There they sat down and studied the layout. The full moon shone brightly, casting its hazy light upon the creek and valley below as though it were dawn or late evening. Moonlight reflections danced off the creek, casting short shadows from the trees beyond.

Thomas sketched a plan in the dust on the ground, which was barely visible. The three decided that each would take a separate position on the two hillsides overlooking the area where Skully kept his fish traps in Richland Creek.

They waited for an hour or so until they could see the first rays of dawn. It seemed like forever.

Then each boy quietly took his gun in hand and the three of them spread out across the hillside.

"Be careful," Nathan warned as he walked toward the creek.

Each cautiously took up his position in hiding on the hillsides overlooking the creek. From these positions they could move in on Skully and surround him when he came down at daylight to check his fish baskets. Then they would demand his surrender.

Thomas would be first to shout at Skully. Then Nathan and Steven would immediately repeat the command, yelling at him to raise his hands and throw down his pistol and knife. They believed that their yelling from three different directions would convince Skully that he had no chance of escape. They would then move in on him, force him to lie on the ground where they would tie his hands and feet.

If anyone was forced to shoot, the other two would hold their fire unless it was necessary to convince Skully to give up. If a shot was fired, they would all stay hidden until they could be sure no one was in the house. They would then force Skully back into the house.

Just as soon as they found Calvin and Herman, they would release them and quickly head back up Purgatory Mountain to their hideouts. They planned to leave Skully tied to a chair in his house and hope no one would come soon to release him. This way they would be long gone before he could begin his search for them up on Purgatory Mountain.

Nathan, Steven, and Thomas sat like crouched statues. None of them could see the others. The pale moonlight slowly gave way to glimmers of daylight in the eastern sky as a light haze rose from the ground and glistened in the first rays of morning. The fragrance of spring's first honey-suckle blossoms permeated the crisp dawn air through the morning dew.

The boys were so nervous they had to force themselves to hold their guns still. The morning was very quiet, save for an occasional mockingbird call from the treetops. Overhead the skies were brightening as the first rays of sun lit the dawn. The landscape was becoming more visible, but the light morning mist made details a little fuzzy.

Nathan could feel sporadic trembling in his right hand as it gripped the musket. The only way he could stop it was by shifting the weight of the gun to the other hand.

As the morning light washed over the valley below, it gave a clear picture of the meandering creek. The three boys sat quietly on their perches, each trying to mentally prepare himself for the task ahead and stay calm at the same time.

In a few minutes they could hear a noise coming from the direction of Skully's house. Someone was walking in the woods leading down to the creek. The crackle of dry twigs beneath his heavy feet left no doubt: This was a large man walking in their direction and it was probably Skully.

Their tension heightened. They looked toward the house and could see the figure of a man moving briskly in their direction. In the dim light of dawn, they could barely make out the form of the object moving toward the creek.

Nearly five minutes passed. The large slinking form of the person they'd been watching earlier was now making his way onto the rocks along the creekbed.

At this point Nathan, Steven, and Thomas could all see a second, smaller figure walking closely in front of the larger one. A sinking feeling hit each of them as they realized a real complication had set in. They had not calculated that Skully might not be alone when he went to check his fish baskets in Richland Creek.

Both figures stepped cautiously from rock to rock. As the figures moved toward them, the boys could tell this large hulk of a man was definitely Skully himself. But who else was along? Soon they could see it was a small girl, maybe seven or eight years old.

The hearts of this nervous trio pounded in unison. Their eyes were locked on every move these two made. Nathan immediately wondered what to do next. He felt that the best course of action would be to scrub the mission, but how could he communicate this to Steven and Thomas? Then he realized that was impossible at this point.

The boys were still a good distance from Skully and the girl, who they had all now surmised was his daughter. They all realized that had this mission gone as planned and had Skully been alone now was the time to make their move.

Nathan hoped that Steven and Thomas would realize that their best course of action would be to lie quietly in position and hope that Skully and his daughter would quickly check the fish baskets and return to the house. Maybe this could happen without their presence ever being detected.

Thomas was closest to the creek. Nathan and Steven eagerly waited, wondering if they would hear him shout for Skully to surrender. Using the original plan, Thomas would wait until Skully walked all the way out to his fish traps before making his approach. As soon as Skully pulled his fish traps out of the water, his mind would be occupied and he would be less likely to cut and run or take out his pistol, if he even had one, and start shooting. But now there was the complication of his small daughter being along.

Skully walked out onto a big rock, which jutted into a deep pool of water in the middle of the creek, nudging his daughter ahead of him. He reached out to grab a rope tied to a small overhanging tree. The other end of the rope was attached to a fish trap underwater. His small daughter by now had stepped onto a big log above the rock and begun walking toward the opposite bank of the creek.

Skully, no longer paying attention to the girl, pulled the fish basket out of the water onto the big rock. Two large catfish flopped around inside the basket.

Thomas was about ready to yell at Skully and move in on him. His hands were trembling and his heart pounding like an Indian war drum. He gripped his musket tightly.

Just then a shot rang out and echoed across the valley. Skully slumped over his fish basket on the rock. His body slid partially into the water and went limp.

Thomas stepped quickly back into hiding behind his clump of briars and vines. He looked around and saw the young girl running hard into the woods in the opposite direction from the house. Thomas was not sure where the shot came from.

Nathan immediately glanced around to see from which direction the shot came. He couldn't tell nor could he tell where the girl went.

Oh, my God, what has happened? Nathan said to himself. *They weren't supposed to shoot him. Which one did it? And that poor little girl may have been hurt or killed.*

All three boys could see the rocks where Skully lay motionless. They knew instinctively they should lie low in their thickets for a few minutes, even though they felt the urge to give chase to the little girl. At first, fear motivated them to stay quiet. Then a sense of their situation told them that if anyone else had spent the night at Skully's house he'd, no doubt, rush right out to see what happened.

For nearly twenty minutes no one moved. The three boys seemed to be stunned at this turn of events. Things weren't supposed to happen just this way, yet everything had exploded before them so quickly that no one was quite sure what their next action should be.

Then Thomas stood up and signaled to Nathan and Steven. They each glanced cautiously toward Skully's motionless form lying on the rock partially submerged in the cold creek water. Then from their three vantage points with their guns at the ready position in front of them, they cautiously converged on the spot where Skully lay across the big rock in the middle of Richland Creek.

Blood streamed across the rock. Pools of creek water had now turned pink with Skully's blood as the three boys rolled him over. His lifeless body flopped across the rock and his feet dangled into the water.

The three boys stood speechless over Skully's dead body, each watching their surroundings for anyone else who might approach. They stood for a few seconds, first staring at Skully's body and then at each other. No words appropriate for the moment came to their minds. Their lips were silent.

"Should we try to find the girl or go to the house and see if anyone else is in there?" Nathan finally asked nervously. No one answered as the three of them stood nearly petrified by this experience.

Finally Nathan motioned for Thomas and Steven to follow him toward the house. They walked cautiously along the wide path with their guns fixed in front of them.

They paused as they approached the edge of the farmstead and then slipped quietly into the yard, carefully scanning their surroundings as they went. Nathan crept cautiously around to a side window while Steven sneaked to the other side of the house.

Thomas then boldly shoved the front door open. "Is anybody in there?" he bellowed.

There was no answer. However, Nathan could hear

faint groans coming from the back room.

Again Thomas yelled, "Is anybody in this house?"

Nathan could hear the deep grunts and groans growing louder. He peered over the window ledge into the back room. He could see Calvin tethered to a chair with a rag tied over his mouth to keep him quiet.

After several calls, the three boys cautiously climbed through the window into the house. Their guns remained carefully fixed in front of them. They could now see both Calvin and Herman tied, bound, and gagged in chairs. They quickly cut the ropes, releasing the two, and told them what had happened.

"We've got to get out of here fast," Nathan commanded. "We don't know what might happen next. Skully is dead, lying on a rock over at the creek, and we don't know who might come this way and find us here. There was a little girl with him and she disappeared into the woods."

Calvin and Herman explained that this was Skully's seven-year-old daughter and that she had been the only other person with him here in this house for several days. Skully's wife and other children had left a few days earlier in fear of their lives. This small daughter went everywhere Skully went and he kept her close by his side. He believed that no one would shoot him if his daughter was close to him. She was supposed to be his shield.

"Let's go back over to where Skully was shot before we leave," requested Steven.

Nathan was a little hesitant to grant this request, but Thomas chimed in. "I want to see for myself that he's dead. After the way he treated us, I want to know that he's really dead. I also feel we should try to locate the little girl. But we must be careful in doing it, because someone might be out to get us when they find out what has happened."

Herman and Calvin joined in the request and asked to

be allowed to see Skully's body before leaving the scene. Nathan could detect a bit of revenge in their voices, but he quickly realized that it would be best for all to honor their wishes.

So the five of them walked ever so cautiously back to the creek. They examined Skully's lifeless body carefully and decided to take the three brass buttons off his coat. Thomas took his knife and cut the three buttons from the top of his coat. He noticed that the three bottom buttons were missing.

Thomas gave Nathan and Steven each a button and kept one for himself. "We can keep these to remind us of the most dangerous thing we ever did in our lives," Thomas said. "I just hope we live to remember this day."

Then the boys began searching the wooded area near- by for the little girl. After an hour or so, they decided to give up the search and return to their hideout. They took off almost in a slow trot back up Purgatory Mountain. They knew, or at least hoped, the other boys were waiting for them there. There was very little conversation as the five frightened young men walked through the woods in a single line still in a daze from the morning's events.

Herman tried once to fire a volley of questions about what had happened, but none of the other boys would talk about it. The deep gnawing pain inside them, coupled with an almost overpowering fear, left them nearly speechless. There would be time for questions and answers later, Nathan reminded Herman, but for the moment the other four boys preferred good Quaker silence to ponder their next move.

When the group of five arrived back at the Panther Creek meeting place, they found all fifteen of the other boys waiting anxiously for them. Their jubilance at seeing Calvin and Herman was quickly quelled by Nathan's immediate call to order to explain the current state of affairs.

Nathan quickly described what had happened. He felt it best not to say what was really on his mind. He knew in his own mind that his strategy of taking only Thomas and Steven on this mission had failed. The plan that he had worked out so carefully did not include killing. Yet the very thing he tried so hard to prevent happened anyway. He just didn't know which one of them had pulled the trigger. And there was still a little seven-year-old girl left behind somewhere in the woods near her father's dead body.

They talked at length about where the group should go now to hide and how soon they should leave. Finally it was decided that since Skully was no longer a threat, they would stay here at least one more day. Each of the boys would return to his own hideout.

As the group was ending its discussion, Herman felt compelled to ask the inevitable question. "Which one of you shot him?"

Nathan, Steven, and Thomas looked at each other in silence. After a long pause Nathan replied, "Why don't we just let that go unanswered for now? What's done is done. Herman, you and Calvin are safe back here with us and Skully is dead. Nothing we can say will change anything that's happened, so let's not talk about it now. Perhaps it is best that we not talk about this to anyone outside this group or ever tell what really happened last night."

After a period of silence that seemed to last for several minutes, Nathan felt he must speak further. "War is dreadfully wrong. Hopefully this war will be over soon and we can all put this entire incident behind us. No one had malice in his heart. Intentional killing is wrong, no matter when or where it happens. In time of war men do things that they wouldn't at other times. Killing is part of war and let's all pray that God will forgive us for anything we have done wrong."

That night Thomas went back to his home, hoping to get new information for the group. He stayed until morning and slipped back to the mill to talk with Raymond Kemp. Later that day he returned to the hideout and reported his findings to the group.

"Raymond says the news is out that someone shot Skully and that the entire community is speculating on who did it. They have found his daughter and she is living with her kinfolks. Some people are saying they think we did it," Thomas reported. "They say that tall, skinny man with a beard who had been helping Skully buried him. Then he took off back to Moore County.

"That means the threat to our lives is probably over. In this desperate time of war, it is not likely that anyone in the community will even try to solve the mystery of who killed Skully, much less attempt to bring charges against the killer. This being wartime probably means no one is likely to press for action. Skully will be looked upon as just another war casualty.

"The community is rejoicing over this, according to Raymond. But they have more to celebrate than Skully's death. They are saying that General Lee may surrender to General Grant any day now. The two men plan to meet in central Virginia today or tomorrow and sign the surrender papers to end this war.

"Raymond also had some other news from the war that should interest you. He said that three weeks ago there was a major battle at Bentonville, North Carolina. General Joseph Johnston led thirty thousand Confederates against General Sherman's sixty thousand Union soldiers. Johnston's men were no match for Sherman's. After three days of fighting, Johnston and his men fled to Goldsboro in the middle of the night, thus ending the battle.

"The fighting Nathan and I saw from the treetop on our trip home was a small battle at a place called Averasboro. These men who faced off there were going to join this big battle at Bentonville. They first engaged in the smaller battle we saw, which lasted only a short time. If we had not escaped, we would have been part of General Johnston's army fighting at Bentonville."

Thomas's news brought some relief to the group, but they were still too upset to take any chances. They knew their battle with Skully had been won, yet the uncertainty of the war still hung over their heads. Would they be safe to walk the roads again? Would the Confederacy send someone in Skully's place to hunt them down and punish them? Had they committed unpardonable war crimes? Would they ever be able to live in society again? Would God forgive them for what they had done? Were their young lives ruined almost before manhood began? Would the ghost of Skully haunt them for the rest of their lives?

All of these questions now plagued the group of young boys who found their lot in life that of fugitives. They hoped for the best, but found little comfort in their discussions and thoughts on the subject.

The boys decided they would stay in their hideouts one more night. The next day they would all return to their homes. Their war with Skully was over, but somehow Nathan felt no honor in the victory.

Nathan, Thomas, and Steven simply refused to talk whenever Skully's name came up in conversation. The whole incident had taken something out of them that they could not explain. It had also built a feeling of mistrust and uncertainty among the three of them. Each had questions in his mind about the events that took place that night of the full moon over Purgatory. No one of them dared bring the subject up in the presence of the other two. Perhaps in time they would talk about it, but not now.

A sadness gnawed at their innards each time even the thought of Skully crossed their minds. They did what they had to do to save Calvin and Herman from hanging. Yet they felt responsible for the death of another human being and it weighed upon them heavily. They felt Skully's blood was now on their hands.

The three of them also wondered if being part of the group of twenty boys believed to have killed Skully would provoke a hearing at the Friends meeting. They knew they could be removed from the Quaker faith for this.

Finally, after a few days had passed, Nathan, Steven, and Thomas discussed the possibility of their being brought to trial before the Friends Meeting. They knew that if anyone in their group told that they were the ones sent on the rescue mission, they'd probably all be kicked out of the religion. There might even be criminal action by the state.

They agreed to keep everything about this incident a secret as long as they lived. They begged the rest of the boys to do the same.

Just as Thomas had reported, Gen. Robert E. Lee did surrender to Gen. Ulysses S. Grant at Appomattox Court-house, Virginia, the next day, April 9, 1865.

The boys all returned home and jubilation spread across this beleaguered community. Celebrations took place across the land.

The Society of Friends gathered at its meeting house to pray and thank God the war had ended. People were talking and laughing as they hadn't done in years.

Nathan, Steven, and Thomas huddled in one corner of the churchyard with just the three of them talking solemnly. Somehow they just hadn't been able to share the joy and jubilation that seemed to have captivated the rest of the group.

Several of their friends tried to chat with them, but they just didn't have much to say. All attempts to cheer them up ended mostly in silence. Even when Sarah Pugh came by to chat, Nathan could only make polite conversation. Everyone could read that something was seriously troubling these three young men who had now tucked their lives in their own little shells.

Yancy Pugh walked over and spoke to them in a consoling tone of voice, a gesture in which they found some comfort because they felt he knew what had happened. They also believed that he knew much more than he was telling. They felt that Yancy was a strong pillar of support for them and their cause, yet he didn't know the whole truth about this incident nor would he ever.

Nathan, Steven, and Thomas knew in their own troubled hearts they had done what Quakers could never in good conscience do. And maybe that is why they had not confronted each other even once since about who actually fired the fatal shot that killed Skully. Each of the boys had hidden his musket back in the thicket after the incident, and no one had been back to collect them. Thus, none of the boys knew which musket had been fired and which ones were still loaded.

They all knew that the one who pulled the trigger could never face the meeting in good faith. Sooner or later the one who shot Skully would have to confess his sin of killing another person. And he would probably be removed from the Quaker faith when he did. Wartime would not be accepted as an excuse for killing in the eyes of the Society of Friends. But which one of them was the killer?

Just then a wagon drove up and stopped beside them.

A stern-faced, one-armed man stepped down from the buckboard and walked over to them. It was Herman's father.

"I have something for each of you," he said with a quiver in his voice. "Here are three buttons from Skully's coat. You each have one like them. I fired the shot that killed Skully because I just couldn't let you face that evil man with your guns. I slipped in the night before, knowing that Skully went out on those rocks every morning at the same time. I hid in the mountain laurel thicket behind those rocks and waited. I had to get close because shooting a gun with just one arm isn't easy. I saw you three take up your positions and I just couldn't let you do it. He might have killed one or all of you. I felt that your Quaker faith might keep you from doing what had to be done. I cut these three buttons off his coat while you went to the house to rescue Calvin and Herman.

"After you left and I could see that Herman and Calvin were safe, I formed a search party to find the little girl. We found her and took her to her mother who was staying with relatives near Carthage. While Skully's wife was scared and grief-stricken, she was not surprised at his death. She told us the whole story about him.

"Skully managed during the first three years of the war to escape the fighting by hiding from recruiters in his county. Then one day while walking down a wagon trail he happened upon a traveling merchant he'd met a few years earlier. This man had stopped to water his horses at a creek near the road, so Skully talked with him.

"The merchant happened to mention that John Stone would be leaving his Randolph County recruiting post due to poor health. Skully quickly worked out a scheme to seize the opportunity and muscle his way into that role. He even asked the merchant to tell Samuel Brown in Randolph

County that he'd be taking John's place. Skully knew the Confederacy was a lost cause, so there'd be no opposition from its ragtag government once he established himself as a bully rounding up war deserters and draft dodgers. He moved his family into the abandoned house where you rescued Herman and Calvin.

"Then Skully convinced two younger Moore County draft dodgers he knew to join him in Randolph County under the assumed names of Ralph and Floyd. They later persuaded three other Moore County boys to pose as Corporal Smith and Privates Carter and King and paid them to march you boys to Wilmington. Skully hired a local seamstress he knew to make rebel gray uniforms for all of them. The army folks at Wilmington were so glad to have twenty more warm bodies that no one questioned the three uniformed men who delivered you.

"Back in Moore County, Skully had been known by his real name, Peter. After moving to Randolph he forced his family to keep a low profile and tried to change his looks by altering the way he trimmed his beard. Thus, he managed to elude the Moore County vigilantes, who he really didn't believe would come looking for him, anyway.

"Skully legally was never a war recruiter, and he had no authority to induct you boys into the army. He thought that when he settled in Randolph County he had escaped the Moore County vigilantes. But they were closing in on him.

"Skully obviously thought that by rounding up war deserters, draft dodgers, and even you Quakers he would somehow find himself back in the good graces of the Moore County people who detested the fact that several hundred people in Randolph County were hiding out from the war.

"Thus, Skully had planned to be a hero to his Moore

County folks by rounding up you boys and sending you into the war. Your escape messed up his plan, and he felt he had to correct the wrong you'd done. When he saw the vigilantes closing in on him a few days ago, he sent his wife, who was pregnant, and all their children except one daughter back to hide out with relatives in Moore County. He kept the little girl close to him wherever he went hoping that none of the vigilantes would shoot at him with her by his side.

"The biggest mistake Skully made was thinking he could force you Quaker boys into a war that you didn't believe in. You outlasted him and he lost this little war within a war. This may have been the only real battle fought in Randolph County.

"Skully was a casualty of the war that killed two of my sons and took away my left arm. As for me, I'll learn to live with my guilt and hope God understands. Nobody in this community wants to talk about it, so can we just let this remain our secret? Forever.

"Let's hope the ghost of Skully doesn't come back to haunt us every year when the April full moon rises over Purgatory Mountain."